Broken Beginnings

USA TODAY BESTSELLING AUTHORS

J.L. BECK & C. HALLMAN

PROLOGUE

Claire

6 Years Ago

Pain. I feel it in every cell of my body.

It's all I can feel while I lie on the floor, unable to get up. I try to make sense of what is happening. Why is my dad so angry? Why is he hurting me? Is he going to kill me?

All the questions swirl in my head, but the pain won't let me conjure up an answer.

"Do you have any idea what you've done? Who he is?" my father spits, confusing me even more. "He's going to tell his boss where I am. He's going to kill me because I can't pay back the money. Is that what you want, Claire? Do you want me dead?"

The feeble attempt I make to shake my head and tell him no sends a sharp pain shooting down my neck. I open my mouth to speak, but my throat is so raw from crying for help. My lips are dry and cracked, and I taste the coppery tinge of blood on my tongue.

"This is all your fault. Everything was great before you were born. Your mother loved me. We were happy, and then you had to come along." He says it like I chose to be here.

He paces through the room, a beer bottle in his hand. I follow him with my eyes since that's the only part of my body I can actually move without causing more pain.

I want to tell him I'm sorry, beg him to forgive me and stop hurting me, but my body is so weak that I can barely keep my eyes open, let alone speak.

Everything hurts, and all I want to do is close my eyes and sleep.

"You destroyed my life!" he yells.

My eyes fly back open just in time to see the beer bottle fly my way. I squeeze my eyes shut and try to turn away, but I'm too slow. The bottle hits me in the side of the head, the glass shattering around me.

Agonizing pain erupts, like a million little bombs going off, crushing my skull, and turning my brain to shreds. The room spins around me, and all I can hear is a loud ringing in my ear.

My vision blurs, and I feel myself fading. Something in the back of my mind tells me to hold on, to keep fighting. Forcing myself to blink and keep my eyes open, I stare at the ceiling and try to think of anything but the pain. There's a loud pop in my ear, and the pressure is so great, it feels like my head will explode.

Above me, my father slams his fist against my head. Saliva clings to my skin as he spits words of hate at me. Something warm and wet trickles down the side of my face. One more punch, and I can't contain the scream that's lodged in my throat.

Fracturing like a piece of glass, I don't even recognize the sound that escapes me. I let my eyes drift closed then, and the darkness becomes a comforting balm.

Please, make it stop! I repeat over and over in my mind.

Then, as if God can hear my unspoken prayers, the weight against my body lifts. I force my eyes open, even though it feels impossible to do. The pain in my face is overwhelming, but for a moment, it becomes background noise when I see Lucca hovering over my father.

The world around me is silent, there is no sound, and all I can do is watch in horror as Lucca transforms right before my eyes, becoming someone else entirely.

Fear replaces any happy thoughts I ever had about him.

There is a darkness in his eyes that makes it hard for me to breathe. Terror reignites in my veins as I lie helplessly on the floor and watch my father's head bounce against the ground, over and over again like a basketball.

Lucca's lips move, pulling back into a sinister grin as he speaks, but I can't hear what he's saying. I'm drowning in the chaos. My eyes drift to a dark spot forming on the floor beneath my father's head.

Blood. The puddle grows bigger and bigger, and it seems like forever before Lucca stops. I can't look away from his hands. They're coated in blood—so much blood. I shake when his eyes find mine. His penetrating stare submerges me into icy water. I'm afraid. I want to move, to run before he hurts me too, but I can't make my limbs work.

Pain blankets every inch of my body.

The darkness in Lucca's eyes fades slowly, and he looks

down at my father and back at me as if he's trying to piece the puzzle of what he's done together.

The person I thought he was all along, the white knight, a friend, reappears.

In a flash, he crosses the room, fear overtaking his features while his gaze sweeps over my body. I struggle to move, trying to scoot away from him, but any type of movement makes the throbbing in my head worse. I'd rather die than attempt to move right now.

With his powerful arms, he picks me up off the floor and holds me to his chest. I push with all my strength, trying to escape him, but I'm in too much pain. Too far gone to care what happens next. The coppery tang of blood is all I can smell as I breathe through my nose. Lucca peers down at me, his eyes liquid pools of amber.

"Call an... ambulance," I croak, afraid that my father may be dead before they arrive.

"Everything is going to be okay. He'll never hurt you again. I swear on it. No one will, not as long as I'm breathing."

I want to cry, but the tears aren't there.

I'm broken. The man I thought would never hurt me, that would save me from everything, just took my entire life and crushed it into a million pieces.

1
CLAIRE

Present

I keep my eyes trained to the floor, walking down the long hallway that leads to the double doors ahead. All I have to do is get outside, and I'll be free of this building, and the people inside of it, for the rest of the day.

The dull sound of footsteps and chatter echo around me as the hallway fills with students being released from their last class of the day.

Everything I do is to limit the amount of attention I bring on myself. Today, however, there is no avoiding Cinderella's three wicked stepsisters.

I look up just in time to see the three witches leaning against a nearby locker. My gut tightens like a knot being pulled tight. I hate them. Hate how they make me feel. How they bully me. Making fun of me because I can't hear properly. Because the teacher always makes me sit up front because I have to ask people to repeat questions or look at me so I can read their lips.

They don't like me because I'm different. If only they knew what made me this way, what caused me to lose my hearing. Maybe then they would be a little more compassionate.

Or maybe not.

Arabella sticks her heeled foot out at the last moment, and before I can stop, I trip over it, barely catching myself with my hands; my face nearly collides with the linoleum. Pain ripples up my arms from hitting the floor, and I grit my teeth, holding back a curse.

"Looks like Claire can't walk any better than she can hear." Bethany sniggers, tucking a strand of silky blonde hair behind her ear.

Popular. Gorgeous. Perfect in every way.

Bethany is mean, but nothing compared to the ringleader, Arabella. I shake my head and reach for the book I had clutched to my chest. My fingers graze the cover just as Arabella's pointed heel comes into view.

Like the bitch she is, she presses it against my hand. My jaw quakes with how hard I'm clenching it.

"Oops," she sneers and pulls her foot back a second later.

I bite my tongue, holding back the insult that's building at the tip of my tongue. Nothing I say to them will change how they act. They want to hurt me, and I'm not giving them that type of satisfaction. I grab my book and scurry off the floor and out of the school before they try to do something else to me.

I don't stop running until I reach the bus stop, and my heart doesn't stop racing until I take my seat. My phone vibrates to life in my pocket, and I reach inside my tight jeans to pull it out. *Hope* flashes across the screen.

My best friend. My one and only friend. My lips turn up at the sides, and I answer the phone.

"Hey!" I hold the sleek device to my good ear.

"Jesus, I thought someone kidnapped you. Usually, you wait, and we walk together. Did something happen today?" Her words come out in a rush, and it sounds like she just got done running. *Shit!* It completely escaped my mind to wait for her. Arabella and her posse didn't really help matters, but now I feel like an asshole.

"Sorry. It escaped my mind."

"Are you sure?" Hope doesn't sound convinced. "It's something. I know it. Is someone following you again? I'll kick their ass if they are." At that moment, an image of a five-foot, freckled-faced, Hope, with zero muscle mass and two left feet, appears in my mind. The idea of her kicking anyone's ass is laughable, but it's the thought that counts. The real seriousness lies in the fact that someone is following me, always, wherever I go.

"Someone is always following me, you know that."

"Yeah... I forgot for a hot second, sue me."

A bubble of laughter passes my lips. Hope is everything I am not, and I think that's why we're such good friends. She brings out the best in me, pushing me to do things I wouldn't do without her.

"It's fine. Nothing happened. I'm sorry I didn't wait for you." I lay the apology on thick.

"You better be."

"I am. There is no one I would rather walk home with..."

"Right, other than the stalker that is always following you." She snorts. "When are you going to go to the police, Claire?"

Never. Hope doesn't know the complete story of how I got

here. I've told her what I wanted her to know. Still, she's the only person who knows even a sliver about my past.

The police wouldn't help me, not when Lucca and whoever he works for have control over this city. I mean, how else did he get away with killing my father? He knows people, and those people are so much bigger and powerful than the police.

I know I might not visibly see Lucca, but he is always there. Watching. Waiting.

"It's not a big deal. I'm fine, and nothing has happened to me. I've told you…"

"Not yet," she interjects. "Nothing has happened to you *yet*. You need to tell this guy to get lost."

Ha, I wish it was that easy.

"Look, everything is fine. I'm not scared, which means you have no reason to be." The bus turns onto the street where my stop is. "I've got to go. I'll call you later, okay?"

"Fine, but we're going to get rid of this stalker guy," Hope mutters.

"Sure." I smile and shake my head.

First, we would have to find Lucca, and that in itself would be a mission.

I pop my earbuds into my ears. The bus pulls to the curb, and I'm out of my seat, heading for the front of the bus before it's even stopped. Harold, the bus driver, gives me a tight-lipped smile as I descend the stairs. The air is cooler now, and the chill of it smacks me in the face as I step off the bus. Like clockwork, I do the same thing I do every day.

I adjust my earbuds and pretend I'm fiddling with my cell phone in my pocket, trying to find a song even though I'm not listening to music.

Call it what you will, but I hate making people repeat themselves or them thinking I didn't hear them if they try to talk to me. Plus, I read in a magazine once that people are less likely to talk to you if you have earbuds in.

My adopted parents' house is only two blocks from here, but the same paranoia I feel every day skates up my spine. You would think since I go through this five days a week that I would be used to being watched and followed, but it seems I'm not.

Glancing over my shoulder, left and then right, I find no one there.

Annoyance nags at the back of my mind. Even after all these years, he has never stopped watching me. There is always someone there, being his eyes and ears. In my mind, he's never too far away. I should be grateful, and I am. Lucca helped me get into a nice foster home, which helped me get adopted by two of the kindest people I've ever met, but that doesn't mean that I've forgotten what he did. If it wasn't for Lucca, I wouldn't be in this situation to begin with.

No, you'd still be unloved and beaten. Probably starving and near death somewhere.

I shake the thought away. Before that night, I saw Lucca as a white knight, a man who could do no wrong. The memory of him with blood on his hands refuses to leave my mind.

It haunts me day and night, repeating over and over like a nightmare. He was a savage beast who would not stop until there was nothing left of his prey, and I got to see him unravel. So while he might be my protector, I know he's also capable of terrible things, and for all the good he's done, there is always some type of bad that counteracts it.

Sadly, I haven't seen him in six years, and somehow, I can still recall his features.

Those liquid pools of blue that shined like jewels in the light. I imagine he's even more of a man now, taller and leaner, maybe even fitter with bulging muscles.

Even thinking about him makes my heart race. When I was a little girl, I never would've thought of him in such a scandalizing way.

He was like a brother to me, but the more time that's passed, the more curious I've become. It's probably because of all the romance novels I've been reading.

I remind myself of how wrong it is to think of him in any way that doesn't include hate. A long time ago, I feared him. Now I'm just annoyed and angry. He killed my father, right in front of me, took my entire life, and shook it like it was a snow globe scattering all the broken pieces before I could catch them.

At the end of the day, my father was abusive; he hurt me, but he was still my dad, and I've learned over the years that you can't choose your parents. I watched Lucca beat him to death that night, and there was nothing I could do to forget the absent look that appeared in his eyes. Nothing that would ever make me see him as the white knight again.

He became a different person that night, and I want nothing to do with that man.

The fact he still watches and protects me after all these years is surprising enough, but I don't understand why. I'm not his problem anymore, so why does it always feel like his eyes are on me even when I can't see him?

2

LUCCA

I want to both strangle and hug Markus at the same time. A week ago, the bastard got a hair up his ass and bought some girl at an auction. I don't know all the details, but he took her and dragged her to one of Julian's safe houses.

It wasn't a common occurrence for made men to take time off, but what the hell was Julian going to do? Killing Markus would be more harmful to him than good.

It didn't change the fact that I wanted to sucker punch him in the throat for leaving out of the blue, but it would be a lie to say I wasn't thankful as well. Julian let me take Markus' place in line, which is not only an immense responsibility but also a huge honor.

At twenty-four, I'm younger than most of the men I oversee now. Still, I'm given the same respect that Markus had. Julian has always treated me well, but having him take me as his second in command is a whole new level of trust.

By the time I get to my apartment, it's after two in the morning, and all I want to do is take a shower and hit the hay, but first, there is something else I need to do. The same thing I do every day when I walk into my place.

I open my laptop and type in my password. The screen comes to life, but I have to type in yet another code before my email opens up. Mike has sent me his normal daily update, and I scroll through it to see what Claire has been up to.

Before I read a single word, I pull up the attached pictures. Through the window of the cafeteria, I see her sitting at the table, her best friend occupying the chair next to her as they share some kind of dessert. She smiles, her green eyes shine bright even in the picture.

The second photo is a closeup shot outside in front of her house. Her hair shimmers like fire, the sun reflecting a million different shades of red and orange. Freckles cover the skin around her cheeks and nose, almost as if a painter has put them there artfully, each tiny freckle placed with a purpose.

The third and final image is further away. She is standing on her back porch, stretching her arms above her head like she just worked out. She is only wearing shorts and a tank top, her body lean, and her curves apparent in this outfit.

I'm glad she'd never wear anything like this to school. She dresses modestly for her age, and I'm more than happy about that. It's hard for me to see her as anything besides the little girl next door, but it gets hard to ignore her growing up.

Soon the boys around her will notice too, and then I might have to rough up some sixteen-year-old guy for having indecent thoughts about Claire.

Part of me knows I'm being overprotective. She is a teenager. She is growing up, and yes, eventually, she will date, but it's hard to let that happen. She is like a sister to me, and I need to protect her, protect her innocence.

Shaking the thought away of Claire with a boyfriend, I read the report.

At first, I read nothing out of the ordinary, breakfast with her parents, lunch with her friend, Hope, a math test during third period. It's not until the last paragraph that something catches my attention.

Those girls have been messing with Claire for a while now, but today they have taken it too far. They got physical, and I will not stand for that.

I type a quick message to Mike.

Take care of those girls. I want them transferred to a different school.

Not wanting to wait for an answer, I'm about to close out of my emails when a new one pops up.

Unknown sender: We need to talk.

I stare at the screen for a few moments before deciding to delete the email without responding. I have no idea how they even got this email, but frankly, I don't care enough to find out.

Just as I hit delete, another email pops up. This one has no text at all. It's simply an image that has my blood running cold.

Claire.

A million thoughts and questions run rampant in my mind as I take in the picture. It's Claire on the back porch, wearing the same clothes that she wore in the picture Mike sent me. This one was taken from a different angle, but they clearly took it today.

How can this be possible? No one knows about her. I have kept my distance. I've been more than careful. I stayed away and only had Mike—someone I trust with my life—watch her.

Fuck.

I can't let her get hurt. She's an innocent. Hell, she's as innocent now as the day I met her.

Walking through the living room, I stop when I reach the back door. My fingers graze the cold copper doorknob as I look through the dirty glass. I'm not sure why, but I'm shocked to find a little girl sitting outside in the grass, her eyes glued on my door.

The door creaks loudly as I open it, and the cool autumn breeze slaps me in the face. The little girl doesn't even move or blink. She just remains sitting, staring at me with big green eyes as if she is in awe.

As I step out onto the porch, I get a better look at her and find she can't be much older than ten. Her hair is red, bright red, the kind that would get you made fun of in school. I'm tempted to walk across the grass to see her features but realize a moment later that would probably scare her.

Still, my feet move without thought, and I stop just a few feet from her. She cranes her neck back to continue staring at me, and I notice the smattering of freckles across her nose and cheekbones. I can tell she is poor, just as most people in this neighborhood are. The purple sweater she is wearing is ripped at the cuff, and the colors on the printed butterfly on her chest are faded.

She keeps staring at me, like she can't believe I'm standing here.

"My name's Lucca, and what's your name?" I pause for a fraction of a second, "Butterfly?" I point to her shirt and smile.

She looks down at the butterfly on her shirt and then back up at me. Her gaze never wavers. In fact, the intensity of her stare grows, becoming two weights that press down on my shoulders.

Even though she is a little girl, I can only imagine all that she's been through in such a small amount of time. If she's living here, she's seen things, probably experienced things. There are far worse hardships in life than being poor.

"Do you speak, butterfly?" I ask, even though I should turn around and walk my ass back inside.

Her green eyes glisten like small emeralds in the afternoon sun. All she does is nod her head, no words passing her lips—annoyance tugs at me.

Why hasn't she spoken?

Maybe because you're a stranger, idiot?

"I just moved in next door. I saw you through the window staring at me." I sigh and scratch at the back of my head with one of my hands. "You know, this is a dangerous neighborhood. You shouldn't be sitting outside by yourself."

It's a statement, not a question.

She shrugs, unfazed by my words. Obviously, she knows the type of people that lurk around these places. So why sit here? Does she not care? Or does she think no one will hurt her because she is a girl? Either way, I don't feel comfortable leaving her out here alone.

"Where are your parents?" Maybe if I give them a scolding and scare them a little, they won't just let their daughter sit outside by herself.

At the mere mention of her parents, fear flashes across her face, lighting up her features like a lightning bolt zinging across the stormy night sky. The fine hairs on the back of my neck stand on end. As soon as the look appears, it's gone, and I wonder, for a millisecond, if I imagined seeing it.

My lips part and the next question I plan to ask her is hanging on the tip of my tongue. It's then that the loud creak of a door meets my ears, and I look up and over the girl's head to find a large man about as tall as me, stepping out onto the porch. That must be her father.

His gaze is murderous as it lands on me, and I can tell in an instant that there is something else about him, but I can't put my finger on it.

Butterfly turns and peers over her shoulder at him.

"Get your little ass back in the house right now!" The man glowers at her, and like an obedient doll, butterfly pushes off the ground and strides through the grass.

I clench my hands into tight fists, unsure why I feel a protective pull toward this girl. My eyes remain on her the entire time, and I catch the way her body stiffens just the slightest as she slips past the man and into the house.

Something is off about him and about her, and I don't like it. Not one bit. His gaze narrows, and he stares at me for another second, before walking into the house. The door closes with a creak, and then he is gone, right along with butterfly. I shake off the bad feeling and head back into my house, leaving the nameless girl in the back of my mind.

Whoever this is, whatever they want, I can't ignore it. I need to keep her safe, no matter the cost. I already failed her once. I won't fail her again.

3

CLAIRE

The weekend passes way too quickly. Hope and I spend the entire time locked in my bedroom binge-watching *Riverdale* and talking about winter formal. I'm not going, not because I don't have a date or a guy interested in me. It's because anything with loud music, the dark, or crowds gives me anxiety.

When I arrive at school, I climb the steps and find Hope is waiting for me at my locker. Her blonde hair is like a beacon of light. She smiles when she sees me, and I tighten my hold on my backpack.

"Good morning. I feel like I just saw you." Hope cocks her head to the side. A second passes, and we both break out into laughter.

"It couldn't have anything to do with the fact that you literally saw me yesterday?"

"Nah, definitely not that." She shakes her head.

I slip my backpack off my shoulder and get my books out, putting everything in its perfect spot inside my locker. My first class is English and one that I enjoy a lot, minus the wicked witches in the class.

"I feel like I'm doing something wrong by not coming with you to English. We've been connected at the hip all weekend." Hope pouts as I grab my books and close my locker.

"You'll survive." I smile.

Together we walk to class, Hope waves goodbye when we part ways, and I slip into Mr. Daniels' classroom. As soon as I step inside, I know something is wrong. The usual seats of the three wicked witches are empty. Nervous anxiety twists in my gut.

With hesitant steps, I take my seat, but I'm unable to look away from their desks. It's not likely that all three of them are sick. No, something else happened. More students trickle into the room, taking their time to reach their seats. Mr. Daniels sits in the room's corner behind his desk, his face void of emotion as his eyes move over us. After a moment, Mr. Daniels stands and moves from behind his desk.

"Take your seats. Your time to socialize ended the moment you walked through my classroom door."

A few students shake their heads, but after another minute, everyone's in their seats and quiet. I open my book to the last chapter we read in class and prepare to take notes.

"As you can see, there are three empty seats in the class today. To save you the trouble of figuring out what happened. I'm going to tell you myself." There is a long pause, probably added for dramatics, and it makes the ache in my gut more profound. I already know something bad happened. "The girls have transferred to another school."

Transferred? Ha, no. This is something else. Anger replaces my previous emotions. Lucca had something to do with this. I know it. It isn't the first time he's meddled in my life, and I don't like it. It makes me feel like I can't fend for myself.

Like I need him to protect me when I don't.

The rest of the students don't even blink at what Mr. Daniels said, but I have to wonder if Lucca had them killed or taken somewhere. I've heard stories about him, about what he does and who he works for. The mob doesn't just transfer people. They dispose of them, make them disappear.

Would he kill three girls, who, yes, were mean bitches, but just kids? *Yes, yes, he would.* He killed my father, so he would kill anyone in my eyes. I find it hard to concentrate but force myself to. I can't let Lucca ruin my day, can't let him cloud my mind. I'll never know the answers to the questions I have, so there isn't any point in dwelling on them.

Lucca will never show himself in my life again, and part of me is grateful for that, while another part of me is curious to see him again.

BEFORE I KNOW IT, lunch is here. Hope gets roped into helping a new student, so I grab my tray of food and head outside. I don't have many friends, and I'm not going to subject myself to finding a table in this crowded lunchroom.

Instead, I turn to the right and head out the doors that lead outside. There's a tree a few yards away, and I choose to eat my lunch there. A soft breeze blows through my hair, and I sigh, leaning back against the bark while eating my apple.

My phone buzzes in the pocket of my hoodie, and I half expect it to be Hope calling to yell at me for not being more ambitious and finding a spot in the lunchroom. Color me shocked to see that it isn't her, but an unknown number.

I stare at the screen, wondering if I should answer it. Something tells me to let it go to voicemail, but curiosity nags on me more. Against my better judgment, I hit the answer key. Holding my breath, I bring the phone to my good ear and listen intently.

"Hello, butterfly." The air in my lungs stills and my heart skips a beat. His voice is rich, gravely, and deeper. The maturity of it reminds me of how long it's been since I've heard him.

For a few seconds, I'm rendered speechless, and when I find my voice again, anger has replaced my shock about Lucca calling me. How dare he just call me out of the blue after six years.

"Don't call me that," I growl, holding the phone a little tighter. I should just hang up. Yeah, hang up and never talk to him again.

He breathes into the phone. "I'm sorry. I know you're angry with me."

I snort, but nothing I'm about to say is funny. "Angry? No, I'm not angry. I want you to leave me alone. Don't you think you've done enough? Caused me enough pain?"

"My intentions weren't to hurt you, and I know I did." Why is he admitting these things? I toss my apple down onto the tray of half-eaten food.

"Stop admitting your wrongs. Why did you call me? Why now? What do you want?" I hiss through my teeth. My cheeks feel hot, and I hate the way my stomach clenches every time he speaks. It reminds me of who he used to be, how much those moments with him meant to my young self. I should've known how dangerous he was then, but I didn't. I just wanted a friend.

"I'm only calling to check on you."

"You don't need to check on me, and you've never called before."

"Don't be like that, butterfly."

I grit my teeth to stop myself from lashing out. I hate that he still calls me by the name he called me when I was ten years old. Looking out into the courtyard, I let the silence between us drag on.

"I'm only trying to protect you, Claire." He shatters the silence.

"How? By killing people? Did you kill those girls? They didn't transfer, did they?" I accuse.

Lucca chuckles. "I didn't hurt them. I just made them leave. I'm not that heartless that I would kill three high school kids for bullying, but I made you a promise that day in the hospital, and I'm a man of my word. I'll always protect you, even from a group of mean girls."

His words would be heartfelt if I didn't hate him for ruining my life.

"I don't want your protection." I shove a loose strand of bright red hair behind my ear. "Actually, I don't need it. I'm fine. I want you to leave me alone."

"You don't know what you need," Lucca interjects, annoyance dripping from his voice.

"I'm not a child. My childhood died the day my father did," I bite out, knowing it's a jab that will hit him right where it hurts. Plus, it's a lie. My childhood died long before that day.

When he doesn't say anything right away, I add, "I'm not asking you to stop following me. I'm telling you."

"No."

"No?" I challenge.

"No. I couldn't stop, not even if I wanted to. Your protection is the most important thing to me. I'm not going anywhere, Claire, and nothing you say or do will change that."

The possessive tone of his voice makes me shiver, and I know he's not lying, he's never going to stop following me or protecting me.

"What do you want from me?" Tears form in my eyes, and I blink them away. "I just want you to leave me alone, please," I whisper the last part, trying to keep the emotions from bleeding into my voice.

"I'm sorry, Claire. I can't." His voice is steel, an iron shackle around my ankle locking closed. "Eat your lunch and get inside. I don't want you to get sick."

My jaw clenches, and I pull the phone away from my ear, angrily pressing the red end key. Looking around, I scan the area for him or someone else watching me. He has to be close, or he wouldn't know what I'm doing. Of course, I don't see anyone. I never do, but I know he is close.

I hate him. I hate he saved me and that he still protects me. I hate that I ever said hi to him because maybe if I didn't my father would still be here.

I know it's rude to watch people. To stare at them. I don't like it when people stare at me, but I can't help myself. Ever since he moved in a few weeks ago, I'm fascinated by the man that calls himself Lucca. I wonder if he would like to be my friend. I know he is older, but a friend can be anyone, and I want Lucca to be mine.

A frown forms on my face at the reminder of my lack of friends. I have no one to talk to, no one that likes me. My father only lets me leave the house for school, and the kids at school all think I'm weird because my clothes are old and stained. I wouldn't dare embarrass myself further by explaining to them that my mother left and that my father, even though he works, likes to drink most of our money away.

"I don't want you outside. Stay in the house, Claire. If I come home and find out you've been outside, I'll lock you up." The vein on the side of his head bulges, and his fists tighten. My entire body tenses, and my heart thunders in my chest.

Is he going to hit me again?

The thought makes me sick to my stomach. I keep it a secret, mainly because no one would care anyway, and also because I'm more afraid of losing my father than I am of his fists.

"I'll stay inside. I promise." I let the lie roll off my tongue. He has no way of knowing if I go out, I just have to be careful.

The disapproving look he gives me tells me he doesn't believe me, but he doesn't say anything else. He simply heads for the door and walks out, slamming it closed behind him.

I'm bouncing on the heels of my feet with excitement when I rush toward the back porch and press my face against the cold window to look outside. As soon as I spot Lucca sitting on his porch, I unlock the door and pull it open. Happiness bubbles up in my belly, and it feels like Christmas morning back when Momma and Daddy were both home, and Daddy wasn't drinking or raising his fists to Momma or me.

Taking a deep breath, I stare at the man. I should fear him. I don't know him. He is a stranger to me, and yet he doesn't seem like a stranger.

The moment he hears the creak of the door, his gaze lifts, and our eyes collide. I'm suspended in time for a second, and my chest hurts, my heart galloping like a racehorse inside of it. I told myself that if I got the chance to talk to him this time, I would be better prepared, but it seems once again, I'm not.

He has the ability to leave me speechless, and I don't understand why. He makes me nervous, but not in a scary way.

"Hey, butterfly." He gives me a small wave.

"Hi."

"She speaks!" His lips curl into a smile, and the tension eases from my stomach.

"Claire... My name is Claire," I introduce myself.

"Nice to meet you, Claire." He holds out his hand like he wants me to shake it.

I look at it for a moment before deciding to close the distance between us and put my hand in his. That's when our size difference really hits me. My hand looks so small and dainty as I place it in his ginormous one. For a second, I think he is going to crush my bones, but when his grip closes around mine, it's gentle and soft.

As soon as I let go, I take a step back, feeling like I need to put some space between us. I take a seat on the edge of his patio and watch him take a sip of his beer.

"Where did you live before you moved here?" I ask curiously.

"A lot of different places. I moved from one foster family to the next until I aged out. Now I work and got my own place," he explains.

"What do you do for work?"

"Something different every day. Odd jobs, I guess." His answer is vague.

"What happened to your parents? Why were you in foster care?"

He chuckles. "First, you don't talk at all, and now you come at me with all these questions."

"Sorry." My cheeks heat. "You don't have to answer."

"Nah, it's fine. I never met my dad, and my mom died when I was little. Car accident."

"I'm sorry your mom died. Mine left when I was eight." On my eighth birthday, to be exact, but I don't mention that part. "It's my fault she left."

"I don't believe that, for a second. Why would you think it was your fault?"

Because my dad tells me it is all the time.

I shrug. "I just know."

He looks off into the distance and takes another drink of his beer. Usually, when my father drinks, I'm tense and stay hidden in my room until the morning. I'm not scared of this man, even though I know I should be.

"Well, you're wrong. You're just a kid; if your mom's gone, it's because she chose to leave. Not because you did anything."

All I can do is shake my head and look away. "Maybe, but that's not what my dad says."

"Your dad's stupid," he growls, and I jump, startled by the sound that comes from his mouth. "Sorry, I didn't mean to scare you," he adds.

"It's okay." My voice comes out squeaky.

Turning the conversation around, he asks, "What do you do for fun?" I cock my head to the side and stare at him. If there was anyone I could've pictured as prince charming, it would be him. I feel safe with him, protected.

"Usually, I just read or sit outside. That's when I'm not at school. I'm usually pretty bored, though, especially when my dad is at work."

"Does he work a lot?" Lucca asks.

I nod. "Yeah, but when he isn't at work, he's sleeping or drinking so..." I realize I've said too much and press my lips together to stop myself from saying anything more.

Lucca's features darken, and he leans in, his eyes zeroing in on my face, making me feel like I'm being inspected. "If you need *anything, butterfly, you can come to me. I will help you. Day or night."*

Maybe my life would be different if I had never talked to him, or maybe I would be worse off. I wipe at the stray tears that fall from my eyes and trail down my cheeks.

Why does he continue to do this?

I'm no longer his responsibility.

No longer his problem, and still, he protects me.

I have to prove to him I don't need him anymore. I have to make him go away. There's no other option.

4

LUCCA

My heart slams against my ribcage like it's trying to escape as I pull up to the cabin where Markus has been hiding out. I'm not sure what to expect inside. I can only hope that he doesn't realize anything is off.

Fuck! Not in a million years did I think it would ever come to this. The Moretti family has been the only family I've known. I don't want to cross them, and not only because I know I will die if they ever find out. No, my loyalties are genuine. I don't want anything to happen to Julian and Elena. Just like I want nothing to happen to Markus or any of the guys, but I have no choice. I can't let Claire down.

For the last few days, I've been feeding my mystery blackmailer information. So far, it's petty stuff, but I know it's not going to stay like that for long. He is simply testing me now. Seeing how far I will go and how far I will take it to protect Claire.

I've briefly played with the idea of asking Julian for help, but he already helped me once, and now that he has

Elena, he will not risk any weakness. I have to deal with this myself. I have to take out this threat, and I need to do it fast. Let's just hope Markus is going to help me with this.

I get out of the car and walk up to the cabin. I don't even have to knock. As soon as my foot touches the first step leading up to the door, the door swings open.

"Hey," I greet.

"Come in." Markus nods and gestures for me to come in.

Stepping into the living room, my eyes land almost immediately on the blonde woman standing a few feet away.

"Lucca, this is Fallon. Fallon, this is Lucca," Markus introduces us with a grunt.

"It's nice to meet you," Fallon replies meekly. She is clearly nervous, maybe even scared. Like the bastard I am, her fear excites me.

I wonder what Markus has been doing to her. After all, he bought her at an auction, an auction she certainly didn't attend willingly. He has been keeping her here, locked away from the world, at his mercy.

Letting my gaze drift over her body, I take in every curve. She is beautiful, and I wouldn't mind keeping her locked up for myself.

Her stare turns from fear to terror as she catches me sizing her up with interest.

"Fallon was just going to start the sides for dinner," Markus hisses through his teeth, his eyes shooting daggers at Fallon before giving me the same death stare.

"Oh, yeah." Fallon's voice is shaky, but she tries her best to act normal. "I'll be in the kitchen if anyone needs me."

I watch her scurry away before turning to Markus. I raise

my eyebrows at him, wondering what he is waiting for. I am here for a reason, after all.

"Not yet," he growls under his breath. "Let's go outside so I can tell you the whole plan."

He grabs a plate of steaks from the table and heads out the side door where I assume the grill will be.

"What are we waiting for?" I ask. I don't want to rush him, but I really don't want to stay long either.

"We'll eat first, then we'll do it."

"Got it." Steaks first, interrogation later.

This will be fun.

"Fallon," Markus' deep voice booms through the room, "come here."

Fallon drops the dish back into the water and dries her hands quickly.

She turns around and heads toward us. When she sees us both standing in the living room, her steps falter. I can see fear and dread in her eyes, both valid emotions at the moment. She will not like what we have planned.

Her gaze ping pongs between Markus and me, and I'm positive she is thinking about running. Not that she would have any chance of getting away. She must realize it, too, since she is not making a move.

"Come. Here," Markus orders, sterner this time. "Stand in front of me."

With shaking legs, she follows his command and stops right in front of him. I move behind her, sandwiching her between us with nowhere to go.

She twists her head to look at me, but Markus grabs her by the chin with two fingers and pulls her back.

"Eyes on me, Fallon." His voice is smoke wisping through the air.

"What are you doing?" Fallon asks, her voice small and unsure.

"We're going to play a game. I'm going to ask you some questions, and you're going to answer them truthfully. Each time I think you're lying, Lucca is going to take one item of clothing off your body. If you are naked by the end of the game, you lose, and you don't want to be the loser in this game. Do you understand?"

She doesn't answer, does not move, probably petrified with fear. If I didn't know she is hiding something, I might actually feel bad for the girl.

"I'm going to take that as a yes," Markus says. He doesn't even skip a beat and jumps right into things.

"First question. Did you know the guy with the camera?"

"No." She shakes her head. Markus inspects her for a moment, his eyes narrowing.

"I believe you," he finally says. "So, you didn't know him. Fine. Next question. Do you know who sent him?"

"No."

Even I notice how her shoulders twitch. She is lying. Markus saw it too. He shakes his head, as if disappointed.

"Do you want to reconsider that answer?" Markus warns, giving her one last chance.

She stays silent.

Markus looks past her and to me. We're both so much taller than her, we can easily lock eyes over her head. He gives me the signal, and I grab the hem of Fallon's shirt to pull it up. She automatically raises her arms, letting me take it off, but I don't miss how her arms are trembling with fear.

I drop it on the floor next to us, leaving her in a pair of leggings and bra. Goosebumps spread across her body, and I'm sure it's not only because of the chill in the room.

"Next question. Do you have a boyfriend?"

"No." She shakes her head, strands of blonde hair flying around her head.

"Were you really going to call your parents from my office?"

"Yes." That lie falls from her lips a little easier, but Markus still sees right through her.

Shaking his head again, he motions to me again. I make quick work of undoing her bra. I push the straps slowly off her arms and let it fall to the floor carelessly.

"Were you sent to the auction by someone?"

"No."

Another small shake of Markus's head, and I push my fingers into the waistband of her leggings. I pull them down her toned legs, leaving her in nothing but a pair of thin panties.

"Did someone send you to get to me?" Markus's voice is nothing more than a growl now. He is angry. Really fucking angry. I didn't think he would go through with this at first, but seeing him now, I think he just might.

"No." She shakes her head before lowering it slightly. She knows what's coming, she knows she is lying, the question is why?

I dip my fingers into the sides of her panties and pull them down so roughly, I make her gasp. Her knees are shaking, she looks so weak, and I think she might scramble to the floor soon.

"Get on your knees," Markus orders, just as I hear him undoing his pants.

My cock twitches in my jeans as I take in Fallon's naked body. I wonder if he is really going to share her with me. I certainly wouldn't mind.

I put my hands on her shoulders and push her down gently. She is so scared, I figured she would go easily, but instead of obeying and getting down on her knees, she shrugs away from my hold and lunges herself at Markus. Wrapping her slender arms around his torso, she buries her face into his chest.

"I'm sorry. Please, don't do this. I'm sorry, I'm sorry," she begs, repeating herself over and over again.

For the longest time, Markus doesn't move. He simply looks at me with conflict in his eyes. This girl has him wrapped around her little finger, and I'm not sure if I should laugh about this or simply be worried.

A moment later, Markus wraps his arms around her small quivering body, engulfing her completely while pulling her closer into his chest.

"Go upstairs to the bedroom and wait there for me. Don't do anything else. Don't fucking touch anything else. Go straight to the bedroom and wait on the bed. Do you understand?"

"Yes," she blurts out, nodding her head furiously.

She doesn't bother picking up her clothes. She simply untangles herself from Markus and runs up the stairs without another glance back.

"Wipe that fucking smirk off your fucking face."

"I knew you wouldn't go through with it." I grin.

"Shut up and get out of here." He points to the door.

"Do you want me to do it? While you're gone, I mean." I barely get the words out before Markus pounces on me. His hands wrap around my throat, and he growls into my face like a feral animal.

"Don't even fucking think about touching her again. This was a one-time thing."

I laugh and shove him away. "You told me to, stupid."

"I know!" he roars.

"How would you feel about me offering to *take care* of Claire?"

My body stiffens, and I wipe every trace of a smile from my face. "Don't even talk like that. It's completely different, and you fucking know it."

The only reason he even knows about Claire is because I had to ask him to check on her when Mike suddenly stopped contacting me. He doesn't know much about her or my relationship with her, but he knows enough to keep his mouth shut about it.

"Sure, it is. Now get out. I have things to take care of." He opens the front door, ready to shove me out.

"Whoa, I didn't drive out here just to help you."

"I remember. I was hoping you would forget to bring up whatever it was you wanted to talk about."

"You're an asshole." I shake my head.

"What do you need to tell me or better yet, ask me?" Markus grips onto the wooden door like he is about to take a chunk out of it.

"Your brother, Felix. Are you still in contact with him?" I ask carefully.

"Yes," he replies, a bit annoyed sounding.

"Could you give me his number? I need help with something, and your brother is the man for hacking and tracking down people."

"First, he's not cheap. Two, if Julian finds out you're working with him—"

"He won't. This is none of Julian's business, and it doesn't affect the family in any way. This is for me and me alone."

"I don't want to be dragged into this mess, so keep my name out of it. I'll text you his number, and only because I feel bad for you."

"You won't be. Thanks, fucker. If you need anything, let me know."

"We're not friends," Markus growls.

I can't withhold a snicker. "Sure, we aren't, asshole."

Markus slams the door shut behind me, and I get back into the car feeling lighter. With Felix's help, I'll find whoever is behind this quickly. And then I'm going to put an end to this once and for all.

5

CLAIRE

"I can do the dishes," I offer after we finish eating.

"I've got it, honey," Tracy, my adoptive mom, waves me away. "Why don't you finish your homework, and I'll clean the kitchen."

"Do you need help with that project you were talking about earlier?" Steven, my adoptive dad, asks rather loudly. They are always considerate of my hearing, speaking louder when I'm not looking at them.

Turning to face him, I smile. "Oh, no. I'm already done with it, actually. I have some reading to do, but other than that, I'm finished with assignments for the week."

"That's great, no wonder you're a straight-A student. Always ahead." Tracy smiles. "Maybe tomorrow after school we can do something fun? Get mani-pedis together? Go shopping at the mall? We could take Hope with us," she offers, her eyes lighting up with excitement.

"Sure, that sounds fun." I grin.

When I first came to live with Tracy and Steven, I didn't

know what to expect. I had heard so many horror stories about kids in the system. I figured I would be miserable here until I turned eighteen. My expectations were low, which made finding out how truly amazing they were even more special.

They could never have children of their own, so they were happy to take me in. Tracy quit her job as an accountant so she could take care of my every need. Steven is a car salesman at the local dealership. I don't know their situation with money, but he must sell a lot of cars because they never seem to worry about funds.

If I just mention my need for new clothes, Tracy takes me shopping the next day. If I simply hint at wanting anything, it's mine within the week, which is why I normally keep everything to myself. I'm eternally thankful for all they've done for me, how they took me into their home to care for me, which is exactly why I don't want them to have to spend all their money on me. They've done enough.

"I'll head upstairs then to—"

I'm interrupted by a knock at the door. All three of us look between each other, asking without words if one of us knows who could be at the door. I don't have a lot of friends, and if it was Hope, she wouldn't knock, she'd just come in.

"I'll get it," Steven finally says.

It's not that late, only seven, but normally no one comes by. Curious, I peek around the corner to the front door. Steven opens the door, and right away, a large figure moves inside the house.

"Oh, hey... I didn't expect you to come by." Steven steps to the side, and Lucca's face comes into view. My blood runs cold, and it's not only because Lucca is here.

The way Steven opened the door and allowed him to walk

inside... like he has been here before. There is a familiarity between them, as if they talk regularly. I can tell just by their body language, something I've become very good at reading over the years.

I don't know why I didn't piece it together before.

"Evening," Lucca greets, his hands shoved into the pockets of his leather jacket that's molded to his body like a second skin. His presence makes the room feel small.

A gasp builds in my throat, but I swallow it down. All I can do is stare. Absorbing every inch of the man before my eyes. It's like I'm looking at a different person. I never remember him being like this. He's huge, taller, and his body is filled out. Broad shoulders and a tapered waist give him the lean but athletic look. His amber eyes are very much the same, reminding me of a time when things were different. The contours of his face are angular, with sharp edges that could cut you with a single turn of his head.

His full lips press into a hard line, intensifying his darkness. There is an edge to him that terrifies me.

"How... how do you know him?" My voice wobbles, and my eyes dart between my parents. This is worse than I thought. The apologetic look that overtakes both their faces confirms my suspicion.

Tracy exhales. "We were going to tell you. I..."

My mind shuts down, and all I can feel is the heavy thump of my heart in my chest. Betrayal slices through me and the sharp dagger of it seems to get lodged in my chest.

"I should've known." Disappointment bleeds through me like ink on a piece of paper, and I whirl around, rushing up the staircase to my bedroom.

I make it up three steps before Lucca is trailing me up the

stairs. It's stupid, but as soon as I reach my bedroom door, I slip inside and whirl around to slam it shut. That would work if I weren't going against such a brute of a man. Placing his foot between the door and the jamb, he makes it impossible for me to lock him out.

"A flimsy wooden door will not stop me, butterfly," he grunts as I push against the wood, willing the door to close.

My hands ache where I grip the wooden frame. I don't know why I'm trying to stop him from getting in here. Just like that, I let go of the door and stumble backward. He advances, tugging the door all the way open before marching inside like a soldier heading to battle.

For every step he takes, I take two back, and I don't stop until my legs hit the edge of the bed. It's impossible not to cower when facing a man as lethal as him. A man that kills with his bare hands.

My body trembles, and I suck my bottom lip into my mouth to stop myself from crying out. I've seen this man kill. I know the power he had years ago, and now he's bigger, stronger, and ten times more intimidating.

Like a wolf stalking its prey, he moves closer to me, and I startle, crab walking backward on the bed. He must read my features because a second later, he stops, his features soften, and the dark glint in his eyes disappears. For a moment, he was that man that I didn't know, the man that he is around everyone else.

"I'm sorry. I didn't mean to scare you." His voice is soft, giving off the alluring charm that everything is going to be okay, but it isn't. I know better. If he is here, it isn't going to be okay.

He looks away, running a hand through his dark blonde hair. It's a little longer than it was the last time I saw him.

When he speaks again, our gazes collide. "I'm not going to hurt you. I would never... I wish I were here under different circumstances, but..." He pauses as if he's trying to keep his frustration in check.

"But what?" I croak.

"I need you to leave for a while." His voice is so low, I have to read his lips, but there is no mistake in what he just said.

My eyes widen, and my mouth pops open. "What do you mean you need me to leave for a while? I don't understand."

Lucca steps closer, his eyebrows drawn together, and he looks like he wants to apologize but presses his lips together to stop himself. That's fine. I don't want his apology. I want nothing from him.

"It's temporary. I'm sending you and your parents on a mini-vacation until it's safe to come back."

"Safe to come back?" My lip curls with anger.

"Yes. I'm doing this to protect you. It's the only—"

"I don't care what you want," I yell, cutting him off mid-sentence. "I'm not leaving. I can't. Steven has to work, and I have school. We can't just get up and leave whenever we want."

"You don't have to worry about that. It's all taken care of. Money is not an issue. It hasn't been for a long time."

His words trickle into my brain, and slowly I'm seeing everything around me with new eyes. It all makes sense now. How I could have anything and everything I wanted. How Tracy and Steven adopted me. It wasn't because of fate or because my parents were working overtime to make ends meet. No. It was because of him. *Lucca.*

Another wave of betrayal hits me. This one bigger than the last. I thought they loved me. I thought they actually cared about me.

Was it all just a show? Did they only care because Lucca paid them to?

Disappointment, dread, and anger hit me all at once. I let the anger rise because the other two are simply too hard to deal with right now.

"I'm not going anywhere," I scream, taking all my frustration out at him.

In a second, he is on me, his huge frame caging me in, and I flinch, afraid of what might happen next. He said he wouldn't hurt me, but I don't trust him. I don't trust anyone, and especially not someone who does the things he does.

Pinching my chin between two fingers, he stares down at me with disappointment and a low simmering rage in his eyes.

"You will pack a bag, and you will get on that plane with your parents because if you don't, I'll have to do something you don't want me to do."

My bottom lip trembles. "You said you wouldn't hurt me."

His amber eyes become luminescent. "I won't, but there are other ways of getting to you that don't directly inflict pain on your body."

I want to hit him; I've never wanted to hit someone as bad as I want to right now. I want to hurt him like he hurts me. Maybe even more so.

Turning my head, I break his hold on my chin and lean back, so I can see his face.

"You might be able to get me to do what you want now, but it won't be like this forever. Someday, I'll fight back. Someday, I'll escape you," I grit each word through my teeth, letting him know I will break free of this prison he has me trapped in.

He smiles, and a row of perfectly straight white teeth appear from behind his lips, and I swear it's the most lethal smile ever, like a serial killer smiling before he murders you and your entire family.

"You can try to run, Claire, but I'll always find you. You're mine, and I protect what's mine." The possessiveness in his voice is frightening.

I am his?

What does that mean? I don't get the chance to ask him because he flees from the bedroom and disappears out into the hall, leaving me more confused than ever.

6
LUCCA

Going to see Claire was probably the worst idea I've had in a long time. But I had to make sure they would leave right away, and with Mike missing, I really don't have anyone else I trust with this. When Felix told me that Petro Volocove is behind the threatening emails, I needed to make a move.

Never take Petro lightly. He is a ruthless monster and unfortunately, holds a lot of power. I should have known it was him. The Volocoves' are desperately trying to get to Julian, and I guess they think getting me on their side is the way to go.

The worst part is that he isn't wrong. I'm close enough to Julian that I could inflict some serious damage if I wanted. I don't want to, but to protect Claire, I'd do anything.

Claire's disappointment over seeing me earlier hit me harder than I thought it would. The betrayal in her eyes only added to it. I thought she would have realized by now that what I did was necessary, that killing her father was the right thing to do—the only thing to do.

I wonder if she will ever forgive me for it?

"That's him." Carter's voice drags me from my inner monologue. I look up and across the street where Benny Marone is parking his delivery truck. A moment later, he jumps out and opens the back to unload crates of fruits and vegetables.

"Let's go!" I signal to Carter.

Together, we step out of the shadows of the alleyway and head toward Benny.

Our heavy footsteps echo across the street, causing Benny to look up. As soon as he sees us, his expression becomes somber. He doesn't know who we are, but he recognizes trouble when it stares him in the face.

He pauses and watches us approach carefully.

"Hey, fellas, can I help you with something?" he asks when we are only a few feet away.

"Hey, Benny."

His body stiffens as the realization sets in that we are here for him. "Matter of fact, you can help us with *something*."

I stop right in front of him, so close that it's clear I don't care about his personal space. He takes a step back, but I eat up the space, crowding him more.

"Look, I don't want any trouble." Benny throws his hands up, showing us his palms in the universal sign of surrender. This is my favorite part. When they beg and plead and claim they had no part in anything. I smile, but it's anything but joyful.

"Then you're going to tell us exactly what we want to know, huh?"

"Yes, yes, anything." He nods, his eyes wild.

Fucking pussy.

"You deliver fresh produce to the Moretti Compound?"

"Yes, twice a week," he confirms.

"One of the papayas you delivered last week contained poison. One person almost died, and another *did* die. You wouldn't know anything about that, would you?"

"What? No, no! I know nothing!" Benny shakes his head profusely, but the terror in his eyes tells me he knows exactly what I'm talking about.

I nod toward Carter. "Carter, what do you think? Is Benny here telling the truth?"

Carter rubs at his jaw with two fingers, his eyes narrow as he stares at Benny. "Nope. I'm thinking he's lying."

"Yeah, I agree." Without warning, I grab Benny by the throat. He immediately cowers, and from the way he shakes like a terrified dog, I'm pretty sure he is about to piss his pants too.

"Please," he whimpers, right before I throw the first punch. My fist collides with his jaw, and his head snaps to the side with the impact.

"Tell us what you know," I demand, following up with another punch to his face.

Benny sways on his feet. Carter grabs him by his upper arm and holds him up.

"I didn't know." Benny cries. "I didn't know!"

"You didn't know, what?"

"I didn't know about the poison," he admits.

"But you knew something? Who messed with the shipment?" For good measure, I throw another punch. This one lands on his stomach. I don't want him to pass out, after all.

"I don't know who they are, I swear!" Benny gasps for breath and curls in on himself. "They said all they wanted to do was check the shipment. I thought Moretti sent them. I was going to call to confirm, but the guy said not to. He threatened to hurt my wife if I did."

I shake my head. *Idiot.* I can't blame him for wanting to protect his wife, but in the end, he's now put both of them in danger.

"You should have known better—"

A high-pitched scream behind me cuts off my words. "Nooo!"

I turn to look over my shoulder and stare down the barrel of a gun. Instinctively, I reach for my gun, but a shot rings through the air before my fingers touch the metal. A second shot fires, the bullet whizzing past my head.

Benny lets out a roar that echoes through the back of the alley. He shrugs out of my hold with newfound strength and runs toward his wife, who slinks toward the ground. Blood seeps from the wound in her chest. Benny scoops her up in his arms and cradles her to his chest.

"She was gonna kill you." Distress fills Carter's voice, and I glance over to see him with gun still raised, pointing at Benny's wife. "She was gonna kill you," he repeats, shocked by what he just did.

"I know. You did the right thing," I assure him. Even though this is a major fuck up, I feel sorry for the kid. Killing women is never easy.

"No, no, no…" Benny sobs as his wife takes her last breath.

I see the moment when Benny's fear, sadness, and grief turn into something else.

Blinding Rage.

He pries the gun from his dead wife's hand. But this time, I'm faster. I pull out my gun, aim it at Benny's head, and pull the trigger.

The bullet hits him between the eyes, putting him out of his misery within a blink of an eye. He sags down to the ground, joining his wife on the ground.

"Fuck," Carter murmurs beside me.

"Yeah, fuck." I sigh, placing my gun back in the holster. "This didn't go as planned at all. We've got two people dead and are no closer to finding out who poisoned Elena."

Carter shakes his head. "Julian is not going to like this."

I turn and look over at him. He's just a kid, the same age I was when I started out.

Tonight was only the second time he's ever killed someone, and it was a woman at that. He did good, but I guarantee he won't forget about what he did tonight. The wonderful thing about this job is that it becomes easier with every kill.

"Don't worry about it. It wasn't your fault," I assure Carter, slapping a hand on his shoulder. "You had my back, and I've got yours. Julian will be upset, but we'll figure it out."

"I'm... I'm sorry." Carter's expression becomes anxious.

"Don't." I growl and grab him by the shirt, pulling him into my face. "Do not fucking apologize. This is your job. Dealing out death is what you signed up for. Pull yourself together and move the fuck on. Call for a fucking clean-up crew," I grit through my teeth.

I know the moment I break through his mournful walls because his gaze turns dark once more, and he nods his head. Stepping back, he pulls out his phone and does as I instruct.

I sigh and look up at the night sky. Of course, my thoughts circle back to Claire. If she knew all the things I did to protect her, would she be more understanding?

Probably not.

Claire doesn't understand and never will. Everything I do is for her, even if she doesn't know it.

7
CLAIRE

Even as angry as I am with Lucca, I am in awe of this place. We arrived a few weeks ago, and I'm still in awe. It's secluded, on the beach, and a true sight to see. With my toes in the sand, you would think I'd be a little calmer. I mean, who could stay angry while on a free five-star vacation?

Me. Apparently. I don't want to be here. He forced me here. It was pack a bag and get on the plane or face the consequences, and I've lost enough in my life. I didn't know how unstable Lucca was or what he was willing or unwilling to do.

I couldn't risk my parents' lives, no matter how pissed at them I am for knowing about Lucca all along. Even though I am mad at them right now, I still love and appreciate them. No matter their reason, they cared for me for the last six years.

So, I left my life behind, my best friend, my school, my home. All gone with a blink of an eye. I couldn't even say goodbye to Hope.

A steady breeze blows off the ocean and whips strands of my long red hair around, and the smell of salt makes my nose wrinkle. The sound of the waves crashing against the beach lulls me into a cocoon of calm. I dig my toes into the sand and stare out into the never-ending ocean before looking up at the moon that's hanging high in the sky.

It's a beacon of hope to me, but the crescent shape reminds me of Lucca in that instant. Half shadowed in darkness, hiding from the rest of the world.

Thoughts of Lucca swim through my mind. I shouldn't offer him space in my head, but I can't help it. It's like an addiction, the hate I feel for him. I can't help but need the reminder of how bad he is, especially when he does things like this. I have to remember there is always a hidden agenda.

Pushing to my feet, I grab my sandals and start the walk back to the beach house. Tracy and Steven have been particularly quiet since we arrived, and I'm grateful for that. I don't want to talk about Lucca with them and how they have been talking to him behind my back for years.

I thought they loved me, but now I'm not sure about anything.

I walk up the steps to the house with care. The moon above is the only source of light, and I don't really feel like breaking my neck out here.

I'm surprised when I come in through the sliding glass door and find the kitchen empty and the house silent. My stomach rumbles, reminding me I haven't eaten anything in a few hours. I drop my strappy sandals and walk toward the fridge. There's a basket of fruit on the counter that catches my eye as I pass it, so I turn and grab an apple and then a bottle of water from the fridge.

By the grace of God, I manage to slip into my bedroom without conversation. I let out a long sigh as soon as I see the bed. I'm exhausted. Being constantly angry and trying to avoid my parents for the last few weeks is tiring, but I'm not ready to forgive them yet.

I don't bother eating the apple. Instead, opening the bottle of water, I guzzle the entire thing down. I should really shower, but I can do it in the morning. Once I change into a pair of sleep shorts and an oversized T-shirt, I wash my face and then crawl into bed.

My phone buzzes on the nightstand. I pick it up and find five texts from Hope. I can't help but smile at her usage of emojis. I'm about to respond when a crash makes me pause. It must have been very loud for me to hear it. It takes everything in me to keep my heart in my chest. It beats so loudly that for a brief second, it's all I can hear.

I have no idea what that sound was, but I know it's bad. I can feel it. I'm struck with fear, my body frozen in place, but I can't just stay huddled up in this room. I need to do something. I need to be brave.

Swallowing down my fear, I force myself out of bed and to the door. As soon as I step out of the bedroom, I'm dropped into chaos.

"Where is the girl?" a man screams into Steven's face while another man holds Tracy.

My feet are concrete. I can't move, can't even breathe. What girl? They aren't talking about me, are they?

"Please, don't..." Tracy's plea cuts off as one man backhands her.

A gasp escapes my lips, and the sound dissipates the hazy fear I'm in. I have to stop them before someone gets hurt.

"I'm here, right here," I croak, my fear rising ten octaves when both men turn to face me. Scars cover their faces, and I know without a doubt that this is a fight I cannot win against their huge bodies. "Please, don't hurt them. Please..." I beg because begging is all I have at this moment.

One man looks me up and down and smiles. My skin crawls, and a fresh fear builds there, caused by the way he's looking at me.

"Come here." He gestures for me to walk toward him, and it's then that I catch the glint of a gun in the dim lighting.

No. I won't be responsible for another death. I won't. As afraid as I am to go to him, I'm more afraid of what will happen if I don't. Hesitantly, I walk toward him, doing my best not to look at Steven or Tracy. The moment I do, I know I'll break down.

"Please, she is just a child. She did nothing..." Steven takes a step forward, and I open my mouth to tell him to stop, to shut up, but it's too late. The other man attacks before the words can come, and moments later, Steven is on the ground, huddled in the fetal position. Instinct makes me rush to his aide, but I make it all of two feet before an arm wraps around my middle, and I'm hauled backward into a hard chest.

"Please, don't hurt him. Please..." my voice cracks, and I struggle to break free of the man's grasp. I don't even realize I'm crying till I taste the salty tang of my tears on my lips.

"If you're a good girl and come with us, then maybe we won't hurt him too badly."

"Please..." The world around me spins as I watch the other man kick Steven in the side repeatedly. I swear I can hear bones cracking. Tracy screams for him to stop. Her tear-filled eyes gut me, and all over again, I'm losing someone I care about.

A sudden bout of dizziness slams into me, and I sway on my feet, making my knees knock together. I'm helpless to protect those I love. Panic seizes every inch of my body, and a flashback from the night that changed my life forever replays right before my eyes.

The memory is too much to bear, and it feels like I'm not getting enough oxygen into my lungs. I'm gasping for air, but no one is going to save me.

"We're going to have so much fun with you," the man holding me says into the shell of my good ear. It's the last thing I hear before my eyes close, and I succumb to the panic that's squeezing the air from my lungs.

WHEN I COME TO, I'm groggy, cold, and my teeth clank together. I clench my jaw to stop the chattering. Wrapping my arms around my middle, I take deep, calming breaths to stop myself from having another panic attack.

Looking around the small room, it becomes apparent I'm locked inside a jail cell. I have no clue where I am or what happened to my parents. My clothing isn't ripped, and I don't feel violated in any way, but that doesn't mean nothing happened.

I'm alone in this dark cell with a dirty, musty smelling cot. I'm grateful I didn't wake to find the two men who kidnapped me hovering above me, but I'm still terrified and wondering what the hell is going on?

I've never seen them before in my life, but I'm guessing this has something to do with Lucca. There must have been a reason he wanted me gone and hidden away. That reason must have found me anyway.

After a few minutes, my breathing returns to normal, and I

build up the courage to get up and walk across the cell and over to the bars. I'd be a fool not to test the door, even though I'm certain it's locked.

I wrap a hand around the cold bar and tug, but the door doesn't move. Shadows along the wall alert me of someone approaching. I rush back toward the wall, putting as much distance between myself and the door as I can. The cold brick penetrates through my clothing and skin, intensifying my shivering.

The footsteps grow closer, and my breathing becomes more erratic. They're going to kill me and cut me up and put me in a box.

Okay, thinking like that is not helping.

A man appears from the shadows and stops right in front of my cell. I start at his feet and work my way up. He's an average-looking man, but the scar on the right side of his face that cuts through his eye gives him a dark edge.

Fear bubbles beneath my skin again. I look down at his hand. There is a long chain in it, and at the end, I spot a shiny key.

The lanky man says something as he inserts the key into the lock, but because his head is down, I can't read his lips. I have no idea what he is saying, so I remain pressed against the wall.

"Are you deaf?" he yells as the cell door creaks open.

I remain huddled against the wall, unmoving. The last thing I want to do is walk toward the danger, but what option do I have?

"Yes, I mean partly. I can read lips, but I didn't see yours. So I don't know what you were saying," I ramble on, hoping my explanation is enough to lessen his anger.

"Oh, fuck." He laughs at me. "That's funny. Well, I said, let's go."

I swear part of my heart shrivels in my chest. There's nothing I can do, no one that's going to ride in on a white horse and save me.

Forcing my feet forward, I walk toward the man. Each cold press of my feet into the concrete makes me tremble, and the closer I get, the more afraid I become.

"Don't make me come in there and get you because I promise you won't like it." The man curls his lip, and his menacing eyes cut me to the bone.

I try to move faster, but fear has my muscles stiff. The shaking in my limbs doesn't help. I'm only a few feet away when the man takes a step forward and grabs me, wrapping an arm around my upper arm and dragging me from the cell.

"You fuckin' stupid? When I tell you to do something, you do it now!" the man screams into my face. Droplets of saliva cling to my cheeks, but I don't dare raise a hand to wipe them away. Shaking like a leaf, he drags me down the long corridor. We pass a few other cells, and I wonder where I am? Who it is that kidnapped me, and what they plan to do? That thought alone is enough to make me dig my heels into the ground and fight off this man.

But what would I do after that? Where would I go? How would I escape this place? I wouldn't. As frightened as I am, I have to think smart. I have to go along with whatever is going to happen, at least for the time being.

Ahead is a huge archway, and as we pass through it, I notice we're in a wine cellar. A few feet ahead, I spot a set of stairs, and the man's grip on me becomes tighter. His fingers bite into the sensitive flesh, and I grit my teeth to stop myself from reacting.

When we reach the next floor, we enter a hallway. The flooring beneath my feet is marble, and I whip my head around, taking in every sight and sound.

At the end of the hallway, we enter a dining room that's set for dinner, but that's not what makes my skin crawl, or a tiny cry escape my lips. It's the three men sitting at that table with resentful scowls on their faces.

The youngest one's eyes roam over my body, and when they meet mine, there is a sinister smile on his face that has me taking a step back.

"Sit," one of the older men orders.

"Have dinner with us, or maybe we could have you for dinner?" The young man licks his lips. I shiver, afraid to speak.

The man holding me releases me and shoves me toward the table. Hands out, I barely catch myself on it. I bite the inside of my cheek when my hip slams into the hardwood, and pain radiates up my side.

"Sit the fuck down!" the other man commands.

I trudge to the only open chair, which is across from the younger man. I wish I were wearing something else, wish I weren't here at all.

I feel so naked beneath their scornful gazes.

"Give her to me. I'm sure fucking her will prove a point." His gaze narrows. "I bet she's a virgin. Pure and untouched." The lust in his eyes builds. "We can send the bloody sheets to him just to prove our point."

What? Send the bloody sheets to who? Oh god, they're going to rape me and kill me.

"Please... I don't know what this is about but—"

"Shut the fuck up!" the man to my right yells. His fist comes down on the table, causing the glasses and silverware to jump.

"You will not touch the girl, Igor. Not until after we've heard from Lucca."

Lucca? I knew it. I knew it had to do with something bad, but I never would have expected this. To be kidnapped and held hostage because of him. I'm reminded of how he told me he would always protect me.

But he's not here right now. He's not protecting me. He's hurting me. I knew I should've tried harder to push him away. Nothing good ever happens when he is around or a part of my life, and this is proof of it.

"Please, just let me go. Whatever he did to you... I have nothing to do with it."

The man closest to me grabs a crystal glass filled with an amber liquid that's to his left. Every muscle in my body tightens as he brings it to his lips and gulps it down.

I'm stuck looking between the three men, and my heart feels like it's going to burst inside my chest at any second.

The nameless man places his glass on the table and smiles. The look alone makes me want to sink through the floor. I don't know what Lucca did to these men, but they want to shred me like hungry dogs.

"We need Lucca to cooperate with us, and he won't do that if we hurt his little butterfly. So, you be a good girl, Claire, and don't give us any more of a reason to kill you."

My throat tightens. I didn't give them a reason to do anything. I shouldn't even be here. Whatever beef they have with Lucca, that's on him. Somehow, I've gotten roped into this, though, and now I'm worried I won't escape unscathed.

I look down at my shaking hands.

He's always trying to protect me without realizing his protection comes with a cost, and that cost always falls on me.

Tears form in my eyes, but I blink them away. I don't want to cry in front of these men.

"Don't cry, princess. Lucca is coming to rescue you..." Igor's voice is low, and his gaze terrifies me but not as much as what he says next. "The question is will it be soon enough."

And that's the biggest question of all? Will Lucca save me in time?

8

LUCCA

I've never wanted to kill anyone as much as I want to kill Petro Volocove right now. He fucking took her. He fucking took Claire. They left Steven beaten and Tracy a sobbing mess. I could barely understand her on the phone, she was so distraught.

Not as distraught as the Volocoves' are going to be after I'm done with them.

"Where is she?" I growl at the two guards who open the front door.

"Mr. Volocove and his guests are waiting for you in the dining room. I'll take you there," one of the goons tells me. He leads the way, and I follow impatiently.

He opens a large double door, and the spacious dining room comes into view. The moment my eyes fall onto the head of bright red hair, I shove the guard out of my way and storm into the room.

"You fucking bastard," I growl, heading straight for Petro, who is sitting at the head of the table. Immediately, more guards appear at my side, and two men from the table stand up with their guns drawn.

"Please, gentlemen. Let's have dinner without killing each other." Petro snickers, and the need to fire a bullet into his skull surges up once more.

"Yes, let's be civil, shall we," the man next to Petro says, and I recognize him as Bruno, Petro's brother. The third man at the table is Igor Volocove, Petro's nephew and Lev's brother.

Julian recently killed Lev Volocove, which I'm guessing is the whole reason I am here now.

"Lucca, have a seat." Petro waves at the chair next to Claire.

Igor and Bruno sit back down and stash away their guns. Only then do I allow myself to look at Claire. She is staring at the plate in front of her, her shoulders slouched like she is trying to make herself even smaller.

She doesn't raise her bowed head, letting a curtain of hair shield her face from me. As I step closer, I notice how her entire body is shaking. I grind my molars together and take the seat next to hers.

"Claire, look at me," I whisper. Reaching over to touch her arm, I wrap my fingers around her slender wrist.

She turns her head, and emerald eyes filled with fear stare back at me. Her lip quivers, and her cheeks are tear-stained, but other than that, she looks okay. There isn't a scratch on her that I can see, and they better be fucking glad there isn't.

"I told you on the phone, no one hurts her as long as you do what we want," Petro tells me, as if his words mean anything.

I take Claire's hand in mine and keep holding it between us. Using my thumb, I rub small circles over her skin, hoping to calm her, at least a bit.

"She is coming home with me."

"I'm afraid that's not possible. I need her to remain here, to make sure you will continue to cooperate."

"I already said I would. I'm not leaving here without her."

"She might mean something to you, but you are also loyal to Moretti. Plus, I have to assume you value your life, so I can't risk you not going through with the plan. She is to remain here until Julian is dead, then she is free to go with you."

I want to rip his throat out, drive a knife into his chest and pull out his guts all at once. Unfortunately, I'm wildly outnumbered. There are at least twenty men and only one of me. This is a battle I won't win.

There has only been one time in my life I have felt this helpless.

I stare at my hands, clasped together in my lap. Blood. So much blood. I can still hear her agonized screams, still feel the rage pulsing through my veins, the need to lash out so strong it controlled every thought and action. All I could think was to remove the problem, to hurt the person hurting her. I didn't stop. Couldn't. He deserved it. And even if she hates me for killing her father, I did what was right.

Looking up, I peer around the waiting room, wishing I was back in the operating room with the doctors, making sure they take care of Claire. Instead of sitting in this chair, waiting for a doctor to come to me.

My leg bounces up and down nervously until I shove out of the chair and march over to the front desk. I had to tell them Claire was my sister when I brought her in, or they wouldn't have given me any information on her.

"Can you tell me if there are any updates on my sister?" I grit the words out as slowly as I can. I don't want to cause a ruckus, but I need some answers before I explode.

"Claire, right?" she asks like she doesn't already know.

"Yes."

She makes a couple clicks on her computer and then looks back up at me. "There isn't anything on my side to share. When the doctor is ready, he will come out and see you."

I slam a fist against the counter, causing the woman to jump in her seat. "I want answers now. Is she okay?" I force myself to calm because if I don't, I may rip this entire hospital apart piece by piece.

"I'll... I'll call back to surgery and ask..." The woman squeaks. I nod and drag myself back to the chair, slamming down into it.

I take my head into my hands. All I can think about is how she's just a fucking kid, and now she has no one. I mean, she had shit before, but now she's truly all alone. I knew the moment I brought her to the hospital, I would be the one to step up and ensure they took care of her. Still, the mob isn't any place for a child, and I'm not sure I'd be any better of a parent to her.

The thought of letting her go kills me, though.

"Mr. Torres," someone greets, and I lift my head to find a doctor in a white coat standing in front of me.

I must've been so lost in thought that I didn't hear him approach.

"Yes, that's me." My voice cracks. "Is she okay?" The beat of my heart drums in my ears, and my lungs burn as I hold my breath while awaiting his answer.

"The surgery went well. There was a small amount of internal bleeding that we stopped. Her right arm is broken. However, we set it, so that's good to go. Our primary concern is the damage sustained to her eardrum."

Panic claws at my insides. "What happened?" I barely withhold the growl threatening to pierce the air.

The doctor raises his hand in an I'm-not-the-enemy-here kind of way. "She suffered extensive damage to her inner ear. We fixed it as best as we could, but realistically, only time will tell if she'll make a full recovery—"

I shove from the chair, all the emotions I've been keeping at bay rushing to the surface. "What are you saying? There's a chance she won't recover?"

"What I'm saying is that her eardrum might never heal, or it might not heal right. That means when she wakes up, she might be deaf or partially deaf. We won't know until she is fully awake and can tell us."

Deaf? She might be deaf? I could handle that. Handle anything as long as she isn't dead.

"When can I see her?" I squeeze the arm of the chair to keep myself in place.

"In just a few minutes. The nurses are setting her up in a room right now and once they're finished, I'll have them come out and get you." He smiles, but I can't bring myself to return the gesture. I'm thankful that Claire is okay, but I know she's got a long road ahead of her.

"Thanks, doc."

"You're welcome." He walks back through the double doors and disappears into the E.R. leaving me alone with my thoughts once more.

All that matters is that she is okay. That she won't have to return to that house or her father hurt her ever again.

Thirty minutes and three coffees later, a nurse finally comes to get me. I feel sick to my stomach when I enter the room and find Claire lying there, hooked up to a bunch of machines with an IV protruding from her arm.

Her skin is ashen, in the unbruised spots, and she looks like a fallen angel. Battered and broken. I vow then, in that single moment, to never let something like this happen to her again, not as long as there's air in my lungs and blood pumping through my body.

Moving closer to the bed, I spot her tiny hand cradled near her cheek. I want to reach out and take it into mine, to let her know she isn't alone. Dragging my gaze from her hand, I return to her face and find her eyes open.

They're big and wide with the residue of sleep crusted to them. Recognition takes place in an instant, and the moment it does, she eases as far back on the bed as she can, both terror and fear overtaking her features. The dread in her eyes shakes me to the core. Steals the air from my lungs and makes my heart skip a beat. She's truly afraid of me. Afraid that I may hurt her the way I hurt her father.

All I can do is stare at her, see her delicate face morphed with fear and pain, see the bruising. Her green eyes glisten with unshed tears, and I hate seeing them there, knowing that I'm the cause for them. It eats me up inside.

I feel responsible for her, but knowing she is afraid of me, knowing that I can't even get close to her, tells me everything I need to know.

9
CLAIRE

My fear dissipates for a fraction of a second at Lucca's appearance. He marched into the room radiating anger and fierce determination and has since sat beside me fuming.

Still, he is here, and before any of them had a chance to hurt me.

His negotiations with the men do not go as either of us planned, and when I find out I'm going to have to stay here, my anxiety goes through the roof. Lucca's hand in mine is the only thing keeping me from having a full-blown mental breakdown.

I've discovered that I am the bribe. The object that will keep Lucca in line and get him to do whatever these three sinister men want. I don't care about the logistics of it, who Lucca killed or hurt. I just want out, want to be away from these creepy men who I know will hurt me the moment Lucca is out of sight.

"If she is going to stay here, then you will treat her with kindness," Lucca orders.

"Like you treated my brother with kindness?" Igor snarls,

and I tense in my seat as his chubby fingers wrap around the glass.

"How rude of me. I forgot to offer you my condolences," Lucca shoots back.

Igor's hand tightens on the glass. He's ready to burst at the seams with rage. His face is red, nostrils flared, and his upper lip raised in a rabid snarl.

Lucca must be trying to defuse the situation because when he speaks next, his tone is much calmer and controlled.

"I had nothing to do with your brother's death. He pissed off Moretti and got himself killed. He shouldn't have touched what wasn't his, just like you shouldn't touch what isn't yours."

"Are you threatening me?"

"I'm simply stating a fact."

Before their conversation can continue, the doors open, and maids sidle in with their hands full of serving dishes.

The smell of tomato sauce and Italian seasonings make my mouth water and my stomach rumble. My cheeks heat with embarrassment, and I wonder if the other people in the room can hear it. One maid places a plate in front of me, and I hesitate to reach for my fork.

It looks like a normal plate of spaghetti with homemade noodles and a red tomato sauce, but I can't help but wonder if it's poisoned? I glance over at Lucca, who is still staring at the man across the table.

The man beside Igor chuckles, dragging my attention to him. "If you're worried that it's poisoned, it's not. What would be the point in doing that? We need you to make him comply."

Lucca's gaze narrows, and then in a flash, his features soften, and he turns to me.

"Eat, Claire," Lucca encourages, and that's all the reassurance I need. I let go of his hand and grab the fork resting on the napkin.

I twirl the spaghetti on my fork and act like I'm not as hungry as I feel. Shoveling the food into my mouth, I half chew it and swallow. It lands in my stomach like a block of concrete, and I focus all my attention on filling that deep ache in my gut.

I can feel eyes on me, watching me, but nothing stops me from finishing my food. I wash it down with a gulp of water that I almost choke on when Lucca speaks.

"Before I go, I want to see where Claire is staying," Lucca tells Petro. The reminder of him leaving me here feels like a bucket of ice water being poured over my head.

"I can assure you, her room is adequate." Igor snickers, and Lucca's hand tightens around mine again.

Petro ignores Igor's remark and motions for his guard. "Take her back to her room, let Lucca come, and then make sure he finds his way out after." A sinister smile spreads across his face.

Lucca stands up, pulling me to my feet with him. We follow the guard in silence, but Lucca's hand remains around mine as we walk back to my cell. With each step I take, the dread in my gut grows. Tears well in my eyes, but I force them back, not wanting to show anyone how scared I am.

All too soon, we are at the door that leads into the small room I'm being held in. Lucca curses under his breath when he sees it. I know he wants to say something, but we both know it will be futile.

He leads me into the cell, and I squeeze his hand tightly, not wanting him to let go. Lucca turns to face me, and I have to tilt my head up to look into his face. I take in his features. All I see is regret and sorrow reflecting at me.

"When they took me, they hurt Steven and Tracy..."

"I know, but they are fine now. Steven is okay, just some bruises, that's all."

I suck in a shaky breath as I let that information sink in. I was so worried about them. I would have never forgiven myself if they killed them because of me.

"I barely talked to them the last few weeks. I was mad at them and now…" My voice breaks at the end.

"They know you love them, and they love you, no matter what."

"I just want to go home."

"I know. I wish you could. I wish I could take you home right now, but I can't, not yet. I need you to be brave," Lucca whispers so quietly that I can't hear him at all. I have to read his lips to know what he is saying. "I promise that I'm coming back for you, and I'm going to make them pay."

Lucca lets go of my hand, and immediately I feel cold and alone. The tears I was able to keep at bay fall down my face.

"Don't cry, butterfly," Lucca mouths.

He lifts his hand to wipe away my tears, and I lean into his touch, seeking more comfort. Closing my eyes, I pretend for a moment that he is not leaving, that I am safe, and nothing is going to happen to me.

Lucca wraps his arms around me and pulls me to his chest, where I take a deep breath. His scent surrounds me, swallows me whole, and I let it.

"I have to go," Lucca says in my good ear. He pulls away, and all I want to do is wrap my arms around him and beg for him to stay. It's weird how I didn't want him near me yesterday, and now the thought of him leaving is crushing my chest.

I watch him take off his jacket. He wraps it around my

shoulders and tucks it around me. "I'll be back as soon as I can. Be brave. I know you can be."

He places a kiss on my forehead before turning around quickly and leaving the cell like he can't get away fast enough. The door shuts, and the lock is put back in place.

As the sound of Lucca's footsteps fading away, my strength fades with it.

10

LUCCA

The days pass in slow motion. I don't sleep, I barely eat, and all I can think about is killing every person with the last name *Volocove*. My hatred for them knows no bounds. I want to eliminate them, rid the earth of their bloodline.

Just the thought of Claire in their clutches has bile rising in my throat. I need to get her out of there. I have to protect her, the way I've always protected her.

I just wish it was as easy as it was six years ago...

I push the button to roll the passenger side window down. "Hey!" I call to get Claire's attention. Her head comes up and her eyes connect with mine. "Get in. I'll drive you home."

She gives me an indecisive look, not slowing her step. "I'm fine. I always walk home."

"Claire, get in," I repeat, driving next to her slowly. "You ran away the other day without answering me. Now you don't have an option. I'm not leaving you alone until you tell me what happened to your arm."

"I told you, I fell."

"Claire, get in," I command in a tone I would normally not take with her.

"No." she shakes her head, making a sharp turn into the park and away from the road.

"Claire!" I yell after her, which only makes her feet move faster.

Fuck!

Pulling my car to the side of the road, I park and get out. With long strides, I follow her into the park, hoping I'll be able to catch up with her in time.

The air stills in my lungs as I watch five guys circle Claire like vultures would their prey.

Those fuckers.

"Stop!" Claire's frightened voice reaches my ears and my chest constricts. She tries to pull out of his hold, but the asshole pulls her further away. Someone else grabs her other arm, and they both pull her away from the park path.

I will kill them. All of them.

"Please," she begs desperately, digging her heels to the ground. Her feeble attempt to get away from them only seems to excite them more.

The guys are so busy toying with Claire, they don't even see me approach.

I wrap my hand around the guy's throat who grabbed Claire first. He lets go of her wrist, and his friend lets go a second after.

"You fucking punk," I grit through my teeth. My anger is blinding, my rage all-consuming.

I keep one hand wrapped around his throat while smashing my other fist into his face. I see the fear in his eyes, feel bone crushing beneath my knuckles, I hear his pleas, and I enjoy all of it. I revel in his suffering.

His friends try to get me to stop, grabbing my arms to pull me off, but I shove them away.

I'm vaguely aware of two of the guys running off, leaving their friends behind without a second glance.

All the while, I pummel down on this fucker's bloody face until his body goes slack. Only then do I let go of him and watch him crumble to the ground.

"Fuck, man! You killed him," one punk yells as he pushes himself back on his feet.

"He isn't dead, but he will be, and so will you. If one of you fuckers ever touch her, talk to her, or even think of her, I will end you," I growl, already thinking about all the ways I can hurt them. "I will find you, and I will kill you in the most painful way I can think of, and trust me, I can think of a few."

The guy on the ground is coughing and gasping for air, while his two remaining friends look at me with pure terror in their eyes. With pale faces, both nod before helping their friend to his feet and dragging him away.

Reining in the remaining anger, I turn to Claire. She is staring at me like she doesn't even know me. Her whole body is trembling, and she folds her arms over her chest in a protective manner. Shit, I terrified her.

"Are you okay?" I ask, taking in her frightened face. "Claire, talk to me. Did they hurt you? Let me see your arms, kiddo."

Keeping my voice low and soothing, I step in front of her and reach for her wrists. Gently, I push up her sleeves and inspect her wrists one by one.

I catch the blood on my knuckles and silently curse myself for losing my shit. She shouldn't have seen that. I should have taken her away and dealt with these punks later.

"This will never happen again," I say, keeping my voice even and calm. "You should have told me. I could have scared them sooner. They won't bother you again. I'll make sure of it."

"I thought you were going to kill him," Claire admits, still a bit shaken up.

"I just wanted to scare them, Claire," I lie. I wanted to do so much more. Hell, I still might. "He'll have a bruised face, and a bruised ego, but that's all. Hopefully, he learned his lesson. Come on, let me take you home." I hold my hand out to her. She looks at it for a moment before reaching out and placing her small hand in mine.

I sigh in relief. She isn't scared of me. She still trusts me, and I won't ever break that trust.

I will always be here to keep her safe.

I haven't broken my promise, I'm still here. The only difference is now the monsters I'm fighting for her are more vicious and dangerous.

Picking up my phone, I dial Petro's number and hit call. He answers on the third ring.

"Lucca," he greets me with fake cheeriness, "what can I do for you?"

"I sent over what you asked for. I want to see Claire today."

"You coming to the house again is too risky. I don't think that's a good idea—"

My blood pressure spikes. "I don't give a fuck what you think. I want to see her today, and you're going to make that happen."

"Don't forget who you are talking to."

"Don't forget who *you* are talking to," I quip. "You might have been born into this world, but I've killed my way into it. There is more blood on my hands than you will ever see in your pathetic lifetime, and let's not forget that you still need to get to

Julian. So let's not play games. I'm seeing Claire today. Make it happen."

The line goes silent for a few seconds, and I briefly wonder if I took it too far. I don't know what the fuck I'm going to do if they hurt her. There is only one person on this fucking planet I would give anything and everything for, and it's her.

"Come back to the house tonight," Petro tells me, his voice eerily calm. "I'll tell my men to let you in." The line goes dead, and I drop my phone onto the passenger seat before I crush it with my bare hands.

11

CLAIRE

The cell is where I remain, scared and alone. Two men guard me at all times, so while I'm not *really* alone, I might as well be. I'm still wearing the pj's they kidnapped me in, so I'm grateful for the water bucket and wash rag the maid brought down last night. At least I have Lucca's jacket keeping me covered and warm. Every time I feel like I'm going to freak out, I tuck the leather jacket closer around my shoulders, using it as a security blanket.

Sitting in the basement's corner on the cot they tossed at me, I await Lucca's return. He said he would come back for me, and I believe him. Whether or not I want it, he is always there, always watching me since the day he made that promise to me.

"I'm not going to hurt you," Lucca says. He is only a few feet away, but it sounds like he is at the end of a long corridor. His voice barely above a whisper.

"Y-youuu..." I croak, feeling the vibration in my throat but having a hard time recognizing my own voice. It seems so raspy and far away.

The nurse told me I hurt my ear badly and that I'll have a hard time hearing, but it's more than that. Everything feels wrong. All the surrounding sounds are off.

Squeezing my eyes shut, I pray everything goes back to normal the moment I open them again.

"Claire, look at me." Lucca's voice reaches me, but only barely.

I shake my head slightly, making the insistent pounding inside my skull worse. I'm so confused, so lost. None of this can be real.

A few seconds later, I blink my eyes open again, hoping my surroundings have changed, but I'm still in the hospital bed. Lucca is still standing in front of me, looking at me like he knows exactly what I'm thinking of him now.

"Please, don't look at me like this. All I did was protect you. He could've killed you. Hell, he almost did."

"I... you're a bad person. You work for bad people. My father told me. Told me you would hurt me."

He takes another step toward the bed, and my entire body trembles. Pausing mid-step, he says, "Claire, I would never hurt you."

"Don't come any closer... or I'll scream."

"Okay." He lifts his hands like he is showing me he's not a threat before he takes a few steps back.

"I'm going to make this right..." The distance between us makes it harder to hear him now, but I don't want him to come closer again. I have to look at his lips and watch them move to make out the words he is saying. "I will protect you, provide for you, and ensure you're always taken care of."

His words are heartfelt, and if he had said them to me a week ago, I would have been over the moon. Now, everything has changed. Now his words make my skin crawl.

I can't shake away what I saw. I can't forget the person he transformed into. He's an evil man. A horrible man. Yes, my father hurt me, but he was still my dad, the only family I had. He didn't deserve to die. He didn't deserve what happened to him any more than I did.

"Claire, I know you're scared right now, but I swear, I'll make this right. I won't ever let you down again. From now on, I'll never let you out of my sight."

His words cause a shiver to run down my spine because I know he is telling the truth. He is never letting me go again, and right now, that's scarier than anything else.

That fear has turned to my salvation. The words that caused me to shiver back then are the only thing that can stop me from falling apart now.

A maid brings down my breakfast and hands it to one of the guards, who opens the cell and enters. My natural reaction to this man is to curl up in a ball and hide. I know that's what he expects, so maybe that's why I don't do it.

"What do you think I can get you to do for a..." his eyes roam the tray and then fall back on me, "a peanut butter sandwich?" The way his tongue darts out over his bottom lip and his eyes gleam with lust, I'm sure whatever he wants isn't something I'm willing to offer.

"I just want my food. Please..." I try not to sound as weak as I feel.

Lucca said to be brave, to be strong. I can't give them the reaction they're expecting. Even if it terrifies me, I have to do the opposite of what my brain says, which is to huddle in the corner and cry.

The guard advances toward me and tosses the tray onto the ground. I jump back and collide with the wall, watching as the pitiful peanut butter and jelly sandwich flies across the dirty concrete.

"You think you're protected because of that fucker, that he's going to come back and save you." The guard grabs me by the throat and squeezes. I freeze, my body becoming a block of ice. He leans into my face, and I can feel his hot breath on my cheek.

Tears spring from my eyes and slip down my cheeks without approval. To cry in front of these men is to give them a loaded gun and beg them not to shoot me.

I can't control my fear, not here, in this place. I'm afraid of what may happen next. The darkness in his eyes sends a shiver down my back.

I didn't want to be here. I wanted to escape, even if that meant I had to crawl inside a dark place in my mind.

Thankfully, the other guard walks into the cell and interferes before anything more can happen. "Let her go, Yuli. She's not worth getting your head blown off for. You heard what the boss said. We have to wait until Lucca is dead before we can have our fun with her."

Yuli releases me, and I sag against the wall. I'd be relieved he let me go, but my fear spirals after hearing what I just did. Are they planning to kill Lucca? Oh god, I have to find a way to warn him. If anything happens to him, I'll never get out of here. I'll never be safe again.

Yuli looks to the other guard and smiles. My heart skips a beat, and I'm tempted to wrap my arms around my middle and make myself appear small. Maybe they won't hurt me then? Maybe they'll forget I'm here.

There isn't a chance, but I can hope.

"Maybe we can take her on a brief walk? Take her to see what awaits her?" Yuli pauses, looking from me and back to the other guard. I don't want to beg, but I will if it means they'll leave me alone. I'll do anything. "What d'ya say, Robert?"

Robert rubs at his jaw like he's contemplating it.

"Please..." The whimper of a word slips free before I can stop it.

Yuli turns on me, his face morphed in rage, and I cower beneath his stare, wishing I had pressed my lips together. He doesn't even wait for the other guard's approval. He grabs me by the arm, his fingers dig into my skin, and I know there will be bruises tomorrow.

Rushing out of the cell, he drags me behind him. I can barely keep up and end up tripping over my own feet. I'm so afraid of what's going to happen next.

Are they going to hurt me? Punish me? Rape me? It won't matter if Lucca returns to save me if they do any of those things. I'm not sure I can mentally survive something like that. I've endured enough in my life—more pain and sadness than most. I don't think my heart can take anymore.

Yuli's boots slap against the marble floor once we reach the landing. Peering over my shoulder, I find the other guard following a few steps behind us.

"Don't do anything stupid," he growls, his face morphed with worry.

We turn down a hall, and then another, and all I feel is dread—complete and utter dread. Yuli stops at a door, and I almost topple over. He retrieves a key from his pocket and unlocks the massive wooden door.

I swallow down the fear as he pushes the door open, and I'm tugged inside. My gaze darts around the room full of whips, chains, and other objects that promise pain and humiliation. The sights before me leave me overwhelmed with fear.

"No!" I scream.

My entire body trembles, and I struggle to break free of Yuli's unforgiving grip. That only causes him to tighten his hold.

"What? Are you afraid of the future that awaits you? Because this is where you will spend most of your time. As a sex slave, used and abused in every unimaginable way."

"Stop! Please, stop." I refuse to believe that this is my future. My struggles intensify, my fear reaching a new height. I can't let them hurt me. My foot connects with Yuli's calf, and I shove away from him.

"You stupid fucking bitch!" he sneers, and his grip on me loosens enough that I pull my arm free of his grasp altogether.

I don't realize the mistake I've made until Yuli's fist is flying at my face, and I can't move out of the way fast enough.

Robert tries to step between us, to stop the train wreck from happening, but it's too late. By the time he's reached me, Yuli has already hit me.

His knuckles collide with my cheekbone, and pain radiates across and up my face. I stumble backward, cradling the side of my face. I sob, uncaring how weak it makes me look or feel.

"Jesus fuck, Yuli! Boss said not to touch the girl."

Robert takes a step toward me, and I shake my head. My vision blurs, and I feel helpless and at the mercy of these horrible people.

"I don't care what the boss said. She fucking kicked me."

Robert shakes his head. "You stay upstairs, and I'll go put her back in the cell." I can already feel my cheek and eye swelling.

I know it shouldn't surprise me, but I can't believe he hit me. Before gesturing for me to walk ahead of him, he says, "Try to run, and I'll drag you back."

The warning is clear, and with a black and blue eye already,

I'm not about to dig myself a shallow grave. I nod and start walking back the way I came, cradling my bruised cheek the entire way. Tears fall like raindrops from my eyes, and I barely hold back the sob building in my throat. I miss Lucca. I wish he never left me alone.

By the time we reach the cell, I'm a sobbing mess. Robert doesn't touch me or even offer an apology. He seems more worried about what his boss is going to say than anything. I rush to the back of the cell, where I always sit, passing the uneaten food on the ground.

I hold myself together, hoping and praying that Lucca returns for me tonight. I don't know what I'll do if he doesn't. In no time at all, he went from being the villain to being my savior all over again.

12

LUCCA

As soon as I arrive, I know something is horribly wrong. Call it intuition or whatever the hell you want, but I know deep in my gut something has happened to Claire. Fuck, I should've pushed for her release. Not that Petro would've allowed that, but I could've tried harder.

My suspicion rises when the guard walking me to her cell won't even look at me. Like it scares him I'm about to rip his balls off, and I seriously might.

He unlocks the door to her cell, and I step inside. Claire sits on the small cot, her knees drawn up to her chest and bundled up in my jacket. Her head shoots up, and her teary eyes find mine.

My blood boils in my veins when I see her black eye and swollen face. *Motherfuckers.*

I'm about to spin around and kill the guard, but Claire is already on her feet, throwing herself into my arms. She buries her face into my shirt, her small hands clinging onto me like I'm going to disappear.

Wrapping my arms around her tightly, I hold her to my chest and let her cry. When she doesn't seem to calm down, I pick her up and sit down on the cot with her on my lap. I stroke her hair and tell her everything is going to be okay until she finally stops sobbing.

"Claire, look at me." I nudge her to move her head, so I can see her face. Her red-rimmed eyes find mine, and my chest aches. "Who did this? Who hit you?"

Her frightened gaze flickers to the door like whoever did this will be there. "I—I don't know."

"Just tell me. Was it one of the guards?"

She nods her head but doesn't give me a name.

"Did he do anything else? Did he touch you?"

"No," she shakes her head, "he just hit me."

I feel a fraction of relief, but not enough to put a dent in the need to kill whoever hit her. No matter if she tells me or not, I will make someone pay before I leave here.

Claire leans her head back against my chest, and I stay a while longer to hold her. I wish I could stay, or better, take her with me, but I can't. Not yet anyway. After a while, I lean my head down, so my mouth is right next to her good ear.

"One more day, butterfly. You need to make it one more day. Tomorrow, I'm coming for you, and I'll take you away from here. We'll go somewhere safe, where no one can hurt you."

She pushes against my chest, putting enough space between us to look up and into my eyes. There is frantic worry swirling in her green eyes.

"They said they are going to kill you."

"I know they are going to try, but they won't succeed. Don't worry about me. I'll be fine and so will you. One more day, and all of this will be a long distant memory."

She wants to believe me. I can see the longing in her eyes, but fear has a chokehold on her. I know how she feels because I've been feeling the same. I haven't been scared in a long time, but I am now. Scared of losing her, scared of seeing her hurt, scared of failing.

"One more day," I repeat, praying to a god I don't even believe in that my words are true.

I give her one more hug and place a kiss on the top of her hair before I tear myself away to rush out of the cell.

My footsteps echo through the long hallway, and I concentrate on that sound and nothing else. It takes everything in me to keep going.

At the very end of the hall, Igor waits for me with crossed arms, leaning against the wall like the world bores him.

When he sees me approaching, he straightens up. "One of my men didn't follow orders. I was going to deal with it, but then I thought you might want to do it yourself. He is in this room." Igor points to the door next to him. "Enjoy."

"That I will." Matter of fact, I will enjoy this very much.

I PLACE the explosive in the closet close to the stairs. My hand is shaking, actually shaking. I haven't been this nervous in a long time, but I've also never crossed Julian, or hurt someone I actually cared about either. At least not continuously.

"What are you doing?" Carter's voice startles me.

I spin around and stare at him as he assesses the situation. "What is that?"

For a split second I think about lying to him, but I know he isn't stupid. He already knows something is off. The suspicious look in his eyes gives him away.

"Explosives," I explain, keeping my voice low.

"Why?" is all he asks. One word that holds at least five questions.

Why explosives? Why here? Why are you doing this? Why are you betraying us? Why are you telling me this?

All these unasked questions deserve an equal amount of answers, but again, I only speak a single word, "Sorry." It's a half assed response but what more could I say?

Carter studies me for another moment before he speaks again. "What do you need me to do? Let me help?" Young and naïve. He doesn't even know what he's asking. Does he want to die? Anger rushes to the surface.

"If you help me, you go against Julian. Do you know what that means? A life on the run… that's *if* you are lucky and we get away."

Carter straightens, standing a little taller. "I know what it means, but I also know you. You wouldn't do this if you didn't have a good reason. Plus, I've already seen you, so there is no way out for me now. Either way, I'm an accomplice."

"I could knock you out." Carter snorts at my remark. "I'm serious. You could tell them you tried to stop me and I knocked you out. No one would doubt that story."

Another snort. "Sounds a bit unbelievable to me, old man. Now tell me how I can help."

Asshole. I hate bringing him into this, but he has a point. He's already seen me, and knocking him out would be a risk. I've done a lot of really fucked up shit, but to let Carter get killed because of my own doings? I don't think I could live with myself.

"Make sure all the other guards are occupied."

The rest of this fucked up mission goes smooth. We leave before anyone knows it was us. My phone keeps ringing, but I ignore the constant buzzing in my pocket for a while. I know it's Julian, and I know what he is going to tell me.

My phone rings again, and I finally find the courage to pull it from my pocket. Julian's name lights up the screen and the pit in my stomach grows. I know I can't ignore his call forever, so this time, I accept it.

"Hello," I answer, knowing that this will probably be the last time I ever talk to Julian.

"Where the fuck are you?" Julian screams into the phone.

"I'm sorry… I had no choice," I say with a heavy heart.

"You fucking betrayed me! You let them in, didn't you?" Julian rarely lets his emotions show, and even though I can't see him, I can hear the disappointment and hurt in his voice. He's given me everything, and I betrayed him.

"I'm sorry," I repeat honestly. I am really fucking sorry. "They have someone I love."

"That's no fucking excuse!" Anger overtakes his sorrow. "You vowed to protect this family. You vowed to protect Elena with your fucking life! You took an oath, Lucca. A fucking oath."

"Long before that, I vowed to protect someone else." I drop the phone from my ear and disconnect the call before he can say anything else. I know everything he was going to say anyway… *I will kill you*, and *you are going to pay for this*, are on the top of that list.

Part of me wishes I could make him understand, make him forgive me for my betrayal, but I know there is no going back now. Julian won't tolerate a man who betrays him, he won't see past this. He will hunt me down for the rest of my life, and I don't really blame him for it.

I just hate that Carter got mixed up in all of this. He involved himself by pure accident.

If it wasn't for him finding me, everything would've gone off without a hitch. Now he is in the same boat as I am. Running for his life.

Thankfully, he got a head start. I shoved a stack of cash into his hand and told him to drive south and don't stop.

I'll contact him as soon as I can, but until then, it's better to stay apart.

I pull up to the Volocove compound. Right away, I know something is off. There are no guards stationed at the front. The normally shut and heavily guarded gate is now hanging wide open.

My hand tightens on the steering wheel. I drive through the gate and park outside the steps that lead to the front door. With my phone and gun in hand, I jump out of the car. I run toward the front door, and I'm surprised to find it unlocked and ajar.

A warning bell goes off in my head. *Something is wrong.*

Shoving the door all the way open, I slowly walk inside. This might be a trap, so I walk in with my guard up and my gun drawn. After doing a quick walkthrough of the foyer, I find the area deserted. Fuck, this is worse than I thought.

I don't think twice about my next move. I can only hope they left Claire here before disappearing. I jog to the basement and descend the stairs as fast as I can.

I just want her to be in her room. I want her to be safe, but the closer I get, the more my heart sinks, and when I come around the corner, I see the open door of her cell. There's a tightness that develops in my chest that spreads outward like a slow-moving cancer.

Fuck. They took her.

Shoving my gun into my holster, I fish my phone out of my pocket and dial Felix' number.

"I told you they would move," Felix says as soon as he answers, knowing what my question was before I could even speak.

Anger and fear rush through me, fucking with my head. *Focus.* Time is everything in this situation if I want to save Claire.

"Tell me you know where they took her."

"Don't worry, I've got the location. Sending everything to your phone."

I sigh, literally fucking sigh. "Thank you."

"Thank me by not contacting me again. Julian already hates me. I don't need him to add another reason to kill me." The line goes dead, and I make my way back to the car.

My phone buzzes again. Felix delivered a location. Now it's time to go on a killing spree.

13

CLAIRE

They're going to kill me and send my body in pieces back to Lucca. When the guards came into my cell and dragged me outside, I didn't know what to think. I hoped they were releasing me. Squeezing my eyes shut, I pretend my hands aren't bound, and I'm not in the trunk of a car, being driven god knows where.

Dread trickles in as the time passes. I've been trying my best to be brave, but after yesterday, and now, I'm not sure being brave is going to cut it. Lucca never came back like he said, and now it's over. I'm going to die. I can feel it with every beat of my heart. It clings to my skin, and by the day's end, that will be my fate.

The car slows, and I slide forward, crashing into the wall of the trunk. Before I can gather my bearings, the driver hooks a right, and I roll the other way, my head slamming into the sidewall of the car. I feel like a basketball being tossed around. The car finally stops, and all I can hear is my heavy breathing and the thundering of my heart.

Doors open and then slam, and I tense, preparing myself for a fight that I know I won't win. The trunk opens, and the light hits my eyes, temporarily blinding me. I'm grabbed by the arm and dragged out of the trunk. My feet barely touch the ground, and we're moving. I glance around, trying to put together what is going on and where I am.

"Please, let me go," I plead, wondering if using my words might make the man dragging me away break down. It does nothing, as he doesn't even react to what I've said.

All hell breaks loose when we reach the steps of the house, and shots ring out through the street. Everything becomes mass hysteria. The guard releases me and reaches for his gun. I drop to the ground and cover my head, too afraid to see what's going to happen next. The guard fires back and bullets rain down onto the pavement.

Bile rises in my throat, and I breathe through the need to vomit. I don't know who the person firing back is, and I don't want to find out. Slowly, I crawl backward, trying to put enough distance between the guard and me so that I can get up and run.

The shooting continues, and then there is silence. The silence terrifies me more than the shooting, and when I peek through my long red strands and toward the guard that was a few feet away, I find him on the ground, blood splattered against the concrete, and a bullet hole in his forehead. *Oh god.* This time I can't stop myself.

I look away, and all the contents in my stomach empty. My entire body shudders with the after-effects of vomiting. Will my life ever be the same again?

Footsteps approach quickly, and I shove up onto my knees,

getting ready to make a run for it. If Lucca isn't going to save me, then I'll save myself.

"Fuck, Claire." Lucca's voice penetrates my thoughts, and I pause, turning just in time to see him rushing toward me with fear in his eyes. "Are you okay?"

I nod because, at this moment, I'm afraid to speak. I look away from Lucca and down to the ground where the guard is lying, dead. Blood, there is so much blood. That's all my life has amounted to, death and chaos, and all because of him.

Lucca interrupts my thoughts, "We need to get out of here."

He frees my hands, his rough fingertips slide over mine, and he drags me down the street. I'm in such disarray that I don't even attempt to stop him. By the time we reach the car, I'm still not any better.

Lucca opens the door and shoves me inside, rushing over to the driver's side. He slides in and shoves the key into the ignition, and the engine roars to life. With his foot to the gas pedal, we rip out onto the road. The only sound inside the car is the quiet hum of the engine and our own breathing, but in my head, I can still hear shots being fired. I can still see the blood, the bullet in the guard's head.

"Talk to me. Are you okay? Did they hurt you?" Lucca's voice is feverish.

"No, I think I'm fine." I make a mental check of my body. Right now, I'm numb, so it's hard to say if I'm hurt or not. My mind is a mess, like a swarm of bees buzzing inside my head.

Leaning my head back against the headrest, I close my eyes and try to calm the storm. Slowly, my heartbeat returns to normal, and my breathing evens out.

When I open my eyes the next time, the world around me

seems a little more normal again. As normal as my world can be.

"Why... why did you kill him?" My voice comes out calmer than I expected.

Lucca looks away from the road and over at me. His eyes are still dark, frenzied. It's a reminder of the night that forever changed my life.

"It was kill him or let him get away with you." He looks back at the road, and his grip on the steering wheel tightens. When he speaks again, his voice is deeper, rougher, "Is that what you wanted me to do? Let them take you."

"N-Nooo," I stutter and hold my head in my hands with defeat. "I'm just tired of all the death. It seems like I'm trying to outrun my past, but I'm a hamster on a wheel going nowhere. I thought I could finally be normal without all of this violence and death in my life."

Lucca sighs. "I'm sorry, Claire, and I truly mean it. I'm sorry you got dragged into this mess. It wasn't my intention. And how they ever found out about you is a mystery. I was always careful and made certain no one else knew anything about you."

I'm both angry and grateful, and I don't know which emotion is going to come out first. If Lucca had left me alone, none of this would've happened in the first place, but if he wasn't there today, if he didn't save me and protect me all those years ago, I might not be here now. It is a fucked up situation.

Ignoring what he said since I do not know how to approach it. I lift my head and ask, "What's next?"

"I'll drive for a bit, and then we will stop at a hotel for the night. I have to put as much distance as I can between the city and us." I nod, and he continues, "To save you, I had to do something, something that will most likely get me killed."

I shouldn't ask, it's none of my business, and the last thing I need is something else to worry about, but regardless of what I say or how I feel sometimes, I don't want Lucca to die.

"What did you do? Does it have something to do with the Moretti guy they were talking about at dinner?"

"You need to forget that name. Erase it from your memory, and what I did doesn't matter. All that matters is that you're okay and safe. I made you a promise, and I keep my promises."

Anger rips through my veins. He's talking to me like I'm a kid. Like I have no right to know what he gave up when his choices affect both of us directly. "I'm not a child, Lucca. I've seen death. I've felt loss, and I deserve to know what you did to save my life."

"You're sixteen, Claire, so yeah, you're a child. And I'm not telling you because it doesn't affect you. You're safe, and you will remain so as long as I'm breathing, and you follow my directions."

"I'm not going to spend my entire life in hiding because of your shitty choices. Last I checked, none of this would be happening if it wasn't for you."

I can't believe the way I'm talking right now, but nothing I've said is a lie.

I won't spend my life running from Lucca's enemies, and I won't let him talk down to me when he is the cause for this problem. I was perfectly fine living with my parents and having him watch me from afar, even if it was annoying.

"I take full responsibility for everything that's happened, but until this point, I've always kept you safe and provided you with everything for a good life."

"I never asked you to do any of those things," I lash out.

"If it wasn't for me, you'd be dead."

Silence settles over the vehicle after that, and I press my lips together and swallow down all the hateful things I want to say. We drive for a long time, neither of us speaking to each other. The tension in the vehicle builds to an almost suffocating atmosphere.

Thankfully, the gas light turns on an hour later, and Lucca takes the next exit and pulls into the first hotel off the interstate, which turns out to be a rundown ma and pop place. There would be no way of knowing the place was open if it wasn't for the blinking open sign hanging in the office window.

Lucca turns to me. "Stay in the car."

"I don't even have shoes. I'm not going anywhere."

He looks down at my feet and grimaces. When he turns to climb out of the car, I notice the dark spot on the back of his shirt. Is that blood? Was he shot?

"You're bleeding?" I ask.

Lucca half shrugs. "The fucker got a lucky shot. It's nothing but a flesh wound. I'll have you clean it once we get into a room."

A flesh wound? He's kidding, right? A flesh wound would not leave a blood spot like that. Lucca's inside for ten minutes before he walks out of the office and approaches the car.

I climb out and wince when my bare feet touch the cold pavement. Suddenly, I realize just how exhausted I am. Lucca goes around the back of the car and opens the trunk, retrieving something before stopping beside me.

In his hand is a duffel bag. At least he came prepared. "I've got some clothing for both of us in here. We can pick up a couple things for you while we're on the road tomorrow."

I nod and wait for him to walk, but he steps closer to me.

Confused, I take a step back, but he reaches out, places his hand on my hip to stop me from moving.

My skin burns where his fingers touch me, and a sensation I've never felt before develops in my lower belly. It's warm and makes me shiver. My nipples harden, and a warm flush works its way up my face. Now I'm confused for other reasons, like why I'm feeling this way and why he's touching me.

"You don't have any shoes, so I'm going to carry you," Lucca says.

I try to cover up the hormonal feelings I'm having by ignoring them altogether. "What about your flesh wound?" Lucca gives me a look that says, shut up. "Seriously, you don't have to hurt yourself for me. My feet are the least of my worries. I've been kidnapped and shot at, and…"

I don't get the chance to finish what I'm saying as Lucca takes it upon himself to grab me by the hips and toss me over his shoulder like I'm a rag doll. I'm not even given the opportunity to object before he is walking, carrying both me and the duffel bag. With a gunshot wound.

His actions would be admirable had he not been the cause for all the problems. When we reach the room, he places me back down on my feet and uses the keycard to unlock the room. The door creaks open, and I walk in, Lucca following behind me.

The room smells of stale cigarette smoke, but I'm happy to find two queen-sized beds and a bathroom. Lucca closes the door behind us, and I walk over to one of the beds and sit at the edge. He tosses the duffel bag onto the other bed and unzips it, pulling out a small first aid kit, as well as a pair of boxers and a T-shirt.

He wastes no time and pulls his bloody shirt off, discarding it on the floor. My eyes bulge out of my head when I see his naked torso, every single indent and sculpted muscle. My throat tightens at the image before me. I've never seen a man naked, not that he's naked but half-naked. His toned body is tan, and the V leading down to his nether region makes my heartbeat pick up. If Hope were here right now... I force myself to look away and think about anything but those well-defined muscles.

"Use the alcohol pads in the kit and clean the wound for me," he says and gives me his back. I take a moment to gather my thoughts before I move from the bed, making sure I don't brush against him when I reach for the alcohol wipes.

Using my teeth, I rip open one and hesitate for a second when I come face to face with the wound. The antiseptic smell makes my nose wrinkle, and I breathe through my mouth as I inspect the wound.

What I thought would be a bullet lodged in his skin is exactly as he said: a flesh wound.

"You were right." I croak and clean the area.

Lucca doesn't even flinch as I press the wipe a little harder, trying to clean the edges of the wound. "Don't worry about hurting me. I can handle it. Pain doesn't bother me. An infection does, so make sure the wound is clean."

What is he, a real-life GI joe or something? He gets shot at, is bleeding, and then doesn't even flinch as he gets the wound cleaned. I guess it shouldn't surprise me.

Not after all that's happened.

Even though I'm afraid of hurting him, I do as he says and cleanse the area, using two wipes.

"Good as new," I say, and drop the wipes into the trash can.

Lucca turns around and smiles at me, and my stomach does this little somersault. It doesn't make sense to me. I shouldn't be attracted to him, but with my hormones racing like Mario in Mario Kart, I don't know what else to expect. He is a man, and I'm a young woman.

These emotions happen, right?

"The shirt and boxers are for you. Go take a shower, and then we can go to bed."

I advert my gaze as best as I can and grab my clothing off the bed before rushing into the bathroom. As soon as the door is closed, I click the lock into place. It makes me feel safe, even though deep down, I know it wouldn't stop him from getting inside.

Exhaustion clings to my bones, and I strip out of my clothes quickly, not even glancing in the mirror and instead moving to the shower. The pipes creak when I turn the water on, but it doesn't take long for the bathroom to fog up.

The feel of water on my skin is heavenly, and I sigh into the misty air. I let my eyes fall closed for a moment while running my hair under the water. It's scalding hot, but it's never felt better. I clean myself as best as I can and step out of the shower, grabbing one of the towels hanging up.

The material is scratchy but does the job. I grab the clothes from the counter and stare at them. I want to sniff them. It's stupid, but I can't help it. The longer I tell myself not to, the more I want to. My resolve cracks, and I bring the shirt to my nose and inhale.

A woodsy scent fills my nostrils and calms me immediately. Goosebumps blanket my skin, and I breathe the scent into my lungs one last time before putting the shirt on. It falls to my knees and looks more like a dress than a shirt. I put the boxers on and roll them to fit my waist.

Lucca isn't a huge guy, but he's a lot bigger than me.

Once dressed, I pick up my clothes and unlock the bathroom door. Lucca is sitting on the edge of the bed in a clean navy shirt and a pair of sleep shorts. His phone is in his hand, and there's this peculiar look on his face, like he's plotting some type of world domination.

"Hey," I say, making my presence known.

His head jackknifes up, and his gaze collides with mine before slipping down my body.

Is he checking me out? I doubt it.

"Ready for bed?" His voice is deeper, almost smoky.

"Sure," I whisper and place my clothes on the floor at the edge of the bed. I pull the sheets back on the mattress and then slip under them.

Lucca moves about the room for a few minutes before shutting the light off.

"Goodnight, butterfly."

Darkness surrounds me, and I panic. I fist the sheets in my hands and blink my eyes rapidly to keep the tears at bay. Ten minutes pass, then twenty, and I'm barely holding onto reality. After being in that cell, having all this freedom, a bed to sleep in, a pillow to rest my head on. I'm afraid it isn't real, that someone is going to pop out of the dark and tell me it's a joke.

Unable to sleep, I roll over and look at the other bed. My eyes have adjusted to the darkness enough to make out Lucca on top of the covers, lying flat on his back. I wonder if he is sleeping? The worst idea ever hits me. Or maybe it's the best idea ever.

As quietly as I can, I slide out of my bed and climb into his. My gaze stays glued on his chest, rising and falling in a slow and steady rhythm. I lift the blanket gently and crawl underneath.

Even with the thin comforter between us, his body heat radiates into my skin. My whole body relaxes knowing Lucca is close. At least for tonight, I am safe. Exhausted, I let my eyes drift closed. I can't hear him, but I can feel his body next to mine, and with that thought, I finally fall into a deep sleep.

14

LUCCA

I wake up oddly hot, like I fell asleep next to a small radiator. Blinking my eyes open, I take in the stained ceiling of the cheap motel room. My brain jump-starts, and all sleep evaded thoughts come rushing back to my mind.

Turning my head, I find Claire curled up next to me. Her small body is swallowed up by the scratchy motel blanket. Her face is only a few inches away from my shoulder. One of her hands is tucked beneath her cheek, while her other hand is flat on my arm. Even in sleep, she is afraid that she might be left alone.

I can't believe I didn't wake up when she crawled into the bed. Normally, I'm a very light sleeper. Part of me is glad to have her close—safe and protected.

Asleep, she looks more like the child I know. Her features relaxed, and her pert mouth ajar. Her red hair is unruly, framing her face. There's a smattering of freckles across her face, but are more prominent around her nose and cheeks. She looks like a little sun-kissed angel.

With a smile on my face, I get up slowly, careful not to wake her. I slip into the bathroom and strip out of my clothes. The pipes creak loudly when I turn on the water, but by the time I step under the spray, it's warm.

I let the water pound against the tense muscles of my back and wash my hair and body. My hand slips down between my legs, and my cock stiffens. Fuck, it's been... I can't even remember the last time I had sex. All I know is it's been too long if the mere graze of my hand against the thick rod turns me on.

There's no point in giving myself blue balls. Still, I hesitate... Claire is just on the other side of that door, sleeping peacefully, unaware of the cruel beast just a few feet away. It feels wrong to fuck my hand, but rationally, I know it's not. I have needs, and all I'm doing is taking care of myself. I'm not exposing her to anything.

Letting my hormones drive my thoughts, I fist my cock in my hand and slide my palm down the thick shaft and back up again, swiping my thumb over the sensitive mushroom-shaped head. A hiss escapes my lips at the primal need that ripples through me. Red fiery hair and soft, innocent green eyes are all I see when I close my eyes. I bare my teeth and lean forward, resting against the shower wall beneath the spray of water.

I cannot, will not, think of the young girl in the other room while I fuck myself with my hand. She isn't old enough for me to be thinking about her while I do this. Despite it being wrong, I can't shake the thoughts away, and even though it's Claire's image that I see in my mind, I force myself to call her something else.

Samantha.

Pink lips and a smiling face are all I see as she looks up at me with longing in her eyes. So innocent and young. If I ever touched her, even in the slightest, I'd risk tainting her.

I'm not a good man, and the fact that the thought of tainting her turns me on more proves that. My cock has never been harder, and that both terrifies and interests me. She's too young, too sweet, too fragile for me and this world.

That doesn't lessen my want.

My grip tightens, and I stroke faster and faster. My breaths come out in shallow puffs, and I know I'm close. A groan lodges in my throat, and I bite my lip until the metallic taste of blood fills my mouth.

Pleasure builds at the base of my spine, and my toes curl.

"Samantha," I growl, slamming my fist against the wall. Even though it's Claire's name, I want to growl.

A second later, the coil in my belly unravels, and my entire body tightens like a bow. One more hard stroke, where I imagine it's her tight virginal cunt wrapped around my cock, sends me over the edge. Spurts of sticky hot cum erupt from my cock and paint the wall while I stand there, my heart thundering in my chest. I can't hear or breathe. All I can do is feel the pleasure course through me, drowning every emotion and thought that isn't centered on her.

I drift back down from my high slowly, like a feather. The guilt shatters the bubble of euphoria immediately. This is wrong. My thoughts are wrong. To even consider thinking of Claire while masturbating is fucked up.

She's like a little sister to me.

The water grows cold and washes away the proof of my wrongdoings. I wish it could wash away my memory of it as well. The shower helped to lessen the tension, but now I feel like a sick fucker.

I turn the water off and step out of the shower, drying with one of the cheap towels. This hotel isn't the worst I've stayed in. I wish I could've taken Claire somewhere better, but I couldn't risk Julian finding us, and I'm not stupid. He's got men looking for me, overturning every rock and trailing every tip given.

He won't stop until I'm dead, and I will not risk putting Claire in that kind of situation, so the shitty hotel is what she gets.

Once I'm dressed, I open the door and step out of the bathroom and into the bedroom. I'm not surprised to find Claire sitting at the edge of the bed. Sleep still clings to her delicate features, and I have to force myself not to drag my gaze down her body.

Who cares if she's wearing my shirt and boxers? Me, obviously. I tell myself it's the proximity and the fact that I haven't been with a woman for a while that has my most basic primal instincts rushing to the surface, but I wonder... if maybe it's something else as well. *No.*

With my jaw clenched, I walk over to the duffel bag and shove my clothes inside of it.

"We should probably get going. We need to stay on the move." I don't mention that I just betrayed one of the most powerful mob bosses of the east coast. The last thing I need is for her to be more worried, looking over her shoulder at every turn.

Claire nods and tucks a few strands of her bright hair behind her ear. "Do you think I could call Tracy and Steven? I know they're probably worried sick about me, and I haven't gotten to contact them. I want to make sure they're okay."

As much as I hate to do it, I have to tell her no. "I'm sorry, but no. It's too dangerous to contact anyone right now. We'll head out in about five minutes, swing through a drive-thru for some breakfast, and then hit the road again."

She doesn't bother trying to hide her disappointment from me. "Okay."

Frustration slithers in my gut. I'm pissed that I put Claire in this situation. If it wasn't for her association with me, she would be tucked in her bed back home, but she's not. She's on the run, barely escaping the clutches of Julian Moretti. Thinking of if he were to get his hands on her keeps me focused. I can handle her disappointment if it means she's safe.

Shelter from the storm that is my life.

I grab the duffel bag and look at Claire once more. She's still in the T-shirt and boxers, but that's just how it has to be. "Let's go," I order with a hint of impatience.

Claire stands, her face still frowning with disappointment. She looks down at her clothing. "I have nothing to wear. I can't be seen like this. It'll draw attention."

I smirk because, for once, she sounds like a typical sixteen-year-old girl. "That's good since no one else is going to see you. Once it's dark and we get close to the next hotel, I'll stop somewhere and get you some pants and a couple T-shirts."

Crossing her arms over her chest, she stares into my eyes, her gaze so concentrated, I wonder if she can see inside my mind. If she knows what I did earlier and was awake and heard me calling another woman's name.

If she did, she hasn't mentioned it, and I'm not about to confess what I did. I need to push the filthy, immoral thoughts I had away. Claire is a kid, and it doesn't matter that she is growing up or that there was something so sweet and pure about her that made me want to dissolve her like a sugar cube on my tongue.

She is off-limits. Completely off-limits.

15

CLAIRE

Another night, another motel. This one seems less of a dump than the last one, but still a dirty place I'd rather not sleep in. Too bad I don't really have a choice.

"You want to wait here or come in?" Lucca asks, putting the car in park.

"I'll come in," I say, already opening the door. I'd rather not be alone, no matter how short of a timeframe.

He nods his head, and we walk into the motel office where a bell chimes above us in greeting. A moment later, a woman walks out of a door behind the small counter. There is a permanent frown on her face that makes it seem like she's annoyed by the prospect of customers.

That look evaporates into thin air when she sees Lucca approaching. She straightens up, puts a smile on her face, and I'm pretty sure she pushes her chest out a little. I stare at her chest, wondering if she has nicer boobs than me.

"Hey ya'll," she greets with a southern drawl, and I wonder

how far we have actually driven. I don't even know what state we're in right now.

"Hey, babe." Lucca grins, showing off his perfect smile. I cringe at the word *babe*. Why is he calling her a pet name? Does he know her?

I inspect her. She is pretty, with long auburn hair and big brown eyes. She seems to be closer to Lucca's age, maybe a bit younger. Her shirt is tight, showing off her petite frame and large breasts.

"What can I do for you, handsome?" The receptionist giggles, and I suppress a gag. I already dislike her, and I don't even know her.

Lucca leans against the counter. "Just looking to crash for a night. You wouldn't have a room at the end available?"

"I might." The girl smiles. "One room? For you and…" she trails off, her gaze swinging over to where I'm standing.

"My sister," Lucca explains. "She's underage, so I'll share a room with her. Two beds if you have any available. I'm paying cash," he adds, placing two twenty-dollar bills on the counter.

"No problem." She types something into the computer that looks like it's thirty years old, at the very least. If I didn't see the screen light up myself, I'd be sure it wouldn't even be running anymore.

"I do have the room at the very end free… and the one right next to it as well. So, if you want to spend some time away from the kid, you could come next door and maybe hang out with me later?"

I don't know what bothers me more, her calling me *the kid*, her trying to get Lucca away from me, or the way Lucca smiles at her like he is actually considering it.

My stomach churns, and my chest constricts. A nasty

feeling spreads through my body. A feeling that takes me a moment to recognize...

Jealousy.

I'm jealous. And surprised that it only now dawned on me... I have a crush on Lucca. It makes sense, the fluttering of butterflies in my stomach, the heat in my core pulsing with its own heartbeat every time he touches me.

"Here is your key. I'm Paula, by the way." Paula grins, sliding the plastic card over to Lucca.

"Thank you, Paula." Lucca smiles back but doesn't offer his name. "Come on, Sis. Time to hit the hay." He turns to me, throwing an arm around my shoulder.

Instantly, I relax. We walk out of the lobby, and Lucca releases me, putting distance between us. We climb back into the car and drive to the end of the building. Getting out of the car, we grab all the bags with the clothes we bought today and head to the room.

"I don't want you to leave," I blurt out as soon as we are inside.

"What are you talking about? I'm not leaving."

Make yourself clearer, Claire.

"I mean, don't go to the room next door with *Paula*." I try really hard not to say her name with venom, but I fail miserably. The idea of Lucca being with another woman is unsettling, and even though I know I shouldn't feel any way about it, I can't help myself.

"I'm not." Lucca chuckles, a sound I haven't heard in a very long time. It warms my body all over like a sip of hot chocolate on the coldest winter day. "I won't leave this room. Don't you worry your pretty little head about that. Why don't you take a shower? I have to make some phone calls."

"Oh, okay..." I nod, feeling a little silly for thinking he was going to leave me. I rummage through the bags for a pair of pajamas and scurry into the small attached bathroom.

Using the hotel provided bar of soap, I wash my body head to toe before rinsing off with hot water. My hair feels dry, and the knots are going to be a pain to get out without conditioner, but at least I'm clean.

Turning off the water, I reach for the thin towel on the rack and dry off.

I stand in front of the mirror and stare at my reflection, wondering what Lucca sees when he looks at me. I'm a little scrawny, my boobs are just now taking shape, my belly is flat, and my hips barely have any curves to them.

I look like a teenager, but I haven't felt like a kid in a long time. I've seen too much evil, experienced a kind of hardship that most people will never know. I lost my childlike innocence the day my mother left, and I haven't seen the world through wondrous eyes in years.

I might live in the body of a teenage girl, but my mind is mature, and I feel like an adult in every way. If only I could make Lucca see it too.

With newfound determination, I quickly pull on my clothes and exit the bathroom. As soon as I open the door, I find Lucca eager to switch, squeezing past me to get into the bathroom. While he is showering, I take a seat on his bed and wait. I try not to think about him being naked in the bathroom.

I do wonder what he looks like... no!

I shake away that indecent thought and count the stripes on the carpet instead.

I'm still counting when the door opens, and a cloud of steam billows into the room. Lucca appears shirtless, droplets of water cling to his tan skin, and I have to tear my eyes from his bare chest before my cheeks burst into flames.

I wonder if he finds me attractive. If he thinks I'm as pretty as that Paula girl.

"Do you think I'm pretty?" I blurt out the question before I can stop myself.

"You're beautiful, Claire. Why would you even ask that?" Lucca's voice is very convincing, and for a moment, I consider not responding, but I can't help myself. If I want him to see me like he sees her, then I need to be different.

"I just... I don't feel pretty at all. I don't look like that girl either."

"Beauty is in the eye of the beholder. It's not just about looks, but what's inside. You can look like a supermodel on the outside and still be a really shitty person. Looks aren't everything, Butterfly."

I can't lie, that makes me feel better, but it doesn't convince me he sees me like he saw her.

"Are you not tired?" Lucca changes the subject, coming to sit on the bed beside me.

"I am. I'm not sleeping yet because I was wondering if I could sleep in your bed with you again?" I don't dare look at him. I simply keep my gaze trained on my fingers in my lap. I feel like a child asking to sleep in bed next to him, but I'm not ready to deal with the trauma I've endured. "I'm just scared of sleeping by myself. The bed feels too big, and the different hotels every night..." I trail off.

"You don't have to explain," Lucca says. "Come on, get under the blanket."

With a smile on my face, I eagerly crawl into Lucca's bed and under the thin comforter. He climbs into the bed beside me but doesn't crawl beneath the covers, leaving the thin blanket separating our bodies. I'm a little disappointed but not surprised.

"Don't you get cold without covering up?" I ask once he turns off the light.

"Nah, I sleep better like this. Plus, this way, I don't have to worry about getting caught up in the sheets if I need to make a quick move."

I don't want to think about what he means by that.

Lucca is so sweet and caring with me, like another person altogether. It seems I keep forgetting what kind of person he is and the damage he can cause. Seconds tick by, the darkness blankets over me. I'm tired, but sleep isn't coming easily. My mind won't shut off, and I'm thinking of what will happen tomorrow and how much longer we will have to do this.

"Is it going to be like this forever? Staying in hotels and hiding?" If that's the case, then I'm not sure I can do this. I'm a mess already, and I just want to fall asleep and never wake up sometimes.

"No. Soon we will slow down, and things will go back to normal. I have to make certain that you're safe first."

A wave of guilt washes over me and clings to me like a second skin. Guilt about feeling safe with Lucca, guilt about liking him even though I know he is a killer. He killed my father, and still, I crawl into his bed, accepting his protection and comfort.

Maybe I'm just as evil as he is?

16

LUCCA

A few days pass by in a blur. I lose track of how many states and cheap hotels we've been in. All I know is that I need to get Claire somewhere safe. I can't keep her on the run with me. She needs stability. She needs her family and to make new friends and be a teenager.

No matter how much I enjoy having her with me, I need to keep her best interest in mind.

"Do you care if I change the station?" Claire asks, pulling me from my thoughts.

"Yeah, sure." I nod. I don't even listen to the radio. How could I with a thousand thoughts racing through my mind?

She turns the knob until some pop song comes on. She leans back in her seat and starts singing along with the song softly. I'm not sure if she even realizes she's doing it, but when she sings about kissing all night, she abruptly stops.

I glance over at Claire and find her cheeks red and her green eyes wide. She quickly looks away and out the window, like she is ashamed about singing those words. Or maybe it's the fact that I heard her singing them at all. Either way, I can't help but smile.

She's so innocent, and even shy, proving her age. I've noticed Claire getting embarrassed about looking at me or doing certain things. I'm pretty sure she has a little crush on me.

It's really cute how she gets all red-faced and flustered. I'm certain this is something we'll laugh about in a few years.

"Hey," I say loudly, so I know she can hear.

Her head snaps back to look in my direction. "I talked to Steven and Tracy this morning. If everything goes as planned, we'll meet them tomorrow."

"Meet them?" Claire asks curiously. "I thought it's too dangerous?"

"It was too dangerous a few days ago. I had to make sure I found a safe place for you to stay with them."

"Wait. You are leaving me again?" Her voice has an undeniably accusing tone to it.

"I can't stay with you for more than one reason, but I'm kind of wanted by some bad men. Terrible and dangerous men, and you can't live your life on the run. You need to go to school, and you need parents. Stability. You need to live your life."

"What if someone comes for me again?"

"They won't." I grip the steering wheel tight.

"But what if they do?"

"Then I'll kill them too," I quip, and that shuts her up.

Crossing her arms in front of her chest, she stares out of the windshield with a pout. I know she is disappointed I'm leaving again, but this is the best thing for her, and I'll always do what's best for her.

"I have to pee," Claire tells me after a while.

"We'll stop for the night soon." The words have barely passed my lips when I spot the sign for a Holiday Inn. "Why don't we stay at a nicer place tonight?"

"Sure," Claire murmurs, a pout permanently etched onto her face.

I pull off the interstate and turn right at the stop sign toward the Holiday Inn. It's a nicer hotel, well, nicer than what we've been staying at. Hopefully, I can make tonight a memorable one, and we can put the last week of chaos behind us. Claire grabs the bag from the back seat while I park, and together, we get out of the car and enter the hotel.

Luckily, the lady at the front desk is an older woman with greying hair and librarian glasses, lessening the likelihood that she'll flirt with me, *hopefully*.

"I need a room with two queen beds for my sister and me," I tell her.

Her brown eyes dart between Claire and me, speculation building before she drops her gaze down to the screen in front of her and types something into the computer.

A moment later, she says, "That's sixty-nine dollars."

Out of the corner of my eye, I notice Claire looking around the hotel. Her eyes are full of amazement, and I swear I see a tiny smile threatening to appear on her lips. I pay for the room with cash, and the lady hands us the keycards without another word.

We take the elevator to the third floor and find our room easily enough. I open the door and flip the light on. Claire rushes in, drops the bag to the floor, and falls back onto the mattress with a sigh as soon as we enter the room.

I walk inside and toe-off my boots next to the bed.

Claire moves into a sitting position and looks over at me.

"This might be a bit dramatic, but this is my favorite bed out of all the beds I've slept in this week."

I don't even try to hide my laughter. "That's not dramatic at all."

"Oh, crap!" Claire rushes from the bed and squeezes past me and into the bathroom. The door slams shut, and I walk over to the bed and lie back against the mattress. Tomorrow, she'll be in her new home and out of harm's way, hopefully, forever.

The sound of the toilet flushing pulls me from my thoughts. A moment later, Claire returns to the room, sitting on the edge of her mattress. She looks down at her hands, a sadness in her eyes, and I don't want our last night together to be one of sadness.

"Do you want to order a pizza and watch a movie?"

My suggestion has Claire opening up like a flower in the sun. "That would be great. It feels like forever since I've done anything normal."

"Let's do it. What kind of pizza do you want?" I ask, pulling my cell phone out of my pocket so I can call one of the local pizza places.

"Anything as long as it doesn't have olives on it." She makes this expression where her nose wrinkles and her tongue sticks out.

"How about sausage and mushroom?"

"That sounds delicious."

I do an online order and toss the tv remote to Claire. She looks down at it with furrowed brows. "What?"

"Pick something to watch. A movie or tv show. Whatever is fine. I want tonight to end on a happy note since it didn't start that way."

"I'm just happy to have a decent bed to sleep in tonight." She giggles, and the sound makes me feel warm all over. When I let her go tomorrow, it will be hard but worth it.

For the next thirty minutes, we get comfortable and wait for the pizza. Claire decides on some superhero movie, and I end up watching her more than the movie. I tell myself it's because I know I won't be seeing her again for a while, but I know that's not completely it. There is something about her that draws me in and makes it hard for me to look away.

When the pizza arrives, I go to the door, pay, and return to the bed.

"Ladies first." I smile and place the box down in front of her.

Claire grins and opens the box, grabbing the first slice. We eat in silence, watching the movie and enjoying one another's company. Over the course of the last couple days, I've come to know more about Claire than I ever did before, and it makes me want to get to know her more. It makes me want to keep her close.

But that would be selfish. She needs to return to her normal life. I need to make sure that I keep us hidden, and her safe. I don't need to be worrying about her.

I'm making the right choice, and I know that as I look over at Claire and she smiles at me.

17

CLAIRE

This is my last night with Lucca, my last chance to make him see that I'm not a little girl anymore. I've missed Steven and Tracy dearly, and I'm happy to be able to see them, but I also can't help feeling sad about Lucca leaving. I feel like I just got him back, and now he is disappearing. I'm losing him all over again.

Part of me knows I should be glad. What he said is true, I need a family and stable home. Unfortunately, there is this other part of me telling me I won't be happy without Lucca. There is a voice in the back of my mind urging me to stay with him. What kind of life would that be, though? I'm not naive to think that it would be great. I mean, look at us now.

He wants me to go to school and be a kid, but I don't feel like a kid anymore. I don't fit in with those teenagers, and I never will. I'm basically an adult. Now I just need to make Lucca see me as one too. All day I've been contemplating what to do, how to make him see me as more than the little girl he saved.

We ordered pizza and watched a movie together, but it wasn't quite how I wanted it to be. He stayed on his bed, and I on mine. Every once in a while, I would catch him watching me, staring at me with a faraway look in his eyes. It's the last push I need to make a move.

He's in the shower when I finalize my plan. I'm terrified of him rejecting me, but I will never know if I don't try.

With shaking hands, I take off my clothes until I'm completely naked. I'm so nervous that I almost get dressed again. Instead, I force my feet to move.

Turning off the light, I climb into bed and tuck the blanket over me. The sheets are cool but soft against my skin, sending goosebumps across my arms.

Excitement and fear swirl around my stomach as I wait for Lucca to finish in the bathroom. A million thoughts enter my mind. What if he rejects me? No, I can't think about that. He just needs to see that I'm grown up now. All he needs is a little push, and that's exactly what I'm giving him.

Just a little push.

My entire body jerks when the bathroom door opens. Light filters into the room for a few seconds before Lucca turns it off, descending the room into darkness once more.

I can't hear his footsteps, but I swear I feel his body moving. The air between us shifts, and my breathing speeds up. I'm hyper-aware of every little movement I make. Every tiny motion shifts the blanket so slightly over my naked skin.

My throat suddenly feels so dry it's difficult to swallow, and when I feel the bed dip, my heart ceases to beat for a moment before picking back up at hyper-speed.

Lucca settles into the spot next to me, and for a long moment, I just lie there, questioning myself and my plan.

Maybe this is a mistake?

A few minutes pass, and I shake all those fears and insecurities away. This is my chance. It's now or never.

Gathering all my courage, I pull the blanket from my body. Cool air washes over my heated skin as I move around the bed. Lucca says something, but I can't make out his words.

In the dark, I reach out to him until my hand lands on his chest. I climb on top of him, straddling his torso while keeping both of my hands planted on his chest.

"Claire," he says my name loud enough for me to hear. His chest rumbles beneath my touch, sending little shock waves through my body. "Claire—"

I lean down, hoping that I can find his lips in the dark. By a stroke of luck, I do. I press my lips to his, and my body tingles.

My first kiss...

For that one moment, everything is okay. Nothing standing between us, not age or morals. No one is hunting us. My parents are alive, and Lucca isn't a criminal.

We're just two people who like each other.

For this single moment, I'm happy. I forget everything around us and simply enjoy Lucca's warm lips against mine. One moment...

I should have known that there is no lasting happiness for me.

Lucca grabs me by the hips and pushes me off him. The next instant, the light flickers on, and the reality of what I've done comes crashing down on me.

"What the fuck are you doing, Claire?" Lucca yells loud enough for me, and everyone else in this hotel to hear. His eyes briefly roam over my naked body before he looks away with disgust. "Jesus, Claire! Put some fucking clothes on."

I can pinpoint the exact moment my heart breaks in two. He doesn't want me. He doesn't like my body. He finds me repulsive. He won't even look at me.

Never in my life have I felt so humiliated and disgusted with myself.

In a haste, I grab my clothes off the chair and put them back on. Even fully dressed, the feeling of being exposed doesn't leave me.

Without facing Lucca again, I get into the second bed and pull the blanket over me. I've turned away from him, so I can only see the wall, but I know he is going to want to talk before he turns off the light.

As predicted, he walks around the bed to stand right in front of me. I close my eyes, pretending to be asleep, but of course, he knows better.

"Claire," he calls to me, touching my shoulder lightly.

My eyes fly open, and I pull away as if his touch burns my skin.

"What?" I ask, like I'm oblivious to the situation.

"I'm sorry I yelled at you. I shouldn't have talked to you like that. You caught me by surprise. It was a poor decision to let you sleep in the bed with me, to begin with. I take responsibility for that."

Way to dig the knife in deeper.

I turn away, unable to listen to him any longer, but he doesn't let me get away. Pinching my chin, he tilts my face, so I'm looking at him. Unable to look anywhere else, I'm forced to stare into his amber eyes.

"Look, you don't have to be embarrassed. You're a teenager. Hormones are making you feel all kinds of things. It's normal to have a crush on someone older than you."

He might as well have slapped me with what he said.

"I'm not a child."

Lucca's gaze turns to steel. "To me, you are."

Not able to take any more of this, I shrug away from his hold and pull the blanket over my head. I know it won't protect me from anything, especially not from Lucca, but for the rest of the night, I pretend it does. I pretend this fluffy hotel comforter is a steel wall protecting me from the world.

Rejection settles deep into my bones. Tear after tear falls from my eyes and runs down the side of my face. I imagine every single one falling onto the mattress and staining it forever, just like my heart.

18

LUCCA

The air is tense, and after the way things ended last night, awkward. I hate that our last day together has come and that we've found ourselves in this situation. Claire can't even look at me and turns her body away from mine when we get in the car to head to the suburbs where she'll be staying.

I try to think of an easier way to approach this, one that doesn't result in me beating her down or embarrassing her further, but I don't know if there is a way around it. No matter what, she is going to walk away from this ashamed of herself, wondering if there is something wrong with her that makes me not want her.

"You know, it's okay, Claire. It's just an innocent little crush, nothing to get bent out of shape about or be ashamed of."

She doesn't respond, and her silence makes my grip on the steering wheel tighten. I have to nip this in the bud, end it before it gets out of hand.

"Look, it's just your hormones messing with your head. Whatever feelings you're having, they'll go away."

She turns in her seat and crosses her arms over her chest. Of course, she would be stubborn about this too.

"And what if it doesn't?"

I grit my teeth. "It will. You'll find someone your own age, someone who likes the same things as you do. Someone special."

"What if I don't want them?"

I clench my jaw, and my molars grind together hard enough to crack. She's not going to stop, not until I make her. Until I drive the point all the way into her little heart.

"Then you don't, but I am not the man for you. I am not a knight or even half of the person you most likely think I am."

"I don't care," she murmurs.

"I do. I care, and I'm not going to tell you again."

"I can have feelings for whoever I want."

She's really going to make me go there. Really going to make me hurt her with my words. How do I tell her I don't want her, but nicely? There is no way.

"I don't want you, Claire. In my eyes, you will always be a child. A little kid. Like a sister to me. Do you understand? I don't care about you or want you in any other way than that."

I'm a bastard. I don't dare look at her. I don't think I could handle seeing the pain in her eyes that I know is there now. I've crushed her spirit, and all but taken her heart out of her chest.

She sniffles. If I could punch myself in the head right now, I would.

"I don't mean to hurt your feelings, Claire." The words taste foul coming out of my mouth, especially because that's exactly what I did.

"Just forget it. I don't know what I was thinking. Obviously,

I'm stupid." Her voice cracks and the pain she's feeling resonates through it.

"No, you aren't stupid—"

"Stop! I already made a fool of myself. I don't need you to continue to explain to me how you feel."

There are so many more things I could say, but would it really change what I already said? Would it really help lessen the hand I dealt her? I don't think so.

Pressing my lips together, I swallow my responses down.

In a couple hours, she'll be back where she belongs, safe with Tracy and Steven again. This time will be different, though. I won't be able to watch Claire every second of every day, so I found a way around it. I found someone to help me.

Claire will not like it, but that doesn't matter to me. All that matters is her safety, and that's not up for negotiation.

The remainder of the drive is pin-drop quiet. Each mile marker we pass, the tenser the air becomes. I roll my window down a smidge, so I don't suffocate on it.

When we're about twenty minutes from Steven and Tracy's new place, Claire speaks again, "So, what happens after this? You're just going to drop me off and disappear off the face of the earth again?"

"I already told you that this is how it has to be. You deserve to live a life that is full and happy. I'm not falling off the face of the earth. I'm just not going to be around. You'll live your life like you did before."

"Like when you had someone following me? Like when you forced yourself into my life? That's what you mean when you say you aren't going to be around?" I can feel her fiery stare on my skin. It burns with the intensity of ten suns. She is pissed, and I understand why, but that changes nothing.

"Yes, it will be just as it was before."

"Which means you'll lurk in the shadows watching me at every turn?"

I have no problem admitting that I had someone watching her from afar. It was only ever for her safety, and so I knew what was going on. This time, I won't have someone lurking in the shadows to watch her.

I'll have someone living with her, someone capable of keeping her in place at all times.

"If you must know, *I* won't be watching you."

"No, someone else will be."

"This time, things will be different."

Claire huffs like a small child in the seat. "Whatever. I'd rather you just leave altogether. If you're gone, then I won't be reminded of how stupid I acted."

She really thinks I care that much? That her actions changed my opinion of her?

"That's behind us, Claire. I don't judge you for having a crush."

Claire turns to face the window, arms folded over her chest. It sucks that this is how today will end, with her pissed off at me, but it is what it is.

A few minutes later, we turn into the subdivision and then into the driveway of the small cookie-cutter house. As if she can't get out of the car fast enough, Claire undoes her seatbelt and bounds from the SUV, the second she spots Steven and Tracy waiting to greet us at the front door.

I take my time and put the vehicle in park and shut it off before I climb out. I wanted to give Claire a moment with her parents, especially after everything that happened the last time they were together.

As I step out of the car and walk up to them, Claire's soft laughter rings through my ears. It tugs at my heart, and I'm reminded why I'm doing this. Why I've done everything I could to protect her. She is too innocent for this world, a butterfly that should be free to fly and never caged by the harsh rules that this life I live brings.

"I was so worried that something had happened to you," Claire whispers and wraps her arms around Steven.

He smiles and kisses her on the head. "Nothing could stop me. I've got a few bruises but nothing serious."

Claire pulls away, taking a step back. It's then that she realizes I'm there, and she returns to her sour-faced expression. The door to the house opens, drawing our attention to it.

"Hey!" Carter walks out with his hands in his pockets. Young, and hopefully, not dumb. He's only a little older than Claire but will be the perfect live-in bodyguard. His dark green eyes pause on Claire. I half expect desire to pool in his eyes, but all I see is curiosity.

"Who is he?" Claire doesn't direct her question at me, but instead, Tracy and Steven.

"Lucca thought after what happened that it would be a good idea to have a live-in bodyguard. Someone that could…"

Tracy doesn't even get to finish her sentence before Claire is turning and shoving her finger into my chest. She's short, her head coming to about level with my pecs.

"If this is what you meant when you said things would be different, then no. No, he isn't staying here. It's one thing to have someone follow me when I leave the house, but this… this is taking it too far." The anger in her eyes ignites a fire in my belly.

I want to push her, make her understand why it has to be

this way, why I am leaving. That this is why I will risk her heart to sever the connection.

"Carter will not hurt you. He will not interfere with your life or bother you in any way. If it's easier, you can pretend he isn't here at all."

Carter snorts, a smirk on his lips that slips off his face when I pin him with a don't-make-me-kill-you-right-here gaze.

"Ha, yeah. That sounds doable." Claire shakes her head. "No, you're taking him with you. End of discussion." The more she pushes, the more I push back. She thinks she can win this argument, but there is no arguing with me about her protection.

"Sorry, Claire, but he's staying. It has to be this way."

My word is final, and she knows it, which is probably why she curls her lips and hisses at me like a kitten.

"I hate you!" She pokes my chest with her finger. "I hate you, and I don't want your protection. I don't want you to be a part of my life. In fact, I wish you never saved my life that day." Each word is a slap across my face, but I stand tall and strong like a lighthouse battered by the salty ocean waves. Claire is just mad. She doesn't mean anything she's saying right now. A response sits on the edge of my tongue.

Angrily, Claire turns around and marches into the house, slamming the door closed behind her. Tracy sighs, and her red cheeks tell me she wants to apologize, but she has nothing to apologize for. Claire's reaction is as expected.

"Carter is here to help with anything you may need. I'll still be available via cell phone."

"Do you want to stay for dinner? Maybe she'll perk up soon."

"No, that's okay." I smile through the pain pulsing in my chest. "I think it's best I leave."

I know Tracy is disappointed, but the only thing that will make things better for Claire is for me to disappear. Once I'm gone, she'll return to a normal routine. I'm sure of it. Especially after what she said about wishing I had never saved her life that night.

"Well, drive safe, and if you need anything, please let us know." Tracy smiles.

Steven waves goodbye and ushers his wife into the house, leaving Carter and me on the front porch.

"I've got this, boss. No worries."

I grit my teeth. I'm putting Claire's life in his hands. He better have a good fucking grasp on everything. Otherwise, this is going to end badly for him.

"You better. I want updates every single day, and when I say this…" I stalk toward him and fist the front of his shirt, forcing him to both hear and see me. "If you touch her or hurt her, I will kill you, and I promise it won't be a simple little bullet to the head. Understand?" I give him a little shake.

Carter keeps it together, only allowing a sliver of terror to slip through.

"Yes. Yes, I understand." Carter clears his throat.

"Good." I release him and take a step back. "Every day. I want a text every day, Carter. If I don't get one, then I'll assume the worst, and show up right on this fucking doorstep."

"I know. I'll give you an update every day, and I won't touch her. I won't have anything at all to do with her."

I nod, satisfied with his answer. "Good, be safe and take care of her. I'm leaving now."

"I will." Carter stands a little straighter.

He's the perfect person for this job. I shove my hands into my pockets and walk down the driveway. Every step that I take away from her is another weight added to my feet, making it harder for me to walk away.

I don't want to leave. I don't want to push her away, but staying with me isn't safe. I can't protect her and be the reason she's in danger. I have to go, even if it's just for her. Maybe I'll see her again someday? I would hope so given the way things ended today, but if I don't, I won't be surprised. Claire wished I hadn't saved her life, so it is better for me to not exist in her life, not in the physical sense at least.

If I ever see her again, I can only hope it is years from now, when she has realized her crush on me was nothing special and that I did everything I could to make sure she had a good life.

19

CLAIRE
TWO YEARS LATER

Eighteen years old. I made it to the big one-eight, but it doesn't seem like I achieved anything. I've done the same thing every day since the night he dropped me off with my parents. He abandoned me that day, shattered my heart into a million pieces by calling me a child, by telling me I'd move on, that it was a silly crush that we would laugh about someday. He broke my fragile, stupid heart and then walked away without looking back.

Now, two years later, there is a package sitting on my bed. It's from Lucca. I don't want to open it, but I'm too curious. He can't come see me, but he can give Carter a package to give to me? That fact angers me beyond measure. Knowing he is near, talking to Carter and my parents, but never to me, makes me furious. I know Lucca pays for anything and everything I want. He made certain I had food and clothes, but none of that makes up for leaving.

He pays Carter to protect me or technically babysit me. Through Carter, I've kept tabs on Lucca. Of course, he never tells me anything I really want to know. But enough to know he is alive and doing well.

I rip open the box and imagine I'm snapping Lucca's neck as I pull back the flaps on the box. There's bubble wrap inside, so I yank it out to see the object on the bottom.

It's a shadow box with purple and gold paper butterflies in it and the quote: *"We delight in the beauty of the butterfly, but rarely admit the changes it has gone through to achieve that beauty."* — *Maya Angelou* printed across the glass.

It's beautiful, but a reminder that even at eighteen, he still sees me as a kid. He still sees that shy, little girl wearing the butterfly sweater that approached him that day. I hate it. Hate that in his eyes, that's all I'll ever be. The pain from that day when he left, when he told me he would only ever see me as a child, comes rushing back.

I look down at the box again, remembering the first present he ever gave me. I was so happy, so hopeful... so stupid.

"I should probably get back." *I look over my shoulder and back to the door, worrying that my father might come walking out the door at any second to yell at me.*

"Before you go..." Lucca stands, placing his bottle of beer down, "I have something for you." *He walks over to the door and disappears inside his house.*

I stand, staring at the door, wondering what he could have for me. A second later, I'm given an answer when the door creaks, and he comes back out with what looks like a notebook. I'm further puzzled until he hands the notebook to me, and I see a blue and black glitter butterfly on the cover.

It's beautiful. "Thank you," *I choke out, shocked that he would get me something. No one has ever gotten me anything, not even my father.*

Lucca's eyes dart away, and he picks his beer back up. "It's nothing. I just saw it, and I figured you would like it. I guessed right."

"Yes, you did." I smile and hold the notebook to my chest.

Hope blooms inside, right over the spot the notebook rests. "Thank you," *I say again, taking small steps backward.*

"You're welcome... and remember if you need anything, let me know."

I nod and turn, walking back toward my porch with a wide smile on my face, never looking back even though I'm tempted to.

For the first time in a long time, I feel good about tomorrow. That maybe things will be better? This has to be a sign. It has to be.

I grip the edge of the box and toss it across the room. The box hits the wall and shatters just like my heart did. Angry, I throw myself down on the bed and bury my face into a pillow.

No matter how much I wished for my crush on him to go away, it never did. I always thought time heals all wounds, but that was a lie. My want for Lucca became stronger, and still, to this day, I want him. Over the last two years, I had numerous occasions to get involved with men.

As my body filled out more, so did the interest of the opposite sex. I couldn't count the number of times I had been asked out. I was quiet and kept to myself. Most people called me a book nerd because I was always in the library or reading, but that didn't deter guys from noticing me.

I wasn't interested in anyone else, though. No matter how much I tried to tell myself Lucca didn't care about me the way I did him, I couldn't make my treacherous heart move on.

Now I'm lying in bed, on the evening of my birthday, moping over a man that will never want me. *Pull it together, Claire.* Screaming into my pillow will not change things, but sure as hell will alleviate some tension.

I pull my face out of the pillow and look up to find Carter standing in the doorway of my room.

"What do you want, Carter?" I growl, unable to hide my frustration.

Carter strolls into my bedroom and frowns. "Were you just screaming into your pillow, Claire-bear?" I hate his nickname for me just about as much as I hate Lucca's. I never told Carter, but my mom used to call me Claire-bear too.

I sit up on the bed. "Haven't I told you half a million times not to call me that?"

Carter smirks, his perfectly straight white teeth remind me of a rottweiler's sharp canines. As funny and charming as he is, I've never forgotten that he is here for one purpose, and that's keeping me in line. "Yes, but that's the reason I call you it because I know it annoys you."

I'm not the type to beat around the bush, so I just come out with it, "What do you want?"

Carter's smile becomes bigger and brighter. "Now, wouldn't you like to know?"

I roll my eyes. "Not really, but because you walked in, I figured you had a reason for coming in here. If not, please get out and take that pathetic gift that *he* sent with you."

Looking over his shoulder, he stares at the mess for a second before facing me, his smile now a frown. "Why did you break it?"

I grit my teeth. I don't want to head down this road with Carter. "It's a stupid gift, and I don't want it. What did you come in here for?"

"I got something for you too, but I'm worried that if you don't like it, I might be the next thing tossed in the corner of the room." Somehow, he always finds a way to make me smile.

My lips turn up at the sides just a little. "I would never do that, and you are way too heavy for me to throw you across the room."

"Wait, did you just call me fat?" Carter fake gasps.

I ignore his comment. "You didn't have to get me anything." *God knows, you've done enough.* Though he was my babysitter for all intents and purposes, Carter slowly became my best friend, maybe even brother. I look up to him, and any time I need something, including a hug, he's there. Even my parents love him and started treating him like a son.

"I did." He reaches into the front pocket of his hoodie and pulls out something. "It ain't much of anything, not really, but for tonight, it'll be your one-way ticket to a night you will never forget."

"I swear to god if you're giving me a condom, I will—"

"Shut up and take it." He tosses the object at me, and I catch it mid-air. I flip the piece of plastic that mimics an ID over in my hand. There's a picture of a girl that looks a lot like me, her name is Kayla, and her birthday is conveniently three years before mine, making her twenty-one.

My brows pucker as I examine it. "What… is this a fake ID?"

I'm a little shocked right now. Carter is always straight-laced. He never veers off the path and always makes certain I'm headed in the right direction. So this, it comes out of left field.

"It sure is, and tonight we're going to go to a party at a club. Together, of course, because I'm not letting you out of my sights."

My mouth pops open. "You're lying." He has to be lying.

He shakes his head. "Nope."

I narrow my eyes to slits. "How? What about my parents? They wanted to have dinner tonight."

"They still are, just without us." Carter grins. "I talked them into letting you enjoy your birthday the teenage way. You're welcome."

"Why? Why all of a sudden do you want to have fun? This isn't like you. Does Lucca know?"

Carter's features darken. "Don't worry about Lucca. Tonight, we're celebrating your birthday. Be ready in two hours."

I want to object, knowing Lucca wouldn't approve of me going out, but he isn't here, and I'm going to do whatever I want, especially on my birthday. Maybe also a little bit to spite him.

"I'll be ready," I tell Carter.

"Good. I'll tell Tracy and Steven we're leaving soon. They don't know about the ID, of course. No one needs to know what we're doing exactly."

I smile. "I like this new version of you. Breaking the rules."

Carter runs his fingers through his dark hair. "Don't get used to it. I just want you to have a good time tonight. Don't make me regret it, okay?"

And just like that, he's back to business, being his typical asshole self. "Fine, now get out." I point to the door.

Carter leaves the room and closes the door behind him.

I fall back onto the mattress and stare up at the ceiling. For two years, I've tried to move on. I've tried to forget about him, but I never could. It hits me then, slapping me across the face and lodging itself in my brain.

Tonight, I'm going to shatter that crush, breaking it like I broke that shadowbox. I'm not his butterfly anymore. Lucca doesn't know it, but I'll be free of him after tonight. If he doesn't want me, then I'm going to make it my mission to find someone who does.

College is on the horizon, and I'm not going to be a virgin

when I leave in the fall. The easiest way to put this behind me is to find some random guy and fuck him.

A guy who doesn't see me as a child, who doesn't call me butterfly, and who doesn't care more about protecting me than my sanity.

"Tonight, I will be free of you..." I whisper to myself, a smile pulling at my lips while a tear lingers in the corner of my eyes.

Letting go is easier than enduring a lifetime of disappointment.

THE INSIDE of the club is loud and smells like cheap liquor and sweat. I smile anyway, mainly because I can't believe the fake ID worked. The bouncers didn't even bat an eye at me. Carter scans the room and places his hand on the small of my back, guiding us toward the bar.

When we reach the enormous bar, I'm struck by a sudden bout of wariness. Should I really be here tonight? What if something happens? The fear from those years ago still lingers at the back of my mind. I look over my shoulder, wondering if someone is after me?

Carter leans into my side, and I tilt my head so I can see his face.

"What do you want to drink?"

"Let's do shots," I yell over the loud music.

"Shots?" Carter arches a brow. "Do you want to remember tonight?"

"Actually, that sounds like a good idea."

"Remembering or—"

"Not. I don't want to remember tonight," I tell him. It's the perfect time to end my conversation with Carter because the bartender saunters up to me. "Hi! Can we have five shots of whatever liquor you choose?"

The bartender smirks. "Whatever you want, doll. I'll get it for you."

I peer over my shoulder, giving Carter a dirty look. The bartender disappears to get our order. I know that if I want to find myself in the arms of a man tonight, I'll have to get rid of him.

The bartender returns with the shots and places them down on the bar in front of me. "Would you like to open a tab?"

"Yes!" I say at the same time that Carter says, "No."

"Yes. Please, open a tab for us," I say sweetly, ignoring Carter's fiery stare that's burning into the back of my skull. The bartender, of course, listens to me and walks away with a smile.

"You're not going to drink all those—"

Carter doesn't get to finish his sentence before I've downed two of the shots. The liquid burns a path of fire down my throat, and my eyes water as it settles in my stomach. I grab another and another, and once I've taken all five shots, I turn to Carter with a smile on my lips.

"What was that you said?"

He chuckles, and I know tonight is going to be a good night. I'll find someone worth my time and let him whisk me away. It's the only thing I can think of to sever the connection I have with Lucca.

20

LUCCA

I'm lying in bed, channel surfing, feeling like an asshole for not being there for Claire today. Eighteen. Another year older, but nothing has changed. I try not to let the guilt bother me. I sent her a gift and have kept every promise I ever made her. It doesn't lessen the temptation I have to go to her every day.

I can still recall her heart-shaped face, fractured with pain after the words I spoke to her the last time we saw each other. I broke her heart. *No,* I didn't just break it, I stomped it into the ground and encased the remains in concrete.

My phone rings on the nightstand, and I drop the remote on the mattress and grab it. I'm surprised to see Carter's name flash across my screen, mainly since I talked to him earlier, and he said they were going to be doing cake and ice cream with Tracy and Steven. Maybe something else happened.

I hit the green key and bring the phone to my ear. "What's up?"

"Look, don't get mad, Lucca, but..." Carter's panicked voice fills my ear, but it isn't his words that are alarming to me. It's the loud noise in the background. It sounds like he's at a nightclub, but surely that can't be right because he wouldn't dare go to a nightclub with Claire. Not if he values his life.

"What the fuck is going on?" I growl.

"I'm sorry, okay? I messed up. I got Claire a fake ID for her birthday, hoping we could go out and have some fun. I didn't want to tell you because I figured I could handle it, but it's gotten out of hand."

"What do you mean, it's gotten out of hand?" The words grate through my teeth. "I swear to god if Claire is hurt or if something has happened to her, you will wish you were dead."

"She's okay, mostly..." There is cheering in the background, and I'm frantic to know what the fuck is going on. "I didn't think she would drink this much, but she's drunk, Lucca, and she's making out with guys. I don't know what to do. I tried to get her out of here, but she called the fucking bouncer on me."

Making out with guys? Drunk? A vein bulges in my neck. I want to fucking slaughter someone and watch them bleed out. Another fucker is kissing her, touching her, and she's too out of it to care, too out of it to make a rational choice.

"Where are you?" I'm already out of bed and grabbing my keys and wallet from the dresser before he answers.

"Houdin's."

"Why the fuck—" I shake my head, stopping mid-sentence. "Don't answer that. I'll be there soon. Don't let her out of your sights, and if something happens to her..." My jaw aches as I clench it.

"I know, you'll string me up by my intestines and feed me my own shit."

I don't even reply. I've trained him well, and he knows he's going to get his ass kicked for this little stunt. It doesn't matter if Claire put him up to it or not. He should've known better.

I BREAK every fucking speed limit and run three red lights to get to the club. The adrenaline pumping through my veins has all my focus on Claire. My only thought is to get to her and make sure she is okay, which I won't believe until she is right in front of me, and I can visibly see her.

When I'm five minutes away, I text Carter, telling him to meet me outside. The last thing I need is for Claire to make a scene and for me to have to kick someone's ass. I don't want to draw attention to myself. I've been doing a good job staying under wraps, and all that could be blown to shit if I have to fuck someone up.

As soon as the club's neon sign comes into view, I pull into the nearest parking spot on the street. I park the car and notice that there's a line wrapped around the building of waiting patrons. I can't fucking believe Carter got her a fake ID. I'm almost at the mouth of the building when the door flies open, and Carter comes walking out with a very intoxicated Claire hanging off his arm.

Pausing mid-step, all I can do is stare. My chest tightens. The cold organ in my chest thumps loudly in my ears. Two years have passed, and though she looks the same with her delicate nose and pert little mouth, she doesn't.

The last time I saw her, she was nothing but a budding flower reaching for the sun, but now she is in full bloom. The tight mini dress hugs her feminine curves perfectly and doesn't help to lessen her appealing appearance.

Instantly, she's no longer the little girl I knew her to be, but a young woman who has grown into her body. A woman I want to touch, possess, and explore. I force my hands to remain at my sides. I won't, can't, touch her. After breaking her heart and telling her I would only ever see her as a child, to show any type of attraction would only lead to more heartache. I'm not what she needs, but everything she should stay away from.

Her green eyes widen with surprise first, flames of fury flicker in their depths. Oh, if she thinks she hates me now, she's really going to hate me once the night is over.

"Serioussslyyy, Carter?" Claire slurs and turns her head to peer up at him.

"Don't blame me. I asked you when we started this night if you wanted to remember it, and you said no."

Claire frowns, and even in sadness, she is still beautiful. "You had to call *him,* though." She shoves her finger in my direction. If I wasn't so pissed off over the shenanigans of these two, I might laugh, but all I can picture is something happening to Claire. Some fucker taking advantage of her or slipping something into her drink. The mere thought of something happening makes me insane.

"I'll take her, and you can follow behind in your car," I tell Carter without looking at him. He already knows I want to punch him in the face, but I'll save the violence for later when Claire isn't around.

He nods and attempts to pass Claire off to me. She squirms like a child, huffing and puffing the entire time.

"Let me go... I hate you. I'm not going with youuu..." She tries to dig her heeled feet into the ground but only trips herself.

I lean down, my lips next to her good ear. "Stop!" Her scent invades me, fresh-picked strawberries, and summer. Her soft body molds into mine.

"No, you stop. Stop pretending you care."

I can hear the raw emotion in her voice, and the sadness seeps into my pores. Yes, I'm an asshole for hurting her, for pushing her away, but I only did it to protect her. Everything I do is to protect her and keep her safe. *Why can't she see that?*

"Stop acting like a child," I growl and tighten my hold on her.

"You stop! You overbearinggg-douchebagish-assholeeee prick!" Each word becomes louder and more slurred than the next as I drag her further away from the club.

By the time we reach the car, she is flopping around like a fish out of water. Her fight, if you could call it that, doesn't bother me.

In fact, it has the opposite effect. My cock hasn't been this hard in, well, a long fucking time, and it's all because of the little temptress struggling to get away.

"Lucca," my name rolls off her tongue, "I'll screammm."

Her struggle intensifies, her limbs flail, and out of nowhere, her elbow connects with my face. Pain radiates up my nose, and all I can do is react. Twisting her in my arms, I grab her by the throat and press her against the car.

She hasn't even seen a sliver of what I'm capable of, but she's about to.

My fingers squeeze the tender flesh in warning. Shock overtakes her features, and her glossy, red-rimmed eyes fill with fear.

I hate knowing I put that fear there, but I'm done with her shit right now.

"You think I care if you scream? I'm not afraid of the cops.

Scream, Claire, scream at the top of your lungs. Nobody's listening. No one cares." My lip curls. "That's exactly why I do what I do, so you don't have to scream for help in some fucking alleyway." I release my hold on her throat and take a step back, even though all I want to do is kiss the skin there. To feel her thundering pulse beneath my lips. Something flashes in her eyes, and in this moment, I can't tell if it's fear or something else. Is she still harboring feelings? God, I hope not.

"Now, stop being a brat and get in the car," I snap. The tone of my voice makes her jump.

Whirling around on her heels, she almost tumbles to the concrete, but her tiny hand grabs the door handle of the SUV just in time to balance herself.

"I hate you... you're nothing. You ass. Go away... you're dumb."

I have to piece her sentence together to make out what she's saying.

"Good, you can hate me some more by getting into the car."

She tugs the door open and jumps into the seat. "I don't like you."

I almost laugh at the expression she gives me. Like a kitten that's been told no and put in time out. I don't say anything and close her door before walking around to the driver's side.

Claire sits with her arms across her chest, making her tits more noticeable. She doesn't look at me, but I can see the anger bubbling up inside of her. I start the SUV and head back toward the house.

"Why did you come tonight?"

I turn the radio down, knowing that she won't be able to hear me with the music on.

"Don't ask questions that are just going to piss you off. Shut up and be quiet." I speak to her like she is a child, and not because I see her as one, but because she's acting like one.

She huffs angrily and leans against the door. I white knuckle the steering wheel, the tension in the SUV rises a degree with each breath we take. I shouldn't be here. I shouldn't have come back into her life, not that I was really ever gone, but I wasn't physically involved.

Leaving her again is going to be harder on both of us.

"I'm done, Lucca. Done being controlled." I grasp the steering wheel a little tighter. "I hate you, but more than anything, I hate myself because even after all this time, even after everything you said and did to me. The way you hurt me. I still miss you..." Her voice cracks, and so does my heart.

A sob rips from her throat, and like a rubber band pulled too tight, I snap. I veer off the side of the road and slam my foot on the breaks. All my pent-up anger and rage rushes to the surface. I'm TNT, and she's just lit my fucking fuse.

Carter's car passes by us, and I shoot him a quick text to keep on going home. I need to deal with Claire right now. I need to fix this.

It's wrong to want her. Forbidden, a temptation that I can't afford. Falling for her, giving in to what we both want, would only lead to more pain. I learned long ago that I could never love, not even her. What does it say about me as a man to have known her for years—since she was a little girl—and now that she's older and more mature, I see her in a different light?

"What do you want from me, Claire?" I speak through clenched teeth. "Do you..."

She cuts me off and moves toward me. "I want you to touch me."

I swallow my tongue. She wants me... fuck, she wants me to touch her? I clam up, my entire body stiffens.

"Touch, Lucca. I want to feel your fingers on my skin."

"You're drunk," I croak, my cock uncaring of anything I've thought over the last hour. I'm coming up with every excuse I can fathom not to touch her, all while knowing nothing could ever stop me. My obsession with her is maddening. There is nowhere in this world she could hide from me I wouldn't find her.

"I want you," she whispers and crawls across the seat and into my lap. Straddling me, she wraps her arms around my neck and pulls me close.

I'm consumed by her, swallowed whole, and I can't stop the desire from seeping out of me. I want her so badly; it fucking hurts. I can almost taste her on my lips, feel her against my skin.

I'm at a crossroads. I have to stop this, but I can't.

"Touch me, Lucca, please," Claire whimpers.

Taking my hand in hers, she guides it to the apex of her thigh. My heart beats so loudly, it's the only thing I can hear in my ears. Her movements aren't hesitant. Or timid. In fact, they're experienced and precise, which leads me to wonder if she's been with someone.

Carter has been watching her for me, and until tonight, I trusted him completely, but apparently, he has been doing shit behind my back, and I'm not so sure anymore.

The thought leaves me feeling an irrational rush of jealousy. My cock grows harder as she grinds herself against it, taunting me, edging me toward a breaking point that I'll never come back from. A tiny groan escapes my lips.

"Do it. Feel how much I want you."

Her sultry voice, coupled with her scent, is enough to push me over the edge, but the nail in the coffin is when she spreads her legs a little wider and presses my fingers closer to her warm heat. In a flash, I forget the world around me. I let the worry and fear of what may happen tomorrow fall to the wayside.

She is my greatest sin, and I will sin a thousand times over for her. Inching my fingers closer, I graze the edge of her underwear. At that single touch, she lets out a content sigh. I'm tempted to slip beneath the underwear and sink my fingers inside her tight channel to see if she's given herself to another man, but at the last second, choose not to.

If she is still a virgin, I'm not sure I'll be returning her to her bedroom tonight as one. My control is threadbare with her. Half of me wants to break her, twist her, and push her to her limits. The other half wants to keep her at arm's length because I know what a man like me will do to her. She's pure innocence wrapped in a tight bow, and I want to unwrap her like a little boy on Christmas morning.

"Tell me you don't want this," I growl into the shell of her good ear.

Her head is resting against my shoulder, and I can just barely make out the outline of her face. "Tell me to stop," I beg, moving my finger over the center.

Her arousal has soaked through her panties, leaving a wet spot against the fabric.

I can feel her engorged clit already. When I don't touch her right where she wants, she whimpers and turns, burying her head into the crook of my neck.

Her tongue darts out, and I feel it on my skin. She licks the side of my neck, pressing the tip of her tongue against my throbbing pulse. Fuck, if that doesn't turn me on more.

I know she's ready for me, waiting for me to claim her, but I don't know if I can push myself over the ledge.

Then she whispers into my ear, "If you stop. I'll find someone else. Someone who will finish what they start."

I should stop, that would be the right thing, the proper thing, especially since she is drunk, but I can't. I can't stop. I'm too far gone.

Just like that, my resolve snaps completely, and I grip the edge of her panties and pull. The cotton gives way under my grip, and the audible tear fills the SUV. I was keeping her underwear on to protect her, but it seems she doesn't want protection from me. She wants me to ravage her, devour her from the inside out. Little does she know, once I'm finished with her, there will be nothing left.

I give her no warning and slip a finger between her folds. She is drenched with need, making it easy for me to slide over her clit. The feel of her soft body writhing against mine is my undoing. As soon as I rub circles against her swollen nub, she lifts her hips, seeking an orgasm that she knows is on the horizon.

"Don't stoppp." I don't. I couldn't, not even if I wanted to. Not even knowing that this is wrong. That nothing but pain will come from this.

Adding more pressure to her clit, I move faster, and like a shooting star, she gains speed, getting closer to soaring through the night sky.

"Fall apart for me. Coat my hand. Leave me with a reminder of you because this is the only time we'll ever get."

"Oh, Lucca," she sighs and digs her nails into my wrist and thigh, making me hiss with both pleasure and pain. I want to fuck her so bad, to push deep inside of her, to fill her with my cum, and ensure she will never have another man, but I can't. *I won't.* I'm not the man for Claire. I'm not her savior. I'm not anything.

"Don't stop! Please, don't stop."

Claire's entire body tightens, and a second later, she clamps her legs together, trapping my hand between her thighs as shudders of pleasure rip through her. My heart gallops in my chest, and I've never been more turned on in my life. I'm visibly shaken, and if she asked me to fuck her right now, I would. I don't care that she's been drinking, that her judgment may be off. I'd throw being a good man right out the window to sink deep inside her.

Like a doll, she sags against me and shifts enough so that I can pull my hand away. I rub the two fingers together that are coated in her release before bringing them to my lips. Her sweet taste explodes against my tongue, and I swallow down a groan.

I shouldn't have fucking done that. Now all I see is her pussy pressed against my face, my hands wrapped around her, holding her in place as I feast on her until she begs me to stop. A fantasy that will never come true because I won't let it.

Claire remains molded to my body for a few more moments before I lift her over the center console and place her in the passenger seat. Coldness sweeps over me in the absence of her body heat. Leaning against the window, she doesn't say a single word. Neither do I. Then again, what is there to say? I'm sorry for touching you. I'm sorry, I want to fuck you until you scream my name loud enough for the entire world to hear it.

I hate myself a little more for what I've just done, but there are no take-backs in this life. By the time I start the SUV again and pull out onto the road, Claire is passed out in the passenger's seat, and I'm left with my thoughts, wondering if I just made the biggest mistake of my life by hurting her again.

"Happy birthday, butterfly," I whisper. "I wish I could give you what you want, but I can't. I just can't."

I'd rather die a thousand times over than hurt her, but I'm not the hero she thinks I am. It's time she saw the real me. It's time she realized the man that killed her father that night is the man I am every day, the man I hide from her, so I don't risk hurting her again.

Maybe in protecting her, I'm only elongating her pain? Maybe if she sees the *real* me, her own obsession will die?

21

CLAIRE

There is a moment just before I open my eyes where I actually wonder if I was in an accident last night. I half expect to be in a hospital bed since I feel like I got run over by a bus. When I do open my eyes, I'm inside my room.

Without turning my head, I can see the ceiling and the very top of my dark blue curtains. I've never been so glad about having blackout curtains before. The heavy material is only letting partial light filter into the room, and that is already enough to make my eyes hurt.

Now that I think about it, everything hurts—my eyes, brain, throat, stomach... everything.

"Ugh," I groan, and even that hurts.

If my throat wasn't so dry and my bladder wasn't insisting on me using the bathroom, I would probably not move at all. But as is, I'm forced to make myself move.

With my eyes closed, I slowly turn around and prop myself up on my elbow. The room spins, and I suck in a deep breath before blinking my eyes open again.

I stare at the man sitting in the chair in the corner of my room. I blink a few more times. Then stare again.

"Good morning, butterfly," Lucca greets me like it's the most normal thing for him to be in my room, watching me sleep.

I don't know how long I sit there and stare at him, but it feels like a very long time. Slowly, very slowly, my brain wakes up, and bits and pieces of last night come back to me.

The club... shots... Lucca... the car ride home...

Did he?

No. I must have dreamed that. There is no way he touched me. Only the more I think about it, the more I think he did.

"I..." I start, not sure what to say. I sit up a little more, making the blanket slide off my chest and making me realize that I'm basically naked. Scooting around a bit, I conclude I am only wearing panties. Frantically, I fist the blanket and clutch it to my chest.

"You puked on yourself on the way in," Lucca explains.

Oh, great. Just great.

"I'm gonna take a shower," I announce.

Keeping the blanket tightly wrapped around my body, I get up slowly and make my way into the bathroom. Only when I'm inside with the door closed, do I feel like I can breathe again.

Fuck, what a nightmare. This is not how I imagined seeing Lucca again.

I drop the blanket and strip out of my panties. The moment I bend down to get my legs out of the silky fabric, the entire room spins again, and I have to hold on to the edge of the counter, so I don't fall over.

I'm never drinking again.

Turning on the shower, I wait until it's hot before I step

under the spray and let the scolding water wash away the broken up memories of last night.

I normally don't take long showers, but today, I stay in until the water runs cold and my skin is all wrinkly. I dry off just to realize I didn't bring any clothes with me. *Shit.*

When I finally build up the courage to leave the bathroom, I open the door just a smidge and stick my head out. I'm both disappointed and relieved to find my room empty.

Did he just leave?

That would be something Lucca would do. Come barreling back into my life just to disappear as fast as he barged in.

I get dressed into the most comfortable thing I can find and shove my feet into a pair of fuzzy socks. Since I feel slightly more human after my shower, I decide to go downstairs and face whatever the universe has to throw at me today. I don't think my parents are home, but I'm sure Carter is downstairs, and possibly Lucca.

I leave my room and make my way to the kitchen. Every step I take rattles my brain slightly and sends another burst of pain through my skull. If it wasn't for that, I would pick up my speed, so I can yell at Lucca sooner.

I'm not even halfway down the stairs when I hear Carter's voice, but it's not until I'm right in front of the kitchen that I can make out what they are saying. "I just wanted her to have some fun. I didn't think she would go overboard like that."

"Why didn't you stop her?" Lucca growls.

"I tried."

When I finally enter the kitchen, I find Lucca and Carter sitting at the table. Both of their heads snap up the moment I enter.

"Stop yelling at Carter. Actually, stop yelling in general. My head hurts."

"That happens when you drink half the bar's liquor," Lucca murmurs so low I have to read his lips.

"Exactly. I did it. I made that choice, so there is no reason to bite off Carter's head for something I did."

"You wouldn't have been there if it wasn't for him. Giving you a fake ID is on him."

"You know what, you're right. Sorry for being a normal teenager for once in my life. Sorry that Carter actually cares enough to spend time with me on my birthday."

At my words, I see Lucca flinch. A painful expression crosses his face, and I'm almost sorry I mentioned it. *Almost.*

"I care," Lucca defends. "I fucking care about your safety. You put yourself in danger, making out with random guys at a club. Do you even know the stuff that could have happened to you?"

"I could have had sex, you mean? Like every other eighteen-year-old—"

"You are not every other eighteen-year-old! I don't give a shit how grown up you think you are. You will not put yourself in dangerous situations like that ever again, or so help me god, I'll lock you up somewhere."

"You don't get to decide anything for me!" I yell back. "I don't understand why you can't just leave me the hell alone?"

"Is that really what you want? For me to leave you alone?"

"Yes!" I lie. I want the opposite of that, but I want it in a way Lucca doesn't, and I'm not going to make myself vulnerable to him again.

"Well, too bad. That's not going to happen. You are mine to

take care of, and you will do what I say. Starting with no more funny business with random guys."

"You can't control me, and you sure as hell will not control who I make out with."

"I don't need to control *who* you make out with because there is not going to be anyone else to make out with, *ever* again," he sneers, making me wonder if that's jealousy I hear in his voice or if my ears are deceiving me.

Is he jealous of me kissing someone else? My heart rate picks up at the thought. No, don't be stupid, Claire. He broke your heart before. He made you feel stupid, told you it was nothing but a crush. Testing out that theory, I dig the knife a little deeper.

"I kiss guys all the time, Lucca. It's not a big deal."

His stupidly gorgeous face turns bright red, and his hands ball into tight fists on the table. I'm guessing he is either jealous or angry for some other reason. I'm going to bank on the jealousy, though, since he looks like he wants to rip my tongue out of my mouth.

"I know you're lying. Did you forget Carter keeps me up to date on everything you do? Everywhere you go, everyone, you see. I know everything."

A sudden surge of anger fills my veins. Carter has become my friend, and to be honest, he is the only friend I have, but like all things, Lucca just ruined that. He reminded me that Carter is only here to babysit me. I knew Carter reported back to Lucca.

Still, the reminder feels like a betrayal all over again. Like a knife in my back that I can't reach to remove, so I feel it there all the time.

Betrayal and anger sting so bad, but nothing is as bad as the sadness. It fills me, suffocating me, making it hard to breathe, to think rationally.

I'm not sure which one of those feelings brings me to what I say next. Maybe it's a combination of all three that pushes me over the edge, or maybe it's that I want to hurt Lucca the way he's hurting me.

"Did Carter also report back to you we've been fucking for the last year?"

As soon as the words leave my lips, I know I've made a terrible mistake.

I want to take it back, force the words back down my throat and erase them from existence, but I can't. I can't, and that is the terrible truth. Before I have the chance to explain myself, Lucca is on his feet.

The chair he was sitting in falls to the ground; the crashing sound it makes is dull compared to the sound the table makes as he grabs the edge and flips it over, and tosses it aside like it weighs two pounds. Lucca's face morphs into something else.

His blue eyes burn with rage, his body vibrates with animosity, and with the snap of my fingers, he becomes a different person.

Memories stir...

He looks like the person from my nightmares. The man that I could never forget.

The man in front of me isn't the one who saved me, who called me butterfly, or gave me a ride home from school. This is the man who killed my father.

22

LUCCA

My brain shuts off. All rational thinking is gone and replaced with pure unbridled rage. I shove the table aside like it weighs nothing. Carter jumps up from his seat, his eyes wide with fear like I've never seen. He knows what's going to happen next. That's why his hands go up to protect his face, but we both know it's no use.

His hands will not stop me from beating the fuck out of him.

"Lucca, I swear—" he starts, but I cut him off with a fist to the face.

I'm vaguely aware of someone screaming. My anger is not only blinding, it is deafening as well. All I can think about is hurting the man who touched Claire. The man who took her innocence. The man who claimed a piece of her. A piece he didn't deserve.

With one hand, I grab onto Carter's shirt, holding him in place while I punch his face with the other. His arms flare out to defend himself, but I easily dodge him and continue my assault.

My heart beats against my ribcage furiously, blood pumping through my body at double speed. I feel someone's hands on me, trying to pull me from Carter. I shrug the unknown person away, ignoring the constant screaming echoing through the room.

Only when I see a head of red hair out of the corner of my eye do I tear myself away from Carter. I glance to the ground beside me, my eyes falling on Claire, and I freeze. My fist stops mid air as if time itself pauses.

My vision adjusts back to reality as the fog of rage lifts from my ears and eyes.

Claire is sitting on the floor, cradling her arm to her chest like she is hurt. Her eyes are red, and her face is tear-stained.

"It's not true," she croaks. "I lied. I'm sorry, I lied... I lied." She repeats it over and over again, almost frantically.

She lied. Her words sink in like a slow-moving creek.

"You and Carter...?"

"We're just friends. I swear. He never touched me. No one has. I just said that to... I don't even know," she shakes her head, "make you jealous, I guess... It was stupid. Really stupid."

While I'm still working on getting my ragged breathing under control, I swing my gaze back to Carter. His head lulls to the side, his face already swollen, and his lip and nose bloody.

Fuck.

I release his shirt, and he slumps back into the kitchen chair with a groan. Claire gets up from the floor and scurries past me to check on Carter. Her concern for him fuels my anger, like gasoline to a simmering flame.

"Leave him," I growl, grabbing her arm to pull her back. "He is fine."

"He is not fine!" She tries to pull away, but I don't budge.

"He will be, and now you know what will happen to anyone who I think touched you, so don't go around flirting because I will hurt them."

"You're a monster," she spits out with venom dripping from her voice.

I curl my lip and give her the same ominous look she gives me. "You're right, Claire. I am a monster, and I'm glad you finally see it."

"I hate you," she hisses. Her rage only turns me on. "Just leave again. Go wherever you've been hiding for the last two years and leave me be."

"No can do, butterfly. Clearly, Carter cannot keep you safe. You're coming with me. Go pack your bag," I order.

"No! No fucking way are you doing this to me *again*. I'm not going with you. You can't make me."

I raise an eyebrow at her, and if I wasn't still angry, I would probably laugh too. "We both know I can make you do whatever I want to." At my threat, her body visibly shivers. I'm not completely certain if it's from fear or something else.

"What about my parents? I can't just leave. I'm about to start college. I won't leave." She keeps shaking her head as if she actually has a choice.

"I'll call them on the way. Let's go. Pack some stuff."

"No!" She stomps her foot before trying to pull away from me once more. I tighten my grip on her arm, making her wince.

"Fine. No bag then." I let go of her arm so suddenly, Claire stumbles forward.

As soon as she realizes she is free, she tries to make a run for it, but I'm faster. I scoop her off the ground and throw her over my shoulder. She beats her small fists against my back, which reminds me to teach her some self-defense when I get a chance.

I quickly carry her out to the car, hoping none of the neighbors are going to come out and try to stop me. I'd hate to be forced to kill someone else in front of Claire.

As gently as I can, I shove her into the front seat. "If you don't stop fighting me, I'll tie you up and stuff you in the trunk.

"You wouldn't..." She looks at me wide-eyed and in disbelief before I see realization settle in. *I would. I absolutely would.*

Crossing her arms in front of her chest, she settles into the seat while I walk around and get into the driver's seat.

"Where are we going?" she asks as soon as I pull out of the neighborhood.

"My place, in the city," I explain.

"What city?"

"St. Louis."

"*St. Louis?* What do we want there?"

"I live there. You're staying with me from now on."

"You can't—" she stops herself from finishing, knowing that I can and will make it happen. She turns her head away from me, silently signaling that she is done talking to me for now.

The drive takes only an hour and a half. We spent the entire time in silence, which I was fine with at first, but once the anger about Claire lying to me passes, something else enters my mind. I can't get the image of Claire coming all over my hand last night out of my head.

My cock strains to get free, pressing uncomfortably against the zipper. Claire squirms around in the seat next to me, and I wonder if she is thinking about it too. Of course, I don't even know if she remembers last night, and I'm not about to ask.

When we finally pull up to my apartment complex, I feel relieved and somewhat excited to have Claire in my space. Glancing over at her pouting and staring daggers at me, I gather she feels anything but.

"Are you going to walk in there like a normal person, or do I have to throw you over my shoulder again?"

"What do *you* know about being normal?" She snorts.

"I know how to *act* normal. I'm great at it, or I would have been thrown in prison a long time ago."

"That's where you belong."

"Probably, but I can't protect you from a jail cell, so I'll make sure I'll stay out of it."

"Great. I'll walk inside. Like a *normal* person." Claire opens her car door and steps out into the parking lot. I do the same, walking around the car quickly just in case she has the dumb idea to make a run for it.

Surprisingly, she lets me walk her into the building without problems. I unlock the door of my apartment and motion for her to step in. She walks in front of me, arms crossed in front of her chest and a frown plastered all over her face. She isn't happy to be here, and she is going to be even less happy with what's coming next.

Walking to the kitchen first, I open the fridge and grab some bottles of water and a protein shake. From the pantry, I snag some granola bars and an apple. With snacks in hand, I walk to my bedroom, passing a confused Claire on the way.

I dump the snacks on my bed and go back to the living room where Claire still stands awkwardly.

"Come on." I take her wrist gently and tug her toward the hallway.

"What are we doing?" I don't miss the slight nervous tone in her voice.

"I'm sure you want to lie down a little more. You must be tired."

"I'm fine," she tells me, tugging her wrist away.

"Well, you'll still rest for a little bit." I pull her into my bedroom. "Drink a lot of water, eat some snacks." I point at the bed. "Take a shower," I say, pointing at the attached bathroom. "But most importantly, relax. I'll be back in a few hours."

"Where are you going?"

"Just taking care of something. Nothing to worry about," I tell her, and before she has the chance to read too much into it, I leave the room.

Closing the door, I take out the key from my pocket and lock her in. She is not going to like this one bit, but this is for her safety. She'll be safe in there. Safe from everything except me.

23

CLAIRE

I'm tempted to get up and pound my fists against the door until he opens it. I doubt he's on the other side, though, so it would only leave me with bruised hands.

Who does he think he is to kidnap me and bring me here? I pushed him too far. The way he attacked Carter, all because of one little lie. All I wanted to do was hurt him, but that set off a chain of events I never would have expected. I can only hope Carter is okay. Lucca proved to me all over again who he was beneath the shiny knight he tried to put on display.

I look around at my prison. There's a queen-sized bed with grey sheets and pillows in the center of the room. A dresser against the wall in front of the bed, and a small flat-screen TV mounted in the room's corner.

One whiff, and I know it's Lucca's bedroom. The scent is woodsy, like cedar and clove, and I breathe it deep into my lungs. As always, the smell of him leaves me calm. I scoot the snacks and water aside and sit on the bed. Pulling my knees up to my chest, I wrap my arms around them and stare at the door.

I know I should be worried, maybe even scared, and I guess a part of me is since I know when it comes to me, Lucca is a loose cannon. More than any of those other emotions, I am excited. There is a hum in my blood and a swarm of butterflies in my gut. Still, I'm angry. Angry that he took me. Angry that he tries to control every aspect of my life as if it's his job to ensure my safety. Angry that he broke my heart and refused to see me as more than his kid sister.

I let that anger push to the forefront of my mind. Why am I sitting here like a damsel in distress waiting for him to return? Why am I not saving myself?

I scoot to the edge of the bed and glare at the door. I'm on my feet and standing in front of it a second later. The cold metal handle makes me shiver as I wrap my hand around it.

I jiggle it just to be certain it's locked and grow even angrier, finding it is. I mean, I don't know what I was expecting. The door was locked as soon as he closed it. Stomping back to the bed, I pause and look out the window.

The window. Slapping myself in the forehead, I march over to the window and pull back the curtains. I press on the glass with my hands, trying to open it, but it doesn't budge, not even an inch. I realize when I see the small lock at the bottom near the lip of the window there is no escape.

Did he plan to take me all along?

I wouldn't be surprised if he did. It seems he's set on controlling me in any way he can. A smile tugs at my lips, lifting them at the sides. Jokes on him. Now is my chance to make him see me, the real me, the one who has always wanted him.

Even if I had to use Carter to get here, it will be worth it once this is all over. Walking back over to the bed, I sit at the edge and prepare myself for what's coming. He set this up, and when all the pieces fall, he'll have no one to blame but himself.

Lucca is mine.

～

AN HOUR LATER, he returns and unlocks the door but doesn't engage in any type of conversation with me. I leap from the bed and follow him out into the hall.

"You can't just leave me locked in bedrooms while you do whatever you want. That's not what normal people do," I scold, following on his heels.

Jesus, he's basically jogging through the house.

He halts, and I barely catch myself from smacking right into him. Whirling around, he stares down at me like a misbehaving child. "I can do whatever I want, Claire. Also, I never said I was normal. I said I know how to act normal. Remember, I'm a monster?"

The condescending tone he gives me makes me want to slap him.

"Oh, I haven't forgotten." I curl my lip.

His blue eyes flash with an unreadable emotion. "I got us dinner. Come and eat. It will be the only time you get to eat until morning, so don't push me, Claire, or you'll end up locked back in that bedroom. Except, this time, I'll tie you to the bed for safe measure."

I can't explain why, but my nipples harden, and my core heats at the thought. Before last night, I've never considered letting a man touch me, let alone tie me up, but the anticipation of Lucca doing it makes me want it all the more.

I swallow around the golf ball-sized lump in my throat

and press my lips together. What am I supposed to say to him? Yes, please, tie me up? I don't want to push him again too soon.

The heat between our bodies smolders until it becomes unbearable, and only then does Lucca turn around and start walking again. I resume following behind him, but at a much slower pace.

For the first time, I actually inspect the apartment. It is clean, sleek, and updated with neutral-colored paint and furniture. How long has he lived here?

As soon as we walk into the kitchen, and I see the bag from Olive Garden, I nearly squeal. I love that place.

"Sit," Lucca orders, pointing at the stools on the opposite side of the long island. "I will dish out the food."" I bite my tongue, knowing whatever response I have won't help me, and instead, do just as he says.

As soon as he sets the plate of food down in front of me, I eat. I don't care how unladylike I might look. I didn't want to eat the stupid snacks in the bedroom, but now that I smell this, I'm actually starving. Once I've filled my stomach enough to stop the insistent growling, I look up from my plate and find Lucca staring at me.

He's holding his plate in one hand while he leans against the counter, studying me like I'm an object under a microscope. I like it but hate it at the same time. I have no idea how he sees me, but I want to find out.

Placing my fork on my plate, I grab the glass of water he gave me and take a sip.

"Is Carter okay?" I ask.

At the mere mention of his name, Lucca's features shift. His jaw becomes sharper, and his eyes narrow to slits. If I didn't know him, I would think he might want to hurt me. At the very least, strangle me.

"Carter is none of your concern," he snarls.

Oh god, he is still jealous of Carter. Even knowing that we haven't done anything.

The question now is... *why?*

"Is there a reason you're acting jealous? I already told you that Carter did nothing to me. He never touched me or even looked at me in a way that was sexual."

"I'm not jealous," he says.

Pfft, could've fooled me. I know I've pushed him enough today, but I can't help myself. I'm going to do whatever I can to make him snap, to make him want me like I know deep down he does.

"It's okay if you want me, Lucca," I purr, trying my best to sound seductive.

A spark ignites in his eyes but disappears when he blinks. "I don't want you, Claire. I just want to keep you safe, that's it."

"You can keep me safe with your cock inside of me." I almost cover my mouth with my hand, shocked that I said such a vulgar thing.

Lucca snickers, the blue of his eyes almost black. "I hate to tell you, but the worst place you could ever be is on my dick. I don't love, Claire. I don't kiss. I don't do flowers and swooning. I don't do dates or call the next day. I just fuck, hard, raw, and fast."

I gulp, taken back a little by his honesty. Surely, he would never be that way with me. I know Lucca. He would never hurt me.

"You were wrong, by the way. You thought my *crush* went away, it hasn't. I still want you."

Lucca shakes his head. "Don't be stupid. Finish your food. I already told you I'm not jealous, and I don't want you."

"Could've fooled me," I mutter before shoving a forkful of food into my mouth. The look Lucca is giving me promises many things, and I shiver involuntarily. He wants me, he's just afraid to admit it. Afraid to look beyond the little girl I once was and see me for the woman that I've become.

When I'm finished with dinner, I follow Lucca down the hall and back into his bedroom. Lucca walks over to the dresser and starts opening drawers. "Since you refused to pack a bag, you'll have to make do with my clothing."

"What if I don't want to wear your clothes?"

A dark shadow crosses his face as he peers at me over his shoulder. "It shouldn't take you long to realize there are no options with me. You've pushed me far enough today. Do you really want to test me further?"

I almost nod my head. He's so bossy and demanding, I can't help but fight him on everything he says or does, especially when they're choices that are made for me.

"Just give me the clothes."

"That's what I thought," he says while handing me an oversized T-shirt and a pair of boxers. I'm reminded of our time together in the hotels while on the run. How I came onto him, and he pushed me away. I had never felt so alone in my life. I wanted his touch, his comfort, and all he made me feel was shame.

I crane my neck to look up at him. His dirty blonde hair is disheveled in a sexy but dangerous way. Just looking at him makes me want things I can never have.

"Why do I have to sleep here with you? I know there's a room next door that I can use."

"I can't trust you not to run off and do something stupid. It's more for your protection than anything."

"Sure." I shoulder past him and stomp toward a door across the room, hoping it's the bathroom. Thankfully, once I turn on the light, I find it is, and I slip inside without further comment. I stand in front of the mirror and grip the edge of the sink. Inhaling deeply, I let the fresh oxygen rush into my lungs. I want Lucca. I want him badly, and I know he wants me.

Even in my drunken state, I remember him touching me and bringing me to orgasm. The bulge of his cock pressing against me, his panting breaths in my ear.

I glance at my reflection; I feel beautiful and ready. My red hair is like a beacon of light in the dark. My green eyes are piercing, and my skin, minus a smattering of freckles, is clear.

I'm young but not dumb, and I know what I want. Now, all I have to do is make Lucca admit he wants it too. I smile like the devil, knowing exactly what I have to do to make it happen.

24

LUCCA

I watch her climb into bed... *my* bed. Just before she slides under the blanket, the shirt she is wearing rides up her thigh, exposing her creamy white skin. My throat tightens.

Did she not put on the shorts I gave her?

Shaking my head and the thought of Claire in my bed half naked away, I head into the bathroom. As soon as I enter, I spot the shorts on the counter.

I grin at her feeble attempt to seduce me. That grin falls off my face when I see the pile of clothes lying on the ground. Because on top of that pile are her panties.

Fuck me.

Her in nothing but a shirt and panties is bad enough, but knowing she is naked underneath my shirt, nothing protecting her from being taken has all the blood draining from my brain and redirecting to my cock.

Now that the image is in my mind, I can't unsee her perky little tits and smooth stomach beneath my shirt. I remember the way her pussy felt as I touched her, bare minus a little landing strip. I scrub a hand down my face in frustration. This is not helping.

With a groan, I strip out of my clothes and turn on the shower, turning it all the way to cold. I step under the icy water, letting it cool my heated skin. My dick shrivels up faster than it got hard, and thank fuck, since that's exactly what I was hoping for.

I take my time in the shower, knowing what awaits me outside this bathroom.

When I'm done with my cold shower, I dry off and put on the pair of shorts Claire left on the counter. My skin is still numb from the freezing water as I return to the bedroom. Claire has turned off the light, and the room is blanketed in complete darkness. Yet, I can still make out the outline of her body under the blanket.

She doesn't say anything when I climb into the bed next to her, and she doesn't move when I pull the blanket up and over my body. For a moment, I think she must be asleep already, and I'm more than relieved about that.

I will my cock to stay down and forget that Claire's bare pussy is inches away.

Just when I close my eyes and let my body relax, Claire stirs next to me. The bed creaks, and in a split second, I'm wide awake again. Her tiny body molds against my side. Fuck, this isn't good.

Her slender arm snakes over my abdomen, and the warm sensation that zings through me causes me to inhale sharply. Then she delivers the final blow and swings her leg over mine until her hot cunt is pressed against my bare thigh.

This little minx is playing with fire, and she's about to get burned.

I lean down and talk close to her good ear, so I know she can hear me.

"What the hell do you think you're doing?"

"Cuddling," Claire whispers, burying her nose into the crook of my neck.

"If you don't scoot over, you're gonna regret what happens next," I warn. Her body stiffens, and a barely audible gasp escapes her lips. I can only imagine what her face looks like right now.

"W-what would h-happen?" She stumbles over the words, but where there should be fear, I find excitement lacing her voice.

"I'm going to expect you to get me off," I half growl, barely able to restrain myself. Fuck, I want her, but I can't. This is wrong.

"What if I want to get you off?"

"You don't know what you're asking for, nor do you have any idea what I would do to you." She deserves so much more than I can offer her, but she pushes me, teases, and tempts me. What the fuck am I supposed to do?

"Tell me then. I want to know." Her fingers feather across my skin. "What would you do to me, Lucca?"

If that isn't the million-dollar question?

"The one question you should ask is: what I wouldn't do to you." I stop myself from touching her, running my fingers through her tousled hair, and rolling her under me, and ravaging her. "If I had it my way, I would use your mouth however I see fit. I would hold your head in place and fuck your face, choking you with my thick cock. I'd make you gag, maybe even throw up, but I wouldn't stop. No matter how much you cried or begged or pushed me away. I would just keep using you like a fuck toy because that's what I do. I take until there is nothing left to take. Is that what you want? For me to use your mouth?"

The room falls silent. So silent, I don't even hear her breathing.

"Okay," she whispers so low that it only just meets my ears, and for a long time, I'm sure I've heard wrong. Did she just say okay?

"Okay," she repeats, louder this time with more confidence. "I want you to."

Christ.

Dumbfounded, I stare into the darkness of the room. I told her what I want from her to scare her off, not so she would offer it to me on a goddamn silver platter. It's like she pushes, I push back, and she shocks me by shoving me back.

When I don't make a move, Claire moves her leg up, so her knee is almost touching my rock-hard dick. Her wet pussy glides against my skin, and my balls are so tight, I could explode from that feeling alone.

It takes every fucking ounce of self-restraint I have to push her away.

"Get off me," I growl at her.

"No." Defiance leaks into that single word.

As I pull her arm aside, she digs her nails into my abdomen, making me hiss out in pain. Like a little kitten, she scratches me, clawing at me. Fighting me.

"I want you. I want you to use me."

Her voice cracks, and so do I. I snap right down the middle.

"Shut up! You don't want this!" I'm full on screaming now,

anger and need making it almost impossible to hold on to my sanity. I don't want to lose control. I don't want to hurt her, but she won't stop. She's poking a bear, and I'm about to attack.

I lose the last shred of willpower I have when her small hand moves south to my cock. She wraps her slender fingers around the shaft, and my chest tightens. There's still a thin layer of fabric between us, but it's enough to drive me insane. My hips thrust into her hand involuntarily, my body craving her touch like the earth craves the sun.

"Please," she whimpers, almost as if she is feeling just as desperate.

In one swift move, I lift my hips and rip down my shorts, letting my cock spring free. I let go of Claire's arm, so I have both hands available to grab her head and pull her mouth to my cock. I'm a starved man, and she is the meal I've been waiting for.

"Open up," I order, my voice distorted.

I drag my thumbs across her cheeks, making certain she is listening to me. When I find her mouth wide open, I pull her down, groaning when her hot mouth swallows the head of my cock. As soon as her tongue runs along the underside of my dick, I lose control. I thrust my hips up, keeping my hands on her head. The tip of my cock hits the back of her throat, and she makes a loud gagging sound. Her tiny hands press flat against my thighs, and any second now, she's going to come to her senses and realize how fucked up I am. How little I care, even for her.

"I told you. I fucking told you what would happen," I grit through my teeth as I fuck her mouth furiously.

I don't let her adjust. I don't let her talk or even breathe.

All that matters right now is my pleasure.

I'm both glad and disappointed that the lights are off. I don't want her to see me like this. But I want to see her choke on my dick. I want to see the spit dribble down her chin, and the tears stain her cheeks. I want to see how dirty this little girl can get.

My balls pull together, and a distinct tingle forms in the back of my spine. I've never come this fast before, but I've never had Claire's mouth either. It's hot and wet, and her whimpers as I take from her like a beast intensify my pleasure.

"I'm going to come. I'm going to fill your throat with cum, and you are going to take it all, my beautiful fuck toy. You're going to swallow every single drop," I demand as I keep pumping into her fiery mouth.

The gagging noise gets louder, and her sharp nails dig into my skin deeper as she frantically tries to escape me. I don't let her go. I hold her in place like the bastard I am.

Her fighting only makes me thrust harder and deeper. Then I slam headfirst into euphoric pleasure. I come. I come longer and harder than I ever have before.

My orgasm seems to go on forever. Claire's nails dig into my thighs so deep, I'm sure she is drawing blood.

When my balls are completely dry, and I finally release her, she sucks in a ragged breath before gasping for air like she was about to suffocate.

"Fuck." I sit up.

The post-orgasmic bliss evaporates and is replaced with a mixture of anger and concern. I flick on the lamp on the nightstand, and the dim light illuminates the room. "I told you. Why didn't you listen to me?"

Her big green wide eyes are watery, and there's a dribble of salvia on her chin. She looks so fucking beautiful and fragile. I'm afraid if I don't get away from her, I'll break her, destroy the good inside of her. She's all that's left of my goodness.

I grab her around the waist and pull her into my chest. Her small body fits into my arms perfectly. I half expect her to fight me, to try everything to get away from me, but she cuddles into my chest, allowing me to cradle her in my arms.

"I wanted you, that's why I didn't listen... and even after what just happened, it might make me stupid, but I still want you."

Speechless, I remain in this position, doing nothing else but holding her. It doesn't take long until her breathing evens out, and I'm sure she is asleep.

Even after she's seen the darkness inside of me, seen the fucked up deprived man I am, she wants me. She still wants me. My warning was no good, and if I have even half a chance of pushing her away, of saving her from my unbreakable grasp, then I'll make a better effort. I'll stop us from heading to a place we can't come back from.

A soft snore fills the air, and I hold Claire a little tighter.

The last thing I want to do is hurt her, but if I don't stop this now, I'll more than hurt her. I'll destroy her.

25

CLAIRE

After last night, I thought maybe things had changed. Rivulets of light peek through the blinds, and I roll over, squinting my eyes to find the bed empty, the sheets cold where he laid hours ago.

It's stupid, but I can't help but be disappointed. The way he used my mouth, owning me, using me. He was rough and didn't treat me like a fragile flower on the verge of wilting away. And I liked that. Liked that he wasn't babying me and that he was showing me another sliver of who he was.

Even if I enjoyed it, it left me feeling confused too. Before, my relationship with Lucca mimicked a brother and sister bond. The crush I had on him shattered last night. Now it's not a crush. It's an obsession. I wanted him in every way he was willing to give himself to me, even if he wasn't ready to admit he wanted me too.

We shared something, and even if I can't describe it, or put it into words, what we did made us closer. It made me feel powerful, like a queen. I held his pleasure in my hands. He wanted me so badly he gave in and crumbled like dry clay in my hand.

I smile while stretching my aching limbs. Lucca might run, but this apartment is only so big, and he can't hide from me forever. Nothing can ruin the mood I'm in. Leaving the bed, I walk out into the hall. I shiver when my bare feet contact the cold wood floor.

I wonder how long Lucca has been awake and what he's doing.

The robust smell of coffee tickles my nose the closer I get to the kitchen, and like a bloodhound, I follow the scent all the way to its source. Lucca stands in front of the stove, completely dressed. I stop in my tracks and stare, remembering him in all his glory last night.

His perfectly sculpted muscles and his thick cock. I bite the inside of my cheek to stop my mouth from watering. If I thought he was attractive before, he's something entirely different now. Like a fine wine, he's aged perfectly.

Lucca doesn't look up from the pan of scrambled eggs he's cooking to acknowledge me. That stings, but not as bad as when I intentionally brush against him while making my way over to the coffeepot, and he merely tucks himself closer to the stove so not to touch me.

What the hell? He acts like I'm repulsive to him. He didn't seem to think so last night when I had his cock in my mouth. Shivers ripple across my skin, and my nipples harden beneath my shirt at the reminder of how roughly he took my mouth, the mushroom head of his cock slipping into the back of my throat. He wasn't lying when he said he would choke me, that he would treat me like I was nothing.

It was degrading and not exactly pleasant, but it ignited a

fire in the depths of my belly. By the time he was done using my mouth, I was left panting, my arousal and need for him dripping down my thighs.

If he was trying to convince me he didn't want me, then he was going to have to try much harder. I get a coffee mug out of the cabinet and pour myself a cup. Lucca is still standing there staring at the eggs like they killed his entire family. I pop into the fridge and grab the milk, splashing a little into my coffee.

The last thing I want to do is let his sourness ruin my good mood, but with him acting so distant, it's hard not to. Moving the eggs to a plate along with some sausage links, he turns and mechanically hands me the food. His eyes are cast down at the ground. He's not even looking at me. *What the fuck?*

I remain standing there, a bit shocked that he's only paying me the bare minimum of attention. Had I not done good enough last night? The question is on the tip of my tongue when Lucca clears his throat and turns to look at me. His features are masked, his face void of all emotion. What the hell is going on?

"I'm preparing the room next to mine for you. You will sleep in there from now on."

He speaks to me like I'm a small child, and I have to wonder if he's deliberately trying to piss me off?

"Did I do something wrong? Last I knew, you enjoyed what we did, or at least it seemed like you did."

Lucca's jaw ticks. "What happened last night will *not* happen again."

"Says who? What happened last night was great. I enjoyed it thoroughly, and I know you did too. Plus, I'm an adult, not a child. I can suck anyone's cock that I..."

The plate in Lucca's hand cracks beneath his grip, and I stop mid-sentence. I look up from the plate and directly into his eyes. Eyes that are not so masked now, eyes that are burning with red hot jealousy.

"If you're half as smart as you think, you will not finish that sentence."

Most women would be wary or afraid, but I'm none of those things. I'm pissed. Pissed that he's still pushing me away. Pissed that he's still acting like I'm a child.

"I can give you a blow job but can't sleep in the same bed as you?" I set my plate on the counter, and suddenly, I'm no longer hungry.

"It's for your protection, Claire," he grits through his teeth.

"For my protection?" I roll my eyes and shake my head. "I don't know how many times I've told you I don't need your protection."

Lucca tosses the broken plate into the sink. The sound makes me jump but doesn't scare me as much as when I look away from the sink and find Lucca advancing toward me. I take a hesitant step back.

Instantly, I'm the prey, and he's the hunter.

Lucca's chest brushes against mine, and sparks of desire form low in my belly. I lick my bottom lip, wondering what it would be like to kiss him or if he would kiss me back? I'm so caught up in him, in his scent, his body, what I want him to do to me, that I lose focus for a moment. I can't let the lust drive me alone.

Dark blue eyes pierce my own, and I break the connection by taking a step back, putting a breath of space between us. It's hard to show him my anger when he's this close.

"I will not be your prisoner here. I will not be trapped in

that bedroom. I'm an adult, but more than that, I'm a human being, not an animal you can keep in a cage."

"I don't care how old you are and what you think is best for you..." His voice is deep and soft, causing me to look up from his chest and directly into his eyes. His gaze has softened to a dull knife, and for once, in all the time I've known him, I feel like I'm seeing him, the real him, for the first time. His thumb brushes against the apple of my cheek, his touch making my skin heat. "Your age doesn't stop me from protecting you, nor does it stop me from locking you up in that bedroom and keeping you there until you learn to listen to me."

That's all it takes for me to snap, and a moment later, I'm swatting his hand away.

"I will never forgive you if you do that to me. I've let a lot of things go, but if you take my freedom from me..."

A flash of pain reflects in his eyes. "I'm not taking your freedom. I'm asking you to behave, to do as I say. It's simple. If you listen, then I'll give you things you want. For instance, I know you want to go to college. I have the means to set that up."

Hope swells in my chest. College? I figured the moment he took me and brought me here, any hope I had of going to college was gone, but now it seems I have a chance.

"Don't lie to me, Lucca. I can handle many things but a liar..."

"I'm not lying. I'll let you go to school. I know you want to go, and I'll give you what you want. I just need... I need you to do what I tell you to do."

There's a certain restraint to his words, almost as if he's forcing himself not to say what he wants to say. A sliver of guilt cuts across my chest. Ever since I got here, I've been pushing him. Is it really my fault he can't see what's right in front of him, though?

The idea of being forced to listen to him doesn't sit well with my plan of seducing him, but there's no way in hell I'm letting him lock me in that bedroom.

"Fine," I hiss. "I'll listen and be the obedient little girl you want me to be."

Lucca smiles sinisterly, like I've just given him the codes to blow up the entire world.

"Do your part and behave, and I'll reward you. Misbehave, and I'll punish you. The choice is and always will be yours."

I can't help but wonder about the type of punishment he will offer me if I choose not to behave? I guess we'll find out because I give it five minutes before I misbehave.

26

LUCCA

We spent the last few days playing a game of cat and mouse. Surprisingly, I'm the mouse in this scenario, and Claire is the cat that stalks me like she is ready to pounce. If she is not actively pouting, she spends her day trying to tantalize me, so I'll lose control again.

It's quite adorable, really.

I don't really want her to stay in the room beside me, but I know it's the only thing to keep sane. There is no way I can control myself when she is in my bed. The first night only proved that.

Flopping down on the couch, I turn on the TV and put my feet on the coffee table. I just start flipping through the channels when Claire's sing-song voice fills the space.

"Lucca..." I turn my head to look at her. "I couldn't find a towel," she explains innocently while standing in the doorway completely naked.

I want to yell at her, cuss her out and send her back to her room to get dressed. I want to be angry at her, angry at myself for being so weak and fucked up in the head. I want to get up and walk out of here, go to a bar and find some random woman, so I can either drink or fuck Claire out of my mind.

Instead, I drop the remote.

A sinister smile spreads across her face.

My brain shuts partly off, and my gaze lowers on its own. I take in her naked form. She is breathtaking. Her tits are just the right size, looking like they would fit into my hand perfectly. Pink nipples I can imagine sucking into my mouth. Her smooth belly and flaring hips that lead down to the land that I refuse to acknowledge.

Fuck me, I want her. I can taste the desire on my tongue.

"You know where the towels are," I try to say, but it comes out more like a groan.

Dragging my attention back to the TV, I pretend to be interested in the cooking show that's playing on the channel I landed on.

I feel her move closer before I see her out of the corner of my eye. She thinks she's smart, that she's going to pull one over on me. That I'm going to break again like I did the other night, and if she was any other woman, I wouldn't have thought twice.

This is Claire, though. Not just any woman.

Burying the arousal as deep as I can, I shove out of the chair, causing her to stumble backward. Her eyes are wide for a second before they return to their seductive nature. Genuine anger mixes with the desire pooling in my gut.

"Get dressed right now!"

Claire's pink lips form a pout. "I can't. I'm all wet."

She thinks she's so smart. She doesn't have a fucking clue what I would do to her.

Shoving past her, I walk into the bathroom and grab the

towel that's in plain sight. I stomp back into the bedroom and shove the towel into her hands.

"Where did you find this?"

I roll my eyes and suppress the grin threatening to appear on my lips. "Hanging on the towel rack. Now go get dressed. The next time I see you, you better have clothes on, and I mean it, Claire." I try to keep my voice stern and serious.

As funny as this might be, she's straddling the line of my insanity. One wrong move, and we're both balancing on the edge of a knife's blade.

"You act like you don't want me, but that bulge in your shorts says otherwise." Her emerald eyes gleam with satisfaction.

My cock stiffens to an almost painful degree. Guess I'll have to drop her down a peg or two. "Yeah, my cock is rock hard, but it would be hard with any red-blooded woman standing in front of me with her tits and pussy showing."

In an instant, her demeanor changes. Her shoulders slump forward, and her eyes divert to the floor. She wraps the towel around her middle, covering herself up.

Almost instantly, the guilt hits. "Look, Claire, you have to…"

She waves me off and tightens her hold on the towel. "No. I get it. I'm good enough to suck your dick, just not anything else."

I'm at a loss for words. What is my response to that? I told you not to push me? I warned you? I have to remind myself that Claire doesn't know what she truly wants. She is still so young and naive to the world. She thinks that I'm the man for her because I'm the only one to have ever paid her an ounce of attention, but she doesn't need a man like me.

"Classes start tomorrow," I tell her to change the direction of our conversation.

"Good. I can't wait to get out of this apartment and away from you!" she sneers angrily and disappears back into the bedroom.

I'm conflicted on how to move forward. Apologizing won't help. Pushing her away is the only thing I can do. I'll never forgive myself if I saved her all these times from the bad men in my life, only to ruin her myself.

Now, I just need to make her realize that I'm not the one for her. I need to push her away, make her lose interest in me. The question is, how?

I stand at the window, looking through the glass at the people walking the streets below when an idea crosses my mind. The only way she is going to let me go is if I twist her misguided love into hate. I need her to hate me. If she hates me, then so be it. At least I won't destroy her life.

Walking to the kitchen, I open my junk drawer and pull out a piece of paper and a pen. I stare at the blank page for a few seconds before I bring the ball of the pen to the paper and start writing…

Claire,

I'm sorry, but I can't let this go on any longer. You know I care about you, and I want to keep you safe at all costs. You are like a sister to me, and that's the way it needs to stay.

I don't want to hurt your feelings, but I've been seeing someone. That's why there can never be anything between us. Because I'm in love with someone else.

I'm gripping the pen so hard it cracks in my hold. My chest aches, and there is a distinct pit forming deep inside my gut.

I imagine her reading this, reading this lie. It would break her heart.

Fuck, I can't do this. I can't let her hate me. It would not just break her. It would break me as well. I'm about to rip the letter up when I hear Claire leaving her room.

The sound of the bedroom door opening has me shoving the paper back into the drawer before slamming it shut.

Claire appears a moment later, now fully dressed. Her hair is still wet, and her mouth is still set into an angry frown.

"You need something?" The words come out much rougher than intended, and I almost apologize.

"Well, I was hungry, but I just lost my appetite," she sneers at me before spinning around and stomping back to her room. The door slams hard enough to rattle the glass sitting on the kitchen counter, leaving the tension in the apartment thick.

One thing is clear now. I don't want her to hate me. I also don't want her to view this place as a prison, even if that's what it is. I want her to be happy, smiling, and enjoying life. Maybe it's time for a truce?

I decide to order some Chinese from a place around the corner. The doorbell rings in under twenty minutes. With a hot bag of food in hand, I close the door and turn around.

Claire's head sticks out of the room, making me smile.

"I thought I heard the doorbell ring. Your doorbell is very loud, by the way."

"There is a doorbell extender in each bedroom. That's why you heard it."

"Oh..." She looks at the bag in my hand as if she is trying to decide whether to go back to her room or come out and eat.

"I got sesame chicken," I tell her, knowing that's her favorite.

"Come on. Have dinner with me. We'll watch a movie or something."

A tiny smile plays on her lips. "That sounds so... *normal*."

I walk to the table and put the food down. Happiness blooms in my chest when I hear her approach. She takes a seat and sits patiently until I open the bag and place the box in front of her.

"I need my phone," she tells me in a stern voice, and I wonder how long she has been thinking about making that demand.

"You could have packed a bag when I gave you the chance, but you chose to be a brat."

"Well, you acted like a psycho, and I still need my phone. I want to call Carter." At the mention of his name, my mood sours immediately. "Lucca, I know you don't want me to talk about Carter—which, as we established, is absolutely not you being jealous—but I need to apologize to him. He got hurt because of me."

A snort escapes my throat. I know she is right. Carter has done nothing wrong. I beat him up, and I haven't even apologized for it myself. Problem is, every time I think about him, I see his hands all over Claire. I know it didn't happen, but it's like once I imagined it, the fake image burned itself into my mind.

"Lucca, please..." She looks at me with her big green eyes and her lip pulling up into a small pout. "He is my friend. The only friend I had in the last two years. I promise we are just friends, but I care about him. I just want to apologize and make sure he is okay."

She keeps staring at me with her puppy dog eyes. Fuck, I would do anything for her when she looks at me like that, which is a fact she can never know about. That little minx will use it on me in a blink of an eye.

"How about we drive over to your house in the morning to grab your phone?"

"Okay." She beams at me, the widest smile spread across her face. "And you'll be okay with me calling Carter?"

"Yeah," I say, but it comes out in a grunt, which only makes Claire giggle.

Fuck me. She has me wrapped around her little finger, and she fucking knows it.

27

CLAIRE

I'm so excited I could squeal like a pig. Lucca is actually letting me leave the house. More than that, he somehow got me into the local university. With his mob connections and all, I wouldn't be surprised if he murdered someone to get me enrolled. I try not to think about that aspect of him. However, it would be just like him to act with violence and ask questions later.

Lucca made good on his promise, and we left the apartment earlier so we could go back to the house. While there, I picked up some clothes and my cell phone. I also gave Tracy and Steven a long hug. I'd only been gone a few days, but I missed them dearly. Carter wasn't there, which I was disappointed about, but at least I could text him my apology.

Like a father dropping his daughter off at school, Lucca pulled up to the university and let me out. That was hours ago.

I'm finished with my first day of classes, and I'm feeling free, not completely free, though, since I know for sure, Lucca is hiding in the shadows somewhere.

I'm not stupid enough to believe he would trust me here alone. He probably thinks I'm going to run away, and maybe I would if I weren't so drawn to him and dead set on having him see me as more than just a *little girl* as he likes to call me.

As I walk out of class, descending the steps from the east hall, I find Lucca standing at the bottom of the stairs. He's watching the students as they walk by, appearing as more of a security guard than a student, assuming that's what he's trying to blend into. Unfortunately, he sticks out like a sore thumb. He's older, more mature, and there is a dark edge to him that is missing from the other guys I've seen on campus today.

I've almost reached him when his gaze gravitates toward mine, and those dark blue eyes flick over my body, making butterflies take flight in my stomach. One look and he has me unable to move or breathe. I feel trapped under his intense gaze.

When he looks away, I can finally move again, breathe again, and by the time I reach him, I've got my emotions and those pesky butterflies in check.

"How was your first day of school?" he asks without looking at me.

I follow his line of sight and discover he's watching a group of guys that are standing outside a coffee shop a few feet away. The way he's staring at them with barely constrained, murderous rage makes me want to laugh. All they're doing is breathing and maybe drinking a cup of coffee, and I bet he's thinking of a million ways to skin them like a rabbit.

"Um, it was good. It would be better if you weren't staring at some of my potential friends like you want to skin them and hang them from a tree."

Lucca moves so fast that all I can do is gasp as he crowds me with his body, blocking my view of the guys. Leaning into my face, he brushes a few strands of hair from my cheek. His touch is gentle, but the look in his eyes is violent.

"If you let another man touch you, I will cut off all their fingers and shove them down their fucking throat. Do you understand me?"

Earlier I was wondering what exactly I could do to make him jealous, to give him the push he needs to make a move, and I think he just gave me my answer.

"You don't have to act so jealous. It's not like I'm with you or your girlfriend."

He drops his hand. "I'm not jealous."

I tighten my hold on the strap of my backpack. "You keep saying that, but your actions say different."

I take a step back, letting the air between us cool my now heated skin. Lucca does things to my body that I don't understand, but that I want to explore only with him. Part of me wishes I was more experienced because maybe then he wouldn't see me as this piece of fine china.

"Let's go to dinner."

"Dinner?" I give him a puzzled expression and check the time on my phone. "It's like three in the afternoon."

Lucca shrugs. "Who cares. We can swing through a drive-thru if you want."

"I mean, I guess. If we have to."

We walk toward the car. "What do you mean? Even the worst of men have to eat."

"That's true," I reply, and a second later, my cell phone pings.

I check as soon as I'm inside the SUV. I can't quite explain the joy I feel when I see it's a message from Carter. Earlier I sent him a long-winded apology, and I didn't expect to hear anything back from him.

"Why are you smiling at your phone?" Lucca asks defensively.

My brows pucker together, but in the back of my mind, I know exactly how to bend this to my winning. "Oh, nothing, just a funny message."

I fire back a quick reply to Carter, who asked how I'm enjoying my time with Lucca.

Me: I'm not.

A second later, my phone pings again. Lucca pulls out of the parking lot, and out of the corner of my eye, I see his hands circling the steering wheel. He's white-knuckling it. I can only imagine what he's thinking.

"Where do you want to eat?" This time his words are gritted through his teeth.

Oh, yes, this is definitely working.

"Oh, I don't know. You pick," I say without looking up from my phone.

I check my message from Carter and let out a soft giggle at the laughing emoji he sent, followed by his message. My heart warms.

Carter: Yeah, I've heard he can be a shit roommate. Let me know if I need to come and rescue you.

I'm still partially watching Lucca and notice his gaze darting between me and the road. It's obvious he is curious, but from the way his nostrils flare and his lip curls, he's also possibly jealous? Maybe? Ignoring him, I type out my reply to Carter.

Me: How about now? I'm going insane.

"Are you going to talk to me or just stare at your phone, smiling?"

I suppress a smile. "Oh, yeah, sorry. Carter is messaging me."

"Fucking Carter..." He grumbles under his breath, but loud enough for me to hear.

I don't think I would find this nearly as funny if Lucca didn't insist he wasn't jealous. It's clear he is. He's just too stubborn to admit it.

"Hey, be nice to Carter. He's my best friend."

Lucca pins me with a glare as he pulls into the Chick-Fil-A parking lot. "You have no best friends. If you want a best friend, then I'll be it."

I bite my lip. I want to tell him that the last thing I want him to be is a friend, but know that right now isn't the time.

"I don't want you to be my best friend," I tell him.

"Too bad. I don't care what you want, in case that wasn't already obvious." He smiles, showing off his perfectly straight white teeth.

It's like looking a great white shark in the mouth and hoping he doesn't bite you. Ten out of ten times, you're going to get bitten. The same applies to Lucca, and for some stupid reason, every time he breaks my heart, I come back for more, hoping for a different result.

As I stare at him now, knowing he is bent up with jealous rage, I wonder if this time will be different. I wonder what it will take to set him over the edge and make him realize he wants this as much as I do.

～

AFTER DINNER, we drive home. Lucca is tense and heads straight for his bedroom upon arrival. I do the same and spend the evening doing homework. Since we ate dinner so early, by the time seven rolls around, I'm hungry and tiptoe out into the kitchen.

Shockingly, Lucca isn't anywhere to be found. He's probably trying to avoid me and my seducing ways. I laugh inside and pour myself a bowl of cereal, shoving spoonful after spoonful of the sugary goodness into my mouth.

I lean against the counter and wait for him to appear in the kitchen, but he never does. I'm disappointed but not shocked. When I'm finished, I put my dish in the dishwasher and shut off the light. The house is eerily quiet, and I stop at the door to my room. I'm tempted to go knock on Lucca's door and see if he's awake but stop before I can build up the courage to do it.

If he wanted to see me or talk to me, he would.

After a quick shower, I climb into bed and wrap the covers around me. The loneliness of my life weighs heavily on me. It compounds like interest, and I don't know what to do.

My life before Lucca wasn't anything special, but at least I had my father. Even if he didn't love me or treat me like he should, he was still there. Lucca protected me, but everything he's done has been from afar. My heart aches, and I can feel tears in my eyes.

I toss and turn in bed for an eternity. No sooner than I've rolled to my back and am staring at the ceiling do I decide I can't stand to be alone tonight.

Even if he pushes me away, at least I tried.

Like a child sneaking from her bed at night, I tiptoe out of the bedroom and into the hall. When I reach the door to Lucca's room, I hesitate but push through the fear of rejection. Taking the knob into my hand, I twist it and push the door open slowly.

The room is blanketed in darkness, minus a few slivers of light from the streetlamp outside, making it possible for me to see Lucca's shirtless back. Closing the door behind me, I move closer to the bed.

I'm trying to figure out how I will get into the bed without waking him when his entire body jerks into a sitting position. I'm rooted in place by fear, and that fear only intensifies when my eyes catch on something silver in his hand.

Gun. He has a gun, and he's pointing it at me.

A scream rips from my throat, and I stumble backward, barely catching myself from falling flat on my ass. The side table light flicks on, emitting a soft glow in the room.

"Jesus, fuck, Claire!" Lucca growls, his deep grumble filling the room. He places the gun in the bedside drawer, and my eyes track the movement.

He almost shot me. My bottom lip trembles.

"I could have killed you! Is that what you want? For me to shoot you?" The anger in his voice pellets against my skin. I can't bring myself to look at him. Would he have done it? Would he have shot me?

"No..." My heartbeat echoes in my good ear as I stare at the floor. "I was... I'm lonely, and I just wanted to sleep beside you."

Silence follows, and I peek up at him through my lashes.

Lucca shakes his head. His chest rises and falls so rapidly it looks like he just got done going for a jog. He fists the strands of dirty blonde hair with frustration.

"Never, ever do something that stupid again," he warns. "If I hurt you, I would've... It would've killed me." The sincere look he gives me tells me he isn't lying.

"I'm... I'm sorry," I manage to get out, still shaken up.

I look toward the door, knowing what's coming. Even after

what just happened, he's going to ask me to leave. He's going to tell me to go back into the other bedroom and go to sleep. I'm prepared to be let down but shocked when his features twist, softening, making him appear more like the Lucca I remember from my childhood.

With a sigh, he says, "Come on. Lie down."

I can't contain myself and run and jump on the bed. I can't imagine how I look to him right now, probably like a small child, and in some ways, I feel like one. I feel fragile and like I'm wearing a sweater with lots of room to grow, but the sweater is suffocating me because I don't know how to wear it.

Rolling onto my side, I grab the blankets and pull them up and over my body. Lucca seems frozen for an instant until the light flicks off. All over again, the room is dark, and when I close my eyes, I see Lucca with the gun in his hand.

Pulling my back to his front, he spoons me. The warmth of his body and his scent flush away the nightmare before it can take root and the loneliness in my heart disappears. As we lie there in the dark with sleep close to the surface, I can't help but play Lucca's words back in my mind. *"If I hurt you, I would've... It would've killed me.*

It reminds me that while everyone else in my life, including my father, had let me down, Lucca, even when breaking my heart, was still there.

He still cares for me, and suddenly, I'm reminded I'm not alone. I have Lucca, really have him, and I have to find a way to keep him by my side. At all costs.

28

LUCCA

I'm not sure how I stayed away from her for so long. Maybe it's because I've kept my distance that I never got this obsessed. Don't get me wrong, I know I've been obsessed with Claire's safety before now. But since she has been staying with me, that obsession has reached a new height.

I used to be okay with watching her through surveillance videos, pictures, and Carter's reports. Now, none of those would quench my thirst for control. The only way to satisfy my need is to watch Claire constantly. I need to know what she is doing every second of the day. I need to see her with my own eyes, feel her skin, fill my nostrils with her flowery scent.

Sitting in the car across from the entrance to the college, I get restless, waiting for Claire to walk out. Checking my watch constantly, I feel like I'm on a stakeout, but instead of killing the subject, I just want to protect it. Maybe I'll kill everyone around her just to be sure she is safe. No one can harm her if everyone is dead.

Solid plan.

That plan sounds even better when Claire walks out, and I spot the guy walking next to her. A guy walking way too close, if you ask me. He is the typical college boy: jeans, sneakers, and the university hoodie. With a backpack slung over his shoulder, he walks like he owns the campus.

My blood boils as I watch the way he leans into her. She giggles and touches his arm like he just said something funny. That's when I've had enough.

I kill the engine and climb out of the car. Her classes are not over yet, and I didn't plan on letting her know I'm here, but I can't stand back and watch this any longer.

Like a man on a mission, I stomp over to where they are. The moment Claire spots me, her eyes go wide with a mixture of shock and fear. Either she feels like she just got caught doing something wrong, or I simply look scary enough for her to worry.

"Hey, Gregg, why don't we grab lunch another day," I hear her say, and my anger reaches a new height. Lunch? Fucking lunch with *Gregg*? Fuck, Gregg!

"Yeah, sure. Maybe tomorrow?" Gregg asks.

"No," I growl. "She won't have lunch with you tomorrow... or ever."

"Lucca," Claire warns, annoyance bleeding through her voice. She grabs my arm, and her touch sends a bolt of lightning through my body.

"Eh, okaaay," Gregg says, looking between us in confusion. "I guess I'll see you in class."

Not if I can help it.

Gregg white knuckles the flimsy strap of his backpack and scurries away from us as fast as he can. I turn my attention back to Claire, who is looking at me with her head tilted, and her hand propped up on her hips like she is about to give me a lecture.

"Seriously? Was that necessary?"

"*Very*. I told you, no funny business with guys."

Mischief twinkles in her eyes, and I already know she is going to do the opposite of what I'm asking just to spite me.

"We'll see—" she starts, but I cut her off by grabbing her upper arm and dragging her across the sidewalk. Pulling her behind the building, I don't stop until we are hidden by some bushes and the shadow of the extensive building. Once alone, I shove her against the wall, causing her to gasp. I lean into her face, letting a mask of menace fall over my face.

"You listen to me. You will not talk to any other guy on this campus."

"What if my teacher is a guy?" She grins like she's fooled me in some way.

"You know what I mean. Don't play games, Claire. You are done acting like a brat. You will listen to me and not flirt with anyone."

"Or what? You're going to pull me back to your cave by my hair?" She laughs without humor.

"No, Claire. I will find every single guy you talk to and kill them."

Her big green eyes grow to the size of saucers with shock.

"That... that is insane." She shakes her head, most likely with disbelief. "Actually, you know what, Lucca, you're insane."

"I know, and I also know you think I'm lying, but I'm not." I lean in, my nose brushes hers, and a strange tightness forms in my chest.

I'm close enough that I could kiss her. Her pink lips are right there, right fucking there, and I'm tempted to do it. Her sweet breath fans against my face. I want to taste her, draw from her, but that would be stupid. She can never be mine. I can never be hers.

"Don't test me, please, don't..." I succumb to the temptation for a millisecond and brush my lips against her bottom lip. A gasp that sounds like a whimper meets my ears, but I can't stop myself. I bite her lip, tugging on it, and then place both of my lips over hers.

It takes a moment for her to catch up, but once she does, she's clawing at me. Her arms come to wrap around my neck, and her petite body presses against mine.

She feels so perfect in my arms, but I'm not stupid. It's all merely an illusion. I'm a criminal with enemies a mile long. What can I offer her besides a life on the run? I've hurt her enough, made her develop feelings. I need to stop this.

Forcing myself to pull away from her, I stumble backward and shiver at the loss of warmth her body gave me. We are polar opposites like the sun and the moon. Like a hero and villain. Like dark and light.

Clearing my throat, I shove my hands into my pockets and try to forget what just happened. I look up and regret it almost immediately. Claire is holding a finger to her lips, her cheeks are rosy red, and her eyes flicker with heat.

"I'm not joking, Claire. Take this as your one and only warning."

She pushes off the wall with determination. "If you don't want me, then why can't anyone else have me?"

I wish I knew the answer to that question, but I don't. Making Claire mine would lead to a life of unhappiness and hate, but letting her go means I have to watch her with someone else.

"I'll pick you up after class," I tell her and turn around and walk back out onto the sidewalk. The tightness in my chest becomes an ache, and I've never experienced this feeling before. It's more than obsession, it's something else, and I'm not ready to face it yet.

29

CLAIRE

For a man that insists he isn't jealous, he sure gets pissed about me talking to other guys or even messaging on my phone. I like it, though. It tells me he cares about me, even if it's in some morphed, fucked up way.

As the days pass, blurring together, it becomes harder and harder to break Lucca down, but I know that I'm causing a crack in his shield. Each day he seems to watch me with a different kind of heat in his eyes. Tonight, however, I'm done playing games.

Tonight, I'm going to put the last nail in his coffin. I'm going to push him hard, and if he doesn't break, then I must face the fact that maybe he really doesn't want me as badly as I want him. It terrifies me to think that he might not, but there is hope that lives inside of me that says he does.

As soon as I hear the shower running, I walk into his bedroom. Rejection from him is something I fear, but I have to try one more time. The courage I need builds as I slip off my clothes, tossing them onto the floor. I'm no longer shy about my body or worried that I'm not good enough for him. I know he wants me.

My nipples become hard peeks when the cool air brushes them, and my core heats, fueled by desire. The countdown to when the shower turns off seems like an eternity.

My heart thunders against my rib cage, threatening to break free from my chest. I'm going to give myself to him, offer him the one thing I've given no one else. To catch him off guard like this will be like offering food to a starved animal. I remind myself of his words from the other night, how if he ever hurt me, it would kill him.

Lucca won't hurt me. He won't.

The door to the bathroom opens, and steam billows into the bedroom. Lucca walks out with a towel slung over his shoulder. His hair is still soaked, and beads of water glisten on his skin. He looks like a damn god, dangerous and sharp.

"What the fuck are you doing?" His voice is filled with venomous rage, but his eyes darken and flicker with desire that burns as it moves over every inch of exposed skin.

I swallow around the knot in my throat. "I want you."

He cocks his head to the side. "You want me?"

"Yes, I want you to be my first."

He's told me before how things are with him, but I'm not any of the other women he's been with. I'm different, and he knows that.

The sides of his mouth tick up, but he's not smiling. It's like he's disgusted, but that can't be right because I know he wants me. Anger takes root in my heart. I will not let him push me away. Not again.

"I know you want me, Lucca. I see it. I feel it. You try to distance yourself, and you lie and say you aren't jealous, but I know you are. You want this as much as I do. You're just afraid," my voice cracks, giving away my emotions, "afraid to feel something for me, afraid to admit the truth."

A war wages inside of him. I see the battle playing out on his face. He's grappling for control.

"If I touched you like I want to touch you, you would never forgive me, and I would never forgive myself."

"You're a good man, Lucca, and you've never hurt me. I trust you."

A sinister laugh that numbs me to the bone slips from his mouth. "See, that's the problem. You're too trusting and too naive for your own good, and I think it's time I proved to you just how bad I am."

The light in Lucca's eyes shuts off, and when he blinks, the man before me is the one that killed my father, the man who murders and kills without care. Like a wounded animal, my first thought is to retreat, but that would do me no good.

If I run, then he will chase, but if I do nothing... I don't know what will happen. I trust Lucca, but do I trust this side of him?

"Run..." he orders. "Do it. I can see you want to run. To hide. Maybe you don't trust me with your fragile heart after all?"

Dropping the towel to the floor, he stalks toward me. Fear zings up my back, and a bright neon sign blinks in my mind, warning me, telling me I've made a grave mistake, but how will I ever know if I've made a mistake if I haven't even tried?

"I..." my voice trembles, "I trust you, and I still want you."

He stops directly in front of me, and his chest brushes against mine. He looks down at me, and I crane my neck back to look up at him. Out of the corner of my eye, I see his hand moving toward my breast. With two fingers, he grabs the hardened tip and pinches it, causing a jolt of both pleasure and pain in my abdomen.

Leaning into my good ear, his teeth graze the sensitive skin there before he asks, "Is this what you want, little girl?"

I normally hate when he calls me that, but this seems different. He is using it in a twisted, perverted way, and I don't know how to process the change. Lucca is not that much older than me. There are only eight years between us, and I've always felt much older than I am. The problem is Lucca is also older than his age in many ways.

Life has aged us, turning the handle on our clock faster than the average person's.

"No. I want more. I want all of you."

With those words, I set into action events that we can never come back from. Before I can grasp what is going on, Lucca pounces on me, shoving me back against the bed. Confusion gives way to fear when he spreads my legs and centers himself between them. I can feel his throbbing erection, and my want glistens against my folds, but I didn't want it to happen like this. I didn't want to be taken by him like all the others before me.

Lifting a hand to his face, I try to get him to look at me, to see me, but he grabs both hands and pins them to the bed above my head. I'm helplessly trapped.

"Is this what you want, Claire?" he hisses through his teeth.

I shake my head, just as tears form in my eyes. He's holding me down with little effort, and no matter how much I buck against him, it's like trying to move a brick wall.

"Say it. Tell me you want me to fuck you..." he taunts, throwing my earlier words back at me.

My body reacts with need because physically, I want him as

the earth wants the moon, but deep down, this isn't the man I've slowly come to fall in love with.

The head of his cock slips between my folds, and I let out a soft gasp at the sensation. I'm wet, my core slick with need. Even so, I don't want it to happen this way.

I want my Lucca, not this monster of a man.

"Lucca..." I whimper, preparing to tell him to stop when something in his features snaps and all control is lost. Like a savage beast, he hitches my leg up on his hip and drives into me, stealing the air from my lungs and cracking my heart into a million pieces.

Pain temporarily seizes my body, and my nails dig into his hand hard enough to draw blood. I can't breathe. I can't think. I can't do anything but see him owning me, taking from me.

For a millisecond, the darkness in his eyes drains away, and his lips brush against mine. Soft as a feather. Like a gentle breeze.

There is still hope, but like a balloon, it deflates at his next words.

"I warned you. I told you I wasn't a good man, and you just kept pushing me." His body visibly shakes, and I can see the effort it takes for him to remain still. "Now, I'll take everything from you. Now, you'll never be free of me, butterfly."

A smile plays on his lips, and he pulls out, slamming back into me, making me feel the pain all over again, making me realize just how wrong I was to trust him.

30

LUCCA

*I*t's like watching a car accident happen right before your eyes. I know I'm destroying her picture-perfect idea of me, ripping at it little by little every time I move inside of her. I'm taking all the good I've done for her and shoving it back into her face. There is no hiding who I am from her anymore. This is me, and now she knows.

"You got what you wanted!" I curl my lip and drive into her once more. Her eyes are wide, and tears slip down the apples of her cheeks. "You pushed me too far.""

I feel like a fucking monster, but her wet pussy calls to me. The sound her pussy makes as I slip inside. She squeezes me so tightly, and even as she resists me, struggling beneath my touch, she still wants this.

Soft little whimpers escape her lips every time I slide deeper, and her nails pierce my flesh, drawing me closer to an orgasm. I'm a bastard for getting off on her pain, for loving that I will be her first and last and that no matter how much she resists me, her tight cunt is going to cream all over me. She is going to come even if I have to force her.

I slip deeper into my subconscious and allow the sick, sinister part of me to take over. I should stop, it's not too late, but I can't. *Won't.* She is mine. Mine forever. Mine for always. I tried to protect her before. Tried to save her from my darkness, but she walked into it with open arms. Releasing her hands, I take both her legs and pin them to her chest and watch with pleasure as my cock bottoms out inside of her, and my balls press against her perky ass.

"Tell me to stop, tell me you don't want this," I taunt.

I might have stolen the choice from her, but it's one that she made long before she walked into the bedroom and stripped out of her clothes.

With her red hair fanned out like a halo and her creamy white skin glowing a soft pink, she looks like a fucking angel. An angel damned to live in the hell I placed her in.

"Lucca," she whimpers and tosses her head back and forth as if she's fighting off the pleasure. With two fingers, I easily find her engorged clit and pinch it between them. Her fingers grasp onto my forearms as I fuck her faster and faster.

"Fuck, come for me. Come on my cock, Claire. Prove to me how much you wanted this. Make it worth my time."

The headboard creaks, and her head tips back into the mattress. Her pussy flutters with the start of her orgasm, which only encourages me to take her harder. I grind my pelvis into her, wanting to be as close as I can to her.

"I... I'm...." She bites her lip, and her legs shake, and fuck me, I can't stop what is happening. Her orgasm causes me to explode, and ropes of warm sticky cum pump deep inside of her. I press my clammy forehead against her and kiss the tip of her nose before rolling off of her and sagging onto the mattress.

The pleasure fades slowly, and the reality of what I've just done blooms. Claire is unmoving beside me, her eyes trained on the ceiling, her hands resting against the mattress.

She doesn't seem to be in any distress, but one look at her thighs, which are stained with blood from her now taken virginity, and my cock, and I know there is an unseen ache inside of her. Anger and guilt clash like bulls in my head. She shouldn't have pushed me, but more than that, I shouldn't have taken from her like I did.

She deserves better, flowers, and sweet whispers. A man that would've prepared her and taken her with finesse. Fuck, I should've stopped.

I reach out and brush a strand of hair from her face. Post sex, Claire is as beautiful as virginal Claire was. Her cheeks are glowing, her eyes brighter.

"Are you... Did I...." I squeeze my eyes shut and grit my teeth. Never have I had to ask a woman if I took her too hard or hurt her. The women I fucked before Claire meant nothing to me. If I hurt them, then I did, but I couldn't look at Claire like that. Even in my haze to get inside of her and claim her, I still took her gentler than I ever had any other woman.

Claire was different, she always has been, and now that I have taken her, owned her body, I can never let her go. My obsession with her will never fade. She is mine, forever.

"Did I hurt you? Are you okay?" I somehow get the question out after a few minutes. Claire rolls to face me, shifting her legs, and pain twists in her features like a barbed wire. She takes her bottom lip between her teeth and stares at me.

"I don't think I'm hurt, maybe a little sore. You were just...

rough." She chokes on the last word, and the light in her eyes diminishes.

"I..." An apology rests against my tongue, but I can't bring myself to say anything. What am I going to do? Apologize for giving her what she wanted? *No.* She wanted me to fuck her, maybe not like I did, but the result was the same.

"I'm going to run you a warm bath. That will help," I say, pushing off the bed, needing to put the distance between us. There is an ache in my stomach that twists, tightening with each second that goes by.

I'm a cruel fucking monster for hurting her, but I know I would do it again. It's why I've been trying so hard to push her away.

In the bathroom, I rinse the tub out and start the bath, making sure the water is warm. Glimpsing my reflection, I pause. The streaks of blood and cum on my cock are a victory of war. Her virginity is mine, and as fucked up as that is, it satisfies me to no end that she is mine and no one else's.

I smile as I clean the evidence from my cock and walk out into the bedroom. Claire is still lying on the mattress, in the same position I left her. The slope of her back has me imagining what it would be like to take her on her hands and knees while I slap her ass. The blood rushes to my cock, and I quickly find a pair of boxers and slip them on.

Even after the damage I've caused her, I could still fuck her again right this second if she begged me to.

"Your bath is almost ready," I say into her good ear and trail my finger down her spine. She moves to sit up and winces. Seeing her like this feels like a dull knife is being shoved into my chest. The pressure to be more for her is astounding. I want to do right by her, but I can't pretend to be something I'm not.

When she winces again, I've had enough and whisk her into my arms, cradling her to my chest.

"You don't have to carry me. I know you don't care that you hurt me," she snaps.

She knows I don't care? She knows nothing.

"Of course, I care if you are hurt. But I won't apologize for giving you what you want, Claire. You basically begged me to fuck you, and I warned you before that I was no good. I told you I can't love you the way you want me to. If you regret what happened, then that's your fault," I say while slowly placing her in the steamy water.

She tucks her chin to her chest, and her lips tremble. I know she is hurting, and I know I am part of the cause, but I don't care. *She is mine now.*

"Do you... regret what happened?"

I sit down on the closed toilet. "No. I don't regret fucking you. I've wanted you as long as you've wanted me, but my want of you is different. It's primal, it's a need to protect, to keep." I look her straight in the eyes when I speak my next words. "Giving yourself to me sealed your fate. You're mine now, Claire. I'm never letting you go."

31

CLAIRE

I wake wrapped up in Lucca's embrace, feeling like I didn't sleep at all. I'm tired and sore. If I didn't have classes, I would stay in bed all day.

After we had sex, he tended to me, and part of me thought he was remorseful, though he didn't apologize. He held me in his arms, and I fell asleep to the sound of his breathing.

The pleasure he brought me was intense, but the pain. It was... unexpected. I'm a little confused by last night, but one thing is clear, whatever it was, it brought us together more. I could feel his walls come down, feel him opening up to me. He let the beast inside of him out to play. I just didn't know he was going to play this rough.

Stretching my stiff limbs, I try to untangle myself from Lucca so I can get up.

"Where are you going?" he asks, his voice deep.

"Bathroom, and then I need to get something to eat. I have class at nine," I whisper. My inside still feels like they have been rearranged, and in a lot of ways, they have been.

Lucca props himself up to his elbow. "Shit. Okay. I'll take you, of course. I've got to do some grocery shopping too, so I'll do that while you're in class."

"Sounds good." I yawn, stretching my arms above my head.

"Are you okay?" he asks almost shyly as I stand from the bed.

"Yes." I give him a reassuring smile. "I promise, I'm fine. Just a little sore."

"You know, I would never hurt you on purpose. Last night was…" He pauses, and I have a million words I could use to fill in the blanks. "It had to happen, was going to happen. There's no way to go back in time. But next time we have sex, it will be better. I lost control, but now I'll be prepared."

Just thinking about having sex again has my thighs clenching together and my nipples tightening. Even feeling raw and bruised, I can feel the wetness building there.

"I'm gonna get breakfast started," I say, trying to distract myself.

"I'll hop in the shower really quick." Lucca gets up, and I have to tear my eyes away from his naked body before I throw myself at him all over again.

With a smile on my face, I make my way to the kitchen, get the coffee started, and pop some bread into the toaster.

As I wait for the toast to be done, I remember how hungry I get between classes and decide to pack a couple of sandwiches. I open a few of the drawers in search of a bag or container I can use when I come across something different entirely.

A piece of paper with my name written at the top catches my eyes, and I stop to read it.

Claire,

I'm sorry, but I can't let this go on any longer. You know I care

about you, and I want to keep you safe at all costs. You are like a sister to me, and that's the way it needs to stay...

I pause, forcing myself to look up from the paper. There is a distinct pain in the center of my chest, and something tells me it will only get worse as I keep reading. I shouldn't be reading this anyway. He didn't give it to me, so he must not want me to have it.

I should close the drawer and finish making breakfast.

I should... but I lower my head and keep reading.

I don't want to hurt your feelings, but I've been seeing someone...

All the air whooshes from my lungs, and I literally feel like I got punched in the stomach. I lay my hand flat on my stomach, physically having to hold myself together. He has been seeing someone else?

Tears form in my eyes, but I blink them back. I need to be strong, and I need to read the last few words, no matter how much it will hurt. I need to know.

That's why there can never be anything between us. Because I'm in love with someone else.

My heart shatters into a million little pieces, and the world around me goes dark. I've never felt so much pain in my life, not when my father beat me, not when my mother left. Nothing hurt as much as the thought of Lucca loving someone else.

One tear escapes. It leaves a cold trail down my cheek and lands on the piece of paper that turned my world upside down.

His words from last night ring in my ears.

"*I warned you before that I was no good. I told you I can't love you the way you want me to.*" I thought he meant he couldn't love anyone, but he just can't love me.

He is in love with someone else, and I gave myself to him

completely. Anger festers in the pit of my stomach. I gave him my virginity. *No, he took it.* He took something from me last night. Stole it right from under my nose.

More than that, he proved to me I was nothing but an object to him, a possession to be owned instead of cherished and loved. I wasn't a lover to him; I was just a quick lay.

I was so stupid, thinking that he could ever love me. I made a mistake in thinking he wanted more.

He will never love me, never care for me beyond protecting me and shielding me from those around me. He wants to control me, use me, and I'm done letting him do it. I'm done being the puppet while he pulls the strings.

Yes, he warned me, and it's my fault for not listening, but I will not be that stupid ever again.

Escaping Lucca is the only way I can protect myself. If he is gone from the picture, then all my problems will be gone too.

For once, I'm not running into Lucca's waiting arms. I'm running away, escaping the shackles that I thought would keep me safe instead of trapped.

He will never dictate my life again.

AFTER BREAKFAST AND A SHOWER, I grab my backpack, phone, and wallet. I won't have my phone for long, but I have to bring it with me; otherwise, it would draw suspicion. Lucca and I drive to the university in silence, and I've never been so glad for the quiet.

I don't think I could hold the tears at bay if I have to listen to his voice.

There are a thousand things I want to say but can't, and my

heart aches because of it. No matter the reason, I am leaving all I've ever known, my protector. The only person who has been in my life since I was eight. The only person who ever gave a damn, but it's not enough. He doesn't love me, and he never will.

As we pull up the school, Lucca seems a little uneasy. "Tonight, I will make dinner, and we can talk about where we go from here. I don't want a girlfriend, but... I can't let you go. What happened between us changed me."

His words only drive the knife deeper because I know he is lying. He wants a girlfriend. He just doesn't want it to be me.

I turn to him, my hand on the door handle. "You just said you don't want a girlfriend. How did it change you if even after I gave myself to you, you still don't want me?"

Pure anguish pinches his features. "It's hard to explain."

"Then explain it to someone else," I reply bitterly and open the door to the SUV. There is no need to explain. I already know. He just wants me as a side piece. To fuck when his girlfriend is not available.

"I'll figure this out, Claire." His words might have fixed things before, but for me, there is nothing left to figure out. I made my choice. I look at his beautiful face one more time, those blue eyes so bright and beautiful, I would've done anything for him.

Without the goodbye sitting at the tip of my tongue, I turn and walk up the steps like I was walking to class.

I don't turn around or do anything out of the ordinary. I walk the same way I always do and disappear into the hall, knowing I have to make it believable.

As soon as I reach the end of the hall, I turn around and speed walk back to the entrance. Students are bustling all around me, but my attention is elsewhere. I scan the street for Lucca's car. He is gone, probably already on the way to the grocery store.

There is a bank on campus a block over, so I jog there. My fingers shake as I glance over my shoulder at every turn. Using my card, I withdraw five hundred dollars in four different transactions until I reach the maximum daily amount at the ATM.

Two-thousand-dollars... How far will I get with that?

It's not a lot, but it will have to do. I shove the money into my purse and order an Uber. The five minutes it takes for the driver to arrive feel like forever. I'm afraid of what would happen if Lucca found me, not so much afraid of what he would do to me, but what he would do to everyone around me.

I have to get away from him. Have to end the obsession.

As soon as the driver pulls up, I sigh with relief and climb into the back seat. He already knows where I'm going, and when he asks me how I'm doing, and I cannot communicate back, he thankfully takes the hint that I don't want to talk. It's rude of me, but my emotions are all over the place. Having a conversation with some random guy isn't what's going to help me.

The drive to the airport goes faster than I anticipated, and I spend the time typing out a message to Steven and Tracy and booking my flight. I know when I arrive at the airport, I will have to toss my phone in a garbage can.

Lucca would track me with it, and I will not let that happen. Still, I wanted to let them know I loved them and that I was sorry to leave on such short notice.

I check the time as we arrive at the airport. Lucca will return to the university soon, and my class will be over. I have to get on a flight and get out here before the opportunity is gone.

"Have a great day," the Uber driver says as I step out of the car.

I tighten my hold on my backpack. Fear wraps around my throat, and for half a second, I wonder if I can really do this. Can I really escape him? I look over my shoulder. Nothing, no one. He's not here. I hit send on the message to Steven and Tracy and turn my phone off. I toss it into the nearest trash can. Taking a huge breath, I straighten my spine and walk into the airport.

I'm ending whatever this was between him and me. He said so himself. He didn't want me, not like that, so why was I there? Why was I letting him control me? The questions linger even after I'm on the plane and soaring through the sky.

I can only hope that Lucca never finds me because for the first time in my life, I am free, and I'm not going to give up that freedom for anyone.

32

LUCCA

Six months, six fucking months, and I still haven't found her. I should have known she would leave. I showed her the worst part of me that night I took her virginity. I should have known it would scare her off.

If I was a better man, I would let her go, but I'm far from it. I won't ever let her go, and I will find her. If Felix would get off his high horse and help me, I would have pinpointed her location the day she left, but the fucker insists on letting her go if that's what she wants. *Asshole.*

I've spent every waking moment either on the run from Julian or looking for Claire. Unfortunately, she has learned too much from me with staying off the grid. I know I need help. I just don't know how to get it.

At least I didn't until Carter called me last week telling me about a gang of Volocove's associates trying to make a move on Julian. I would normally trust that he can handle it himself, but their plan is actually pretty good, and they might have a chance.

That's why I'm here, at a Christmas fundraiser for the rich.

As I had feared, they took Elena, leaving Julian in a frenzy to find her. This is my chance, my only shot at redemption. Either I'll help him and get back into his good graces, or I'll die today.

Julian turns the corner and stops dead in his tracks when he sees me. Shock quickly turns into anger, and I know he is thinking about killing me. I know normally, he would pull the trigger and end me in a heartbeat, but right now, he has more pressing matters on his mind.

He knows I'm not here by chance. He knows he needs me, and that's the only reason I'm not on the floor in a puddle of my own blood.

I can see the moment Julian's temper flares and gets the better of him. He lunges for me, fisting my shirt, and slams my back into the closest wall.

"The only reason you're breathing right now is because I know you have something to do with her disappearance."

"I know you have no reason to believe me, but I didn't touch her. I came here to help. I might be out of the loop, but I've heard the rumors. I heard that some associates of the Volocove's family were going to strike tonight. They are still pissed about you messing with their operation. I came to warn you, but it seems I'm too late."

"Warn me?" Julian hisses before he slams me against the wall once more.

"Let me help you find her. Let me prove myself," I offer, not fighting back at all.

"There is nothing to prove," he spits, looking like all he wants to do is smash his fist into my face.

"I can get her back. I can find her. They think I'm a traitor already. They'll never expect me to be helping you. Let me do this. If not for you, for Elena."

"And why should I trust you? You betrayed me."

"You shouldn't. I did what I had to do for the same reason you're doing what you have to do right now. Love has that effect on people. I didn't want to betray you, but they had her..."

Julian shakes his head, but releases me. He takes a step back, putting space between us. His entire body trembles, no doubt with the need to kill me.

I sag against the wall for a moment before straightening and gathering my wits. "Have they left yet?"

"I have my men posted everywhere, and none have said anything."

"Follow me." I smile, knowing exactly where they are. "They most likely went to the basement. They know your men are here and that they wouldn't be able to get away without you knowing."

His intense stare tells me he is considering this to be a trap. Lucky for me, his concern for Elena overrides his thinking.

"Lead the way," he orders impatiently.

My heart thunders in my chest with each step we take, each beat becoming louder, making it hard for me to hear or feel anything besides that heavy thumping. The door leading into the basement is unlocked, and as we head down into the darkness, I reach for my gun.

It's hard to make out, but several doors lead into what I assume are rooms. I move along the wall, slowly twisting the knob of each one and shoving the door open.

Then we hear it. "Don't cry, sugar. You have nothing to cry about... yet."

Julian springs into action beside me. Taking a step forward, he's ready to go in, guns blazing.

"Whoa, slow down." I hold up my hands, hoping he is going to listen. "We need a plan."

"We go in, kill everyone who is not Elena. Plan over."

"That's too risky. Think about it. Chances are she is going to get caught in that crossfire." He knows I'm right, and he hates it too. "I need you to trust me, okay?" I whisper, knowing exactly what I'm asking him to do.

"Then what's your plan?" he grits through his teeth.

"Be smart. We both don't want anything to happen to Elena. You go in and assess the situation. Make sure she is out of harm's way. I'll come in as a surprise. We'll take them down together." I'm not lying. I might not love Elena like Julian does, but I don't want anything to happen to her either. No matter what happened between Julian and me, I still see him as family, which makes Elena family as well.

"Fine, let's do this," he growls, knowing he's forced to put every ounce of trust into a man that had previously betrayed him. A man that he wants to murder.

I stay back and watch Julian enter the room. Elena sees him first and mouths something I don't catch.

"Well, look who finally made it to the party." One of the men chuckles, while another lifts his gun and presses it against the back of Elena's head. "Julian Moretti himself."

"You made a lot of mistakes today. Taking my wife. Hurting her. Threatening me. You know you're going to pay with your lives, don't you?"

"I don't see how you are in any position to deal out threats. I'm the one holding a loaded gun to your whore's head, aren't I?"

"For every word you speak, I'll add another minute of torture before I finally kill you."

The three men laugh, but I know Julian is deadly serious.

I plaster a smug smirk on my face and walk into the room. "See, I told you he would fall for it."

The room erupts into more laughter.

"We figured he wouldn't fall for it a second time. I'll give it to you, Lucca, you must be one hell of an actor."

"You son of a bitch," Julian growls. His face distorts into a mask of fury as he lunges for me. Before he can even get two feet, two of the masked men tackle him to the ground. A guttural scream rips from Elena's throat, but it's muffled by the gag. I glance over at her just long enough to see the panic in her eyes.

Dread overtakes her features as three men drag Julian to the spot in front of her. The gun that was pressed against Elena moments ago is now pointed at Julian's head instead.

Elena whimpers and tugs on her restraints, making the guy next to her chuckle. "Want to say something, sweetheart?"

He grabs the gag and pulls it from her mouth.

"Please..." she croaks.

She's crying so much now that all I want to do is tell her it's okay. I'm on your side, but I need to keep this up a little longer. Julian stares at his wife, and I can see the profuse love and guilt in his gaze. He thinks he failed her.

"Please... Don't do this. Take me instead," Elena begs for her husband's life.

"How cute that you're willing to give up your life for this piece of shit, but no can do, sweetheart," one man replies.

"It's time to die, Moretti—"

"Hold on. Let me do it," I interrupt at the last second. "He's been hunting me like an animal for two years. I want to be the one to pull the trigger."

"I suppose we owe it to you. You led him right to us." One of the men holding Julian chuckles. "He's all yours. We'll take his wife as payment."

Elena shakes her head profusely, her hair sticking to her tear-stained cheeks.

I move toward Julian and pull my gun from its holster as I let a wicked smile spread across my face. Raising my gun, I aim at Julian's head for a split second before lifting it higher and pointing it at the guy holding the gun in his hand.

I pull the trigger. The bullet flies, hitting its intended target. With a hole between his eyes, the guy falls to the ground. Before his body hits the floor, I fire my gun again, hitting the second guy. Another shot rings out, then another, until every single one of my enemies is on the ground in a puddle of their own blood.

"Open your eyes, Elena," Julian coaxes his wife.

Her eyes fly open, and she takes in Julian kneeling in front of her with wide, teary eyes.

I untie her restraints while Julian runs his hands over her body like he is checking for injuries.

As soon as Elena is free, she falls into Julian's arms and buries her nose into the crook of his neck. He tugs her into his chest, pulling her close into his protective hold.

They whisper something to each other I don't understand until Julian pushes Elena away a few inches. "Baby?"

"Yes, *baby*. I was going to wait until tomorrow morning to tell you. It's hard to give a man who has everything a Christmas gift. I bought some blue baby shoes and wrapped them up." She sniffles.

"Congratulations," I interject, reminding them I'm still here.

Julian pulls Elena to her feet but keeps his arm around her.

I shove my hands in my pockets and watch as they both stare at me for a few seconds. All three of us ignore the dead bodies in the room.

Elena finally breaks the silence. "Thank you." Julian simply grunts, and she gives her husband a little jab in the side, making him roll his eyes.

"You betrayed me... but you saved us today," he finally says. "We both owe you."

I grin. "I was kind of hoping you'd say that. Because I could really use your help with something."

"Is that so?" Julian huffs, clearly not happy about this development.

"Yes. Like I told you earlier, I only betrayed you because Lev's family had someone I cared about. I've been protecting her ever since. Unfortunately, she just ran away from me."

Julian's eyebrows lift, and I know he is wondering why she is running if I'm only protecting her. Regardless, he is considering my request.

"What do you need help with?" Julian asks.

"I need help hunting her down."

33

CLAIRE

*I*t's been six months since I left, yet I still look over my shoulder, expecting Lucca to be there, but he isn't. I thought by now he would've found me. The money I took only lasted me a short time before I had to get a job. Work at the diner is slow tonight. I wiped down the same section of tables three times just to keep myself busy.

"This place is dead. You might as well head home for the night."

Tina's booming voice drags me from my thoughts, and I turn to find her staring at me from the other side of the counter. She was the one who showed me the ropes of waitressing when I first started. She's in her late thirties with soft brown eyes and blonde hair that is always curled. I don't see her as much as a boss as I do a mother figure.

"Are you sure?" I hate to leave, but I won't lie my feet are aching, and the start of a migraine is forming behind my eyes.

"Yes, I'm sure. I feel bad for the tables right now with the amount you're washing them down. Go home, read a book. I'll see you on Wednesday."

"Okay, okay." I laugh.

She knows me so well. All I do now is sleep, read, and work. The library became my best friend and is where I get most of my books, at least until I can afford to buy a Kindle. I bring the rag into the back and toss it in the water bucket.

My hands are all wrinkly, and I dry them on a dishrag before taking off my apron and hanging it up. I keep my purse next to Tina's and retrieve it from the manager's office along with my thin sweater.

"Have a good night," I yell before walking out the back door.

The cool air kisses my skin, and I shiver as soon as I step out the door. I pull the thin sweater tighter around me, knowing that soon I'll have to break down and buy myself something better. That's the downfall of leaving. When I lived with my adoptive parents, I had everything I could've wanted, and now I have just what I need. I found a small apartment with all utilities included and kept low.

I try my hardest not to think of Lucca. I didn't get this far to turn around and go right back to where I was. I'm living my best life here, even if I'm barely getting by. I'd rather have nothing than be trapped under his thumb again.

My apartment is only a block away, and I'm thankful for that since my feet are aching fiercely tonight. The wind howls through my hair, chilling me to the bone, and by the time I reach the complex, I'm an ice block.

The complex itself isn't anything special. There's no elevator and nothing fancy about the place. There's an entrance, and then you walk up the stairs to your floor. I'm on the second floor, so I drag myself up twenty-four steps and turn right to walk another twelve feet before I reach the door to my apartment.

Fisting the keys in my hand, the metal bites into my flesh. For the first time in six months, I feel nervous. Anxious. Like something bad is about to happen.

I shake the thought away and force my fist to unclench the keys. It's nothing. I have no reason to worry about anything. If Lucca hasn't found me yet, then he most likely never will.

The hair on the back of my neck stands on end, and I unlock the door as fast as I can. As soon as I open the door and step inside, I reach for the light switch. My fingers tremble along the wall until they connect with the switch.

I flick it on and off, but it does nothing. Fear trickles in, the floor creaks behind me, and before I can scream, someone grabs me. The scream lodges itself in the back of my throat. I'm dragged backward, an arm locks around my chest, and I collide with a hard chest. A hand slaps over my mouth and presses against my lips.

I struggle for half a second before a familiar woodsy scent invades my senses.

"I told you you'd never be free of me. That I would always find you, butterfly…"

Red hot anger rushes through me, and I part my lips and bite the meaty part of his palm while stomping my foot onto his at the same time.

The combination causes him to release me with a curse, and I rush to the other side of the room, darting for the lamp on the side table. The light turns on, illuminating the soft space, and I grab the nearest object, which is a broom. Under no circumstances do I want to look at him, but that's a little hard, being that he's right in front of me.

"Leave. Get out of my house, or I'll call the police," I yell.

Little does he know I don't have a phone, but that doesn't matter.

My warning must not scare him because he just stands there like a statue, staring at me with his penetrating gaze. He looks the same as he did six months ago when he dropped me off at the university. Not that I expected him to look different. He's still stupidly gorgeous with an edge of danger.

"What are you doing with that?" He gestures toward the broom, amusement twinkling in his eyes.

I adjust my grip on the broom. "If you don't get out, I'll hit you with it."

"Will you now?" He smirks, and that smirk makes me want to hit him ten times more with this thing. "I'd pay money to see that."

His gaze flicks away from me, and I can see him taking in the contents of my apartment.

"You need to leave. I don't want you here." I'm more insistent this time. If I have to, I'll scream, and someone will call the police. Larry down the hall calls the police on just about anything.

"This place is dangerous. I mean, I was able to get in with little effort and could've easily hurt you in the time it would take for someone to call the police here."

"My safety isn't your concern anymore. Get. Out." I punctuate each word, pointing toward the door.

The amusement leaves his face and is replaced with a sober expression. "Your safety always has and always will be my concern."

"I don't need you, and I want you to leave. I might have

meant something to you before, but now I'm not your concern. Leave. Go home."

Lucca must sense my seriousness because he lifts his hands as if to signal that he is harmless. "Fine. Fine. I'll leave. I'll go home."

I almost sigh out loud. That was too easy. This has to be a trap.

He snickers, a triumphant smile overtaking his face, making him seem young and carefree. "By *leave,* I mean for tonight, and by *home,* I mean to the apartment next door."

Fucking asshole!

I'm so angry I toss the broom at him, the tip of it hits the toe of his boot. He looks at the object and back up at me. I want to punch him, ruin his face, tell him how much I hate him for hurting me, but I keep my lips pressed together.

"Word of advice, if you're going to hurt someone with something, don't just throw it at them, and also, before I go…" He takes a leering step toward me, and I don't know if it's an attempt to intimidate me or what, but I stand my ground. "Don't think about leaving because I'll know, and this time you won't get away. We have unfinished business, Claire."

Like always, he leaves me with my mouth hanging open and my still-beating heart in my hand. His footsteps echo as he walks out of the apartment, closing the door behind him. A second later, I hear the door to the apartment beside mine open. The threadbare walls make it impossible for an ounce of privacy, and now I feel even more exposed.

Lucca is here. He found me. There is no running anymore.

I'm a butterfly trapped in a cage all over again.

34

LUCCA

The floor creaks beneath my steps. This entire complex is one dumpster fire away from burning to the ground. To think she's lived here for six months, all on her own, unprotected. It makes me burn with rage. It makes me sick to my fucking stomach.

While I waited for her to return home, I scoured the entire apartment.

She barely has any food, any clothing, and no cell phone. She's living a dirt-poor life, and I can't fucking stand to see her like this.

I take a few calming breaths because my only other option is to stomp into her apartment, toss her over my shoulder, kicking and screaming, and drag her back to where this all started. It seems like a good idea, but giving her space and letting her get used to the idea of me being here seems like a *smarter* choice.

I'll be the first to admit, I fucked up six months ago. When I told her I didn't want a girlfriend, I was afraid. Commitment terrified me. I grew up in foster care. People came and went from my life whenever they felt. That wasn't the biggest thing for me, though.

Knowing I wasn't good enough for Claire was the nail in my coffin. She needed a good guy, a stable home, where she didn't have to worry about any of my enemies.

Where I didn't have to drag her into the dark with me.

I didn't know what the fuck to do, but I was serious about figuring something out with her. I couldn't even give thought to letting her go. I needed her like I needed my next breath.

It was easier for me to tell her I didn't want a girlfriend and break her heart than risk hurting her by association. I was devastated, pissed, and disappointed in myself when I realized she had left. Tracy and Steven contacted me as soon as they got the message from her telling them she was leaving and how sorry she was.

If it wasn't for Julian helping me, I most likely never would've found her.

I can't fuck it up this time. I can't.

I sit on the bed that came with the apartment. The mattress has springs pushing through it, and the walls have peeling wallpaper on them. Every time I look around this place, I'm tempted to put my fist through one of the walls.

Time dwindles away, like grains of sand slipping through my fingers. By now, she has to have cooled off and is probably asleep. I don't like the idea of her being alone in that apartment.

My control wanes. It's been six months. Six fucking months without her scent, without her tempting nature and smile. I need her, or at the very least, to be close to her.

But to be near her and not have her in the way I want is like hanging a steak over a lion's head. He's going to reach for it, snap and bite at it. He's going to devour it whole once he gets his hands on it.

Bouncing my leg up and down does nothing to stop the agitation. All that is going to help me is to go to her. I have to get my fill of her. Unable to contain myself another second, I shove off the mattress and walk out of the apartment and into the hall.

I look at the door to her apartment and wonder if she locked the door. Knowing how angry and shocked she was at my appearance, she probably did.

Glancing down the hall both ways, I check if anyone is coming. Not that it would matter. Even if someone passed by, I'd tell them to mind their own fucking business. I fish the paperclip I used earlier from my pocket. Rattling the knob gently, I discover she locked the door. I smile. With a little finesse, I easily unlock the door and slip back inside her apartment.

Her apartment is identical to the one next door, with a kitchen that shares the space of both the living room and dining room. A door on the far right of the apartment leads into a bedroom, while the door closest to it is the bathroom.

The second I stepped into this place, I had it mapped out. Had every inch of the floor plan memorized. Removing my jacket, my boots follow, making for a quieter entrance into her bedroom. I tamp down desire by breathing through my mouth instead of my nose. Her scent is everywhere, surrounding me, suffocating me.

She smells like strawberries dipped in chocolate. Sinfully sweet and juicy enough to eat.

The door to her bedroom is ajar, so I push it open slowly. I can just barely make out the silhouette of her body from the small slivers of light that stream through the window.

She has nothing but a flimsy curtain blocking the view of any passersby outside. I don't like that. Not at fucking all. It's unlikely that anyone from the street could see inside her room, but the apartments across the street could.

I look away from the window and let my eyes scan over her small body that's curled in the fetal position facing the wall. She's wearing a pair of panties and a tank top. The sight of her before me has my cock hard. I haven't touched or thought of another woman but her. I get naked without even thinking about it.

I'm driven by a deeper, more primal instinct with Claire. I want to hold her and caress her, but at the same time, I need to show her how out of control she makes me and how badly I want her. How much I need her.

Naked, I walk over to the bed and kneel on the edge, looking down at a peacefully sleeping Claire. She's beautiful, so fucking fragile. Really, she is a butterfly. I just have to let her be free because butterflies were not meant to be captured.

The bed creaks beneath my weight, and I worry Claire may wake before I can get in position, but she doesn't even move. I slip behind her and wrap my arm around her, pulling her to my bare chest. I know how fucked up this is, but I don't care. Claire is mine, and I am hers.

She needs this just as much as I do, even if she doesn't want to admit it. She slowly stirs awake, and I slide my other arm beneath her pillow. My fingers drift down the smooth planes of her stomach and sneak beneath the waistband of her panties to splay across her mound.

"Lucca?" Claire's voice is full of sleep, but it won't be for long.

"Yes, it's me," I groan into the shell of her good ear.

As soon as I acknowledge that it's me, she squirms in my arms. I tighten my hold on her, clamping a leg over her calf and wrapping a hand around her throat. I don't squeeze hard, just enough to keep her in place. Her pulse races beneath my fingertips.

A rabbit caught in a trap.

"Don't."

"I won't hurt you," I promise, knowing that the last time I touched her, I caused her pain. I figure that's why she is pushing me away now, which is why I'm not expecting what's comes out of her mouth next.

"I don't think I can survive losing you again if you do this." The words are a gentle whisper, and I feel her pain. She's afraid of losing me again, afraid that I don't want her, but she does not know how wrong she is.

I smile and move my hand lower, tracing the lips of her pussy. "You have nothing to fear, Claire. I'm not going anywhere. I'm not letting you slip through my fingers ever again. I've waited six months to touch you, and I can't wait any longer."

"Please..."

I'm not sure if she is asking me to keep going or to stop, but I don't ask. I dip a finger between her folds and rub slow circles against her clit. My cock is harder than steel and presses firmly against her ass. She continues to fight, pressing her hips back against me and clawing at my skin like a crazed animal.

"Lucca... don't..."

If only she knew how much her struggle turned me on. If

only she knew the things I wanted to do to her—depraved, sinister things. I press my nose into a spot right below her ear and inhale deeply. Her scent calms, and I can think clearly once more.

Tonight is about her, about her pleasure, about showing her how I feel.

"Don't what?" I pant. "Stop?"

Even as she struggles, her folds become wet, and soft little mewls slip past her lips. Her chest rises and falls as her fear becomes pleasure. I work her clit faster, needing her to come like I need air, and the heart in my chest.

"*Stop.* Don't stop!" She sinks her nails into my wrist. "I'm close… so close…" The words rush out of her, and I can feel it, feel her body trembling against mine, building up to a breaking point. Pre-cum beads the tip of my cock, and I can't wait to bury myself inside of her.

"Come for me, Claire…" I squeeze her throat just a little and can feel her hard nipples against my forearm.

Faster and faster, I rub, and then she shatters. She goes off like a rocket, her entire body shaking with aftershocks of pleasure. I tug my hand free of her panties, half tempted to shove my fingers in my mouth and lick her juices off them.

I'm starved for her.

I move to a kneeling position and roll Claire onto her back. She looks up at me with a half-lidded gaze. I'm crazed with need, but I tamp the need down, letting my gaze roam over her perfect body. Vulnerable, soft, a temptation that I cannot deny.

My fingers dip into the hem of her panties, and I drag them down her legs. Claire doesn't struggle further, probably realizing there is no point. Her legs part, and I can make out the contours of her pussy in the shadows. *Fuck.* I can't help myself.

I drop to my stomach, grab her by the hips, and drag her to my mouth.

"Lucca, what are you—" Her words are cut off when I bury my face between her thighs.

I drag my tongue between her wet folds and find the gem hidden inside. She's already drenched, but I want her to be nothing but a heap of her own juices and my cum once I'm finished. I part her folds and alternate between flicking and sucking her clit.

"Oh god. Oh god." Her hands make their way into my hair, and I smile against her pussy. Minutes ago, she was trying to push me away. Now she refuses to let me escape.

When her body tenses, I move south and trace the seam of her pussy with the tip of my tongue. In and out my tongue goes, fucking her when I wish it was my cock that was.

"Don't stop! Don't stop!" Claire cries.

She's close to coming, but the next time she comes, it will be on my cock. With my eyes fixed on her, I pull away and crawl up her body, kneeling between her legs.

A disapproving whine meets my ears but is cut off when I lift her hips and jut my hips forward to nudge my erection against her entrance.

"This is how I should've taken you the first time, and I'm sorry that I didn't." I press a kiss to the crown of her forehead, blanket her body with mine, and push inside of her. Our gazes are fixed on one another, mine wild, and hers shocked.

I hurt her before, and I will never do so again.

I pause my movements and drop my head into the crook of her neck, peppering kisses along her collar bone and throat. Fuck, she's so tight it feels like a vice is wrapped around my cock. A hiss escapes between my gritted teeth, and when I pull back and look into her eyes once more, I find a turbulent amount of emotions there. Then I slide home, moving deeper, feeling our connection grow with every stroke of my cock in her tight channel.

Holding her to my chest, I don't just fuck her. I do something I've never done before. Something I didn't even know I was capable of. I make love to her.

"So tight and perfect," I whisper into her good ear.

She lets out a soft sigh, and I up my pace, driving into her harder and faster. The walls of her pussy grip me so hard stars form behind my eyes.

"Lucca," she rasps, her sharp nails sink into my shoulders.

My control snaps at the sound of my name, it's pure bliss, and I have to hear her say it again. I piston my hips, the slap of our bodies connecting fill the air, and Claire tips her head back into the pillow, showing off the slender column of her neck.

I can't help myself. I latch onto her throat, sucking the flesh hard while maintaining the same rhythm and speed.

Higher and higher we go, twisting together, intertwining with each other.

"Tell me... has another man touched you?" I pull out and slam back into her, grinding my pubic bone against her clit. "Touched what's mine?"

"No." The word comes out as a scream, and with no warning, she explodes, her walls clenching and spasming around me.

Her chest rises and falls rapidly as she gasps for air like she's drowning.

Her orgasm drives me forward, and my muscles quake, my balls draw together, and my impending release hangs above my head, waiting to drop.

Fuck, I don't want this moment between us to end. I peer down into her eyes, hazy with pleasure, and lose myself completely. A few more strokes and my balls ache, my eyes flutter closed, and I hold Claire tighter as a primal roar escapes my throat, and I empty myself deep inside her.

Sweat clings to my skin, and I roll off of her and pull her into my side. Claire nuzzles her head into my chest, and I feel complete. This is right where I belong, right where she belongs, and I was stupid for ever thinking otherwise.

"You're mine, butterfly," I whisper into her hair as her soft snores fill the room.

35

CLAIRE

Every nerve ending in my body tingles, and I roll across the bed, realizing it's empty. In a panic, I sit up, wondering if last night was a dream. One simple stretch of my limbs, and I know it wasn't. The muscles in my legs ache, but in a delicious way. As I lean back against the pillows, I can't believe how different last night was to our first time together. Lucca was still rough and even more possessive, but there was a tenderness to his touch that I didn't understand, and that was definitely not there before.

Every move he made, every swirl of his hips, it was all focused on me. A smile splits my face, and I cover it with my hand. It's wrong to be smiling, wrong to feel any type of joy about having him here. My excitement fades away when I think about the other woman he is in love with. Why find me? Just for sex, or so he can drag me back there, try to control me again?

Suddenly, I'm mad, because if he had come here to talk to me, to see me, to want more from me, or to apologize, maybe I would've thought about it.

Now, I'm going to tell him to get the fuck out.

The door to the bedroom opens, and I jump a foot off the bed when Lucca appears in the doorway with a tray of steamy food in his hands.

"I had to run to the grocery store. You don't have shit to eat here."

The smell of eggs, and bacon along with fresh coffee, waft into the room, and my stomach grumbles in protest of what I plan to say.

"Why did you come here?"

He crosses the room and sets the tray at the foot of the bed. "What do you mean why did I come here? You're mine, Claire. I came here to bring you back with me. I want you in my life. I wanted you in my life before I was just too fucking stupid to put it into words." I pull the thin sheet tighter around me, wishing it could protect my heart from the words Lucca just said.

I'm angry and sad and a little heartbroken. He wants me, but only because he lost me.

"You had your chance to want me. In fact, you had numerous chances. I basically offered myself to you, and you turned me down. Now it's time for you to go."

"There is a life back there for you," he tells me, completely ignoring my words.

"I don't want to go back there, and I don't want you to be here."

Lucca sighs and walks over to me, stopping right in front of me. His blue eyes are soft, and he looks happy. He cups my cheek, running his thumb over the swell. It takes every ounce of resistance I have not to lean into his touch.

"Don't you want to go back to college? Visit your family and friends?" He offers me the world, everything that I could've wanted before, but it's too late. "I can give you that. I don't want you to stay here alone. It's not safe, and you have nothing. The thought of you being hurt by someone, and I'm not here to protect you." A visible shiver works its way down his spine.

"I've been doing it for six months on my own. I think I'll be okay. Plus, that place was never my home. It was only ever supposed to be temporary."

Lucca's hand drops from my face. He seems indifferent to what I've said, and guilt slices through his features. "That's my fault, and I never apologize for anything, mainly because there isn't anything to apologize for, but I am sorry for all I put you through. It's why I didn't give in to my want of you earlier. It's why I tried my damnedest to push you away, again and again."

It dawns on me then that he didn't consider himself good enough for me, but that should've been my choice, not his.

He looks down at his hands. "I got my old job back. We wouldn't be returning to the safe house in Brookfield. We'd be going home. To the place you grew up. You could go to the local college there, and Hope, your friend, still lives there."

"That all sounds perfect, Lucca, but I'm not sure that place would ever feel like home again to me. Everything has changed so much, and I'm not the same person I was when I left that town. I want to close that chapter on my life and move forward."

My heart aches as I say that. The only part of my life I refuse to let go of is my parents, Steven and Tracy. I spent the last six months feeling alone, wanting to call them so badly while scared that doing so would give Lucca a lead right to my doorstep. Turns out, I didn't even have to do that because he found me anyway.

Lucca looks up and right into my eyes. His stare is so

consuming it makes me want to look away, but I don't. "No matter what, I'm not leaving here without you."

"You can't just barge back into my life and act like everything is okay."

"I'm not. I told you how I fucked up and that I want you to be mine, and now you're dragging your feet."

"It took you six months to realize you want me. It took me leaving for you to get the guts to admit it to yourself. Sorry, but if you didn't want me then, you don't want me now. Plus, I've moved on. I don't want you anymore." It's the wrong thing to say. I realize it the moment I say it, but I can't take the words back now.

In the blink of my eyes, Lucca is on me, his hand in my hair, tugging on the strands, making my scalp scream in pain while forcing my attention on him. "Didn't seem you were over me last night as you came on my hand, tongue, and cock. Maybe you should show how *over* me you are right now?"

The skin of my face heats with embarrassment, and I squeeze my eyes shut to hide the tears building there. I want Lucca so much it hurts, but I don't want to risk heartache again. I don't want him to control me. I want to be his equal. I want to be the one he loves, not the mistress.

"I…" Lucca moves closer, and I know this because I can feel his hot breath on my throat. "I want you, Claire, and I'm going to do whatever I have to do to make it happen. What do you want from me? What can I do to make you see it? I know you felt it last night." His lips press against my thundering pulse, and I shiver.

I blink my eyes open, and our gazes collide.

"I want my freedom, Lucca. I don't want to be controlled. I know you're possessive of me, but I can't be your butterfly if I'm trapped in a cage." A single tear slides down my cheek, and Lucca watches it intently. There's a long pregnant pause, and he untangles his fingers from my hair.

Can I do this? Can I trust he won't lock me in the ivory tower the second he has me right where he wants me? Can I trust he will choose me in the end?

"I don't want to trap you, Claire," Lucca finally says. "I've never wanted to hurt you or scare you. Your protection... it just means everything to me. Your safety, knowing you're okay. It gives me life and makes me feel like even with all the fucked up, morally wrong things I've done in my life, at least I did one good thing by caring for you."

He's telling me everything I want to hear, but is it the truth?

I'm about to ask him about the letter, about the other woman he is in love with, but every time I open my mouth, my throat constricts.

My stomach grumbles again, and I'm reminded of the food sitting at the foot of the bed. Lucca smiles. "Are you hungry?"

I nod, and for the first time in a long time, I smile too.

Lucca grabs the tray and places it in front of me. I dig into the eggs and bacon and chug the glass of orange juice down before he's even touched his plate of food.

"Uh, sorry." I giggle.

"No, don't be." He grabs the other glass of orange juice and hands it to me. "I have no idea how you survived here with no food."

Yeah, now would probably not be a good time to tell him I ate whatever I could get at the diner on break and a few crackers with peanut butter here and there.

After I'm finished with breakfast, I hesitate on whether I should ask Lucca if I can use his phone to call Steven and Tracy.

I've wanted to call them since I got here, and now that Lucca is here, there's no reason I shouldn't call them.

"Would it be possible to... um, call my parents, maybe?"

"Yes. I told them I would have you call them as soon as I arrived, but... you know, you tried to beat me with a broom."

I roll my eyes and extend my hand, waiting for him to place his phone in it. He pulls the black device from his pocket and offers it to me. The phone feels like a foreign object after going six months without using one. My fingers move over the screen, and before I can navigate to the dial pad, the phone rings.

The names Steven and Tracy flash across the screen, and I look from the phone to Lucca. "Apparently, they want to talk to you as badly as you want to talk to them."

My finger trembles as I press the green answer key and bring the phone to my ear.

"Hello."

"Oh my god! Is that you, Claire?" Tracy's shriek of excitement makes me pull the phone away from my ear a bit.

"It's me," I whisper. "I've missed you guys so much."

"We've missed you too, sweetheart. When Lucca told us he'd found out where you were, we were excited and scared."

I hate I worried them. That I hurt them. I thought I was making the right choice, and I still feel like I did, but I miss them like crazy.

"I'm sorry if I worried you guys or hurt you. That wasn't my intention at all."

"Do not apologize, sweetie, we understand, and we were only worried because that's what parents do. They worry about their children," Tracy says.

My heart swells. They care about me so much, and I just

left. "I was just about to call you, but you beat me to it," I tell them.

"When we didn't hear from Lucca last night, we got a little worried and called this morning. I'm so glad we did," Steven booms.

I'm distraught, and the guilt I feel presses on my shoulders heavily. They took me in when they didn't have to and helped care for me. They deserved more than just a text message from me saying goodbye.

"I'm going to come and visit soon." It's not a lie, I'm going to visit them. I just don't know under what circumstances yet.

"Yes! We would love that. Are you planning to return home with Lucca?" It's a question I had hoped they wouldn't ask, mainly because I don't have an answer.

"I don't know," I reply, letting sadness drain into my voice. "When I figure out what's going on, I'll let you know."

"Of course, sweetie." Tracy tries to make herself sound joyful, but I can tell she's disappointed. "Yes... yes, hold on..." Tracy suddenly says. A moment later, a different voice comes through the phone.

"Hey, loser," Carter greets.

"Hey, yourself." I smile, only now realizing how much I missed that idiot.

"I was mad at you for leaving, so I farted on your pillow every chance I got." His words make me laugh so hard, I hold my belly and gasp for air.

"Sorry, I just left," I say when I catch my breath again.

"I know, but seriously, come and visit soon. Okay?"

"I promise, but I've got to go now. I'll call again soon."

"You better. Bye, loser."

"Bye, loser," I say and end the call.

My heart is tattered, a bloody pulp of nothing. I've hurt everyone I care about by running away, but I've freed myself too.

Now I have to decide if I want to return with Lucca and see what lies ahead for us or stay here? I look up and find Lucca watching me with a look I don't understand.

"I'm not leaving without you, Claire. I'm tired of fighting us. This, whatever it is between us, is long overdue, and I'm ready to explore it."

"I need to think about it," is what I say, even though I want to scream *yes* at the top of my lungs.

36

LUCCA

Claire has been so quiet since our talk. It was a kick to the ball-sack to hear her say she would *think* about coming back with me, but I wasn't surprised. I've done her dirty, hurt her, and I know she needs time to digest everything that happened over the last forty-eight hours. It doesn't mean I will enjoy it, though. I want to get back to Hillcrest and show her just how much she means to me.

Six months without her was the kick in the ass I needed to see that I couldn't live without her. I am a bastard for doing what I did to her, and she's right. I can't call her my butterfly and then trap her in a cage. Even if it kills me, I have to ease up on the control.

I wanted to protect her against everything bad in the world, including myself, but doing that put *us* at risk. Funny enough, I didn't even know there was an us yet.

Claire chooses then to walk into the bedroom, a towel wrapped tight around her body. It hides all the places I want to see, lick, and taste.

"I need to get ready for work," she announces.

Teeth grinding, I stop myself from replying with the word *no*. She insisted she was returning to work, and as much as I didn't want her to go, I didn't want to risk pushing her away by saying no, and especially not after she confessed her feelings to me.

"Then get ready," I say.

She blinks, staring at me like she can't believe I just told her what to do. "Get out."

It seems I am missing something. "Why?"

"Because I don't want you to see me naked."

My head tips back, and I laugh, and laugh, and laugh, and I don't stop laughing until Claire throws something at me, which is a shoe.

"Stop laughing and get out. I need to get dressed, and I can't with you in the room."

"What? Are you afraid that something might happen?" I tease. "Something you might like, something that may make you scream my name?"

We haven't had sex again since the night before, even though I'm hard every second of the day. I can't help it, Claire has that effect on me.

A deep flush spreads onto her cheeks. "If you're trying to convince me to leave with you, this isn't helping."

I frown, get off the bed, and walk over to her. She retreats like prey, taking a step back for every step I take toward her. Fuck me, I want her.

I want to rip that towel from her body, spread her legs, and place her right on my face, so I can feast upon her like she is my last meal.

Unfortunately, that's not going to happen.

Stopping right in front of her, I can see her pulse fluttering in her throat. Her green eyes are wild, filled with half lust, half anticipation. I lean into her face and watch as her lips part and her pink tongue darts out over her bottom lip.

I am reminded of the very first time I kissed her, the day she was going to go to lunch with Gregg. It had been the only time I had ever kissed a woman, the only time I ever wanted to. Today, I want to kiss her too, so I do. I lean in, my nose brushing against hers, and press my lips firmly to hers, swallowing up every little sound she makes.

She tastes sweet, sinful, and I deepen the kiss, my fingers tangling in her hair. I pull her closer, wanting there not to be even an inch of space between us. One of her hands sinks into my hair, and the other snakes around my neck, and it's about then that we both realize she no longer has a grasp on the towel.

I pull away, panting, ready to fuck her against the wall, but smiling. The towel slips down her body, and the look on Claire's face mimics that of an angry kitten, her nose is snarled, and her eyebrows are drawn together.

"What was that you said about not wanting me to see you naked?"

Snatching the towel off the floor, she gives me a dirty look, and I snicker as I walk out of the room. The door slams shut behind me, and all I can think is I have to get her to come back with me. I have to.

THE CORNER BOOTH in the diner becomes my home for the next six hours. I drink my weight in coffee, forcing Claire to return to my table to fill my cup over and over again. It's amusing as hell. She glares at me each time, but I know she likes the attention.

An hour goes by, and a strange man walks into the diner. I narrow my eyes at him across the room. He's watching Claire with far more interest than I like, and it makes me squeeze the coffee mug a little tighter in my hand. I don't need to make a fucking scene, especially not with Claire here, but this guy better look away, or I'll have to gouge his eyes out.

"Claire, trash," one of the older ladies yells.

Claire frowns and shoves her notepad into the front of her apron.

The guy continues to track her every movement like a hawk. I'm pretty sure he wants me to gut him like a fucking fish. When Claire disappears into the back of the diner, and the creepy fucker rises from his seat and rushes out the door in a flurry, I follow.

I know a sick fuck when I see one, and the way he was watching her, coupled with how fast he ran out of the diner when she disappeared into the back, tells me he was a snake lying in wait. Shit luck for him if he thinks he's going to touch her.

The wind howls through my jacket, and I turn the corner just in time to see him crowding Claire at the back of the alley.

"You're a pretty girl. Maybe give a guy a chance?" I can barely make out what he says, but what reaches my ears has me seeing red. My hand slides into my jacket, and I grab the knife strapped there. I stalk toward them, intent on slitting his throat when Claire notices me out of the corner of her eye and intersects, crossing in front of the fucker at the last second.

It's lower the knife or risk hurting Claire, and I'm not going to fucking do that. Anger surges through me as I drop my hand, pointing the blade at the ground. With both hands against my chest, she pushes me backward and away from the real danger.

"What the fuck?" I growl.

"Don't do this, Lucca. There has been enough death in my life, enough blood on my hands." I look away from Claire and find the creep has turned around and is now walking toward us. My body vibrates with suppressed rage, with the need to kill, to destroy.

"Is there a problem?" the guy questions.

I maneuver Claire behind me easily and hold myself back. I don't know why she cares about this guy, but what she said a second ago pierced my heart. I don't want her to carry the weight of all the bad I have done, so even if I wanted to slit this guy from ear to ear, I wouldn't.

"Yeah, get the fuck out of here."

Lucky for the guy, and myself, he mumbles an incoherent word and stalks away. I can feel Claire pressed against my back, and I place the knife back in its holster and turn and pull her into my arms.

"I.... I thought..." She buries her face in my chest, and I rub a soothing hand down her back. "I thought you were going to kill him."

I lean into her good ear to make certain she can hear me. "I wanted to. I really did, and maybe if you weren't here, I would've, but I couldn't do it. Not knowing it would hurt you."

The dark alley makes it hard for me to see, but when she lifts her head, I swear I see tears swimming in her eyes. I don't want to make her cry anymore. I want her to be happy, smiling. I want to see her like I did the very first day I met her.

"I'll come with you."

Her words are so profound that for a moment, I swear

they're made up. "What did you say?" I ask, just to be certain that I heard correctly.

"I'll go with you. I'll go home."

My heart jolts in my chest; it's beating so loudly it's all I can hear for a few seconds.

"Are you sure?"

"Yes, I'm sure, but I still want my freedom."

"If that's what I have to do, then I will do it. I'll give you whatever your heart desires." I squeeze her a little tighter, grateful that for once, I didn't give into my most basic instinct. Claire changed me and is still changing me.

37

CLAIRE

Most people like going back home, are proud of their roots and long for the place they grew up. The drive back to our hometown has my stomach in knots. So many terrible memories were made here, memories I'd rather forget. I try to shove those down, back to the darkest corner of my mind, and concentrate on the good things.

I'm excited to see Hope again. It's been over two years, and I've missed her dearly. Besides Carter, she has been one of the few actual friends I had.

As we enter the city limits, familiar streets and buildings emerge. I notice right away that we are not going to the part of town we used to live. The neighborhood we are heading to is the upscale side of town. An area I only went to once by accident when the school bus took a wrong turn.

Glancing over to Lucca, I'm close to asking where we are going but decide to just wait and see. We pull into a gated community. The guard waves Lucca through after he flashes some kind of card, and I can't help but wonder if these guards are keeping people in as well as out. I wouldn't be surprised if Lucca is paying them extra to keep an eye out for me.

We pass a dozen upscale homes, one looking more luxurious than the next. Two even have water fountains in the front yards. I'm so enamored with the beauty of the surrounding homes that I barely realize when we pull into a driveway.

Lucca parks in front of the three-door garage, and I gawk up at the breathtaking house in front of me.

"What are you doing? You can't park here."

"Why not?" Lucca chuckles.

"Someone lives here." I sit up a little straighter and look around us, just waiting for someone to come out and yell at us.

"Someone does, indeed."

"Wait! Is this Tracy and Steven's new house? Did you buy them *this* house?" If you can even call this a house. Mansion might be a more accurate term.

"No, Claire. I bought this house for us. For you and me to live in."

I stare at him, speechless for so long that my mouth gets dry. That's when I also realize my mouth is hanging open.

Did he just say he bought a house for us?

What about the woman he is in love with? Does she know he bought a house for *us,* or is he lying to her as well?

"Why don't you let me show you around. I really think you're going to like it." Lucca exits and comes around to open my door for me. The entire time, I remain utterly speechless.

Lucca helps me out of the car, and I can't tear my eyes away from the perfect manicured lawn and flowerbeds surrounding the front entrance. I watch curiously as Lucca gets out a key and unlocks the front door.

I'm still almost certain that the key won't fit, that it can't be our house. This has to be a mistake or a cruel joke. The lock clicks open, and the scale of reality tips closer to me believing it.

I'm back to being certain that this is a dream when I step through the front door and into the foyer. My worn sneakers touch the sleek marble floor, and I instantly feel out of place. Everything in her looks bright, clean, and expensive. I shove my hands into my jacket pocket because I don't think I should touch anything here.

"It still looks a little bare, but I got the essential rooms done. Let me show you the living room." Lucca ushers me through the foyer and into a hallway. I follow him like a lost little puppy while looking around wide-eyed, like a kid in a candy store.

This house is beautiful. I already love everything about it, but when I enter the living room is when I really lose it. The space is fully furnished, decorated in different shades of gray, white, and accented with teal.

My eyes are first drawn to the large modern fireplace with mosaic tiles. A ginormous TV is mounted above, and a fluffy white carpet is on the floor in front of it. My gaze swings to the most comfortable-looking couch I've ever seen, and all I want to do is throw myself into a pile of oversized pillows from that couch.

"So, do you like it?"

Like it? I fucking love it.

I want to squeal, kiss him, jump up and down like a little kid. Instead, I try to tone down my excitement as much as I can. I'm not going to make it that easy on him.

"It's nice, I guess." I shrug as if I'm not that interested.

"Nice, huh? Well, let me show you the bedroom."

"Bedroom? As in only one?"

"Well, there are two furnished bedrooms. But I was hoping you and I could share the master and leave the other as a guest bedroom."

"I want my own room."

Lucca is visibly disappointed by my request, maybe even a little hurt, but he can get over it. I'm going to hold on to whatever freedom I have left. Plus, he gave me the cold shoulder for so long, I'm going to give him a taste of his own medicine.

"I'm going to unpack, so if you could bring my suitcase to the room, that would be great."

"As you wish, your majesty," Lucca mocks but still turns around to walk back to the car.

As soon as he is out of sight, I run up the stairs like it's Christmas morning, and there is a pile of presents upstairs with my name on it. I can't stop the grin from spreading across my face when I make it to the bedroom, which is surely meant to be mine.

Just like the rest of the house, the colors are light. The walls are pale gray, the carpet white, and the drapes covering the large bay window yellow. Only when I get closer to it, I notice the pattern of the wallpaper. It's a paisley design embellished with butterflies. It's subtle and tasteful, making it artistic looking instead of childish.

I run my fingers over the wall, making sure that it's real. It feels real under my touch, but it still doesn't feel right in my head.

Taking off my shoes, I walk over to the bed and climb into it. The bedding is also yellow, and when I throw myself into the pile of fluffy bedding, I sink into it slowly. The scent of fresh linen fills my nose, and I close my eyes, relishing in the smell.

I shoot up into a sitting position when I feel the bed move.

Looking around, I realize Lucca has come into the room and placed my suitcase on the mattress next to me.

"Sorry, I'll try to move louder." I give him a half-hearted smile. I hate when people have to accommodate me, but I hate not being able to hear someone coming more.

"Thanks. I appreciate it."

Lucca nods, running his hand over the footboard of the bed frame. "Enjoying the bed, I see." The suggestive tone in his voice has me jumping up.

Fumbling with the zipper, I open my suitcase and get out my clothes. "I better unpack before I fall asleep."

Lucca stands at the foot of the bed for a few more seconds before he finally leaves. He walks by me, brushing his arm against mine, even though there is plenty of space to go around. I roll my eyes at his antics and continue unpacking, ignoring the tingling on my arm where he touched me and the manly scent he left behind in the air.

When I'm done hanging up all my shirts in the oversized closet, I fold and put away every pair of pants. Lastly, I organize and stash away my underwear and shoes before sliding the now empty suitcase under the bed.

I briefly play with the idea of crawling back into bed and taking a nap, but decide against it. I'd much rather explore the rest of the house.

I make it about three steps down the hall when I come to a stop again. I see him before I hear the faint grunting noise coming from Lucca. His back is turned to me, which means he has been grunting pretty loud for me to hear. Immediately, I wonder if he is doing it on purpose to lure me here.

I want to ask him, but my tongue is super-glued to the roof of my mouth. I watch Lucca's back while he does pull-ups using a bar mounted onto the doorframe. He is only wearing a pair of shorts now. His upper body is bare, the muscles bulge and move as he flexes and pulls himself up slowly. Sweat drips down his skin, making it glisten.

Fuck, I want to run my hands over it. Maybe even kiss... or lick it.

Mesmerized by the show Lucca is putting on, I stand there like a perv and watch him work out. His grunting gets louder and his pull-ups slower until he suddenly jumps down and turns to face me.

"Enjoying the view?"

"Huh?" I ask, like I have no idea what he is talking about. "I was just looking for a towel. I didn't even notice you," I lie, trying my best to play it off.

"Sure." Lucca grins knowingly. "What do you need a towel for?"

"What towel?"

Lucca's smile widens. "You just said you were looking for a towel."

"Yes, yes. Of course, the towel," I say, trying to look everywhere besides his chest. "I was gonna take a shower. So that's why I need a towel. Because you know, to dry off after."

"Got it. So towels are used to dry off after a shower? Huh, I didn't know," he teases. "There are some in your bathroom."

"Okay, great. I'm going to take a shower then." A cold one, probably, to cool the fuck off.

"Cool, me too."

I scurry back to my room, not even noticing that Lucca is following me until I'm already in my bathroom.

"What are you doing?"

"Taking a shower. I told you."

"Yeah, but you can take on in your bathroom. We don't have to take one together."

"We don't have to, but we are going to," Lucca tells me, leaving no room for objections. He reaches for the hem of my shirt and pulls it up. Cool air washes over my hot skin, sending an army of goosebumps across my arms.

My nipples harden under the thin fabric of my bra, and when I catch him looking at my breast, I know he sees it too. Before I can object, Lucca is on his knees, shimmying down my pants and underwear, then tugging off my socks.

Since I'm already mostly naked, I end up taking my bra off myself while Lucca removes his shorts. His already hard cock springs free, pointing at me angrily.

"I'm not having sex with you. I agreed to a shower... well, technically, I didn't even agree to that," I murmur as I watch Lucca's ass while he turns on the shower.

I snap my eyes back up a second before he turns around.

"I didn't ask for sex, even though I'm sure you'd be wet and ready if I reached between those thighs right now. However, I can't help getting hard when you are in the same room naked. Now, get in," he orders.

"Demanding as always." I shake my head but get into the shower like he asks. I step into the hot water and tip my head to the side, letting the spray massage my neck and shoulders. "When are you going to stop?" I ask when I feel Lucca step into the shower behind me.

He touches my shoulder and turns me to face him before answering. "Stop what?"

"Stop pretending there is suddenly more between us."

"You've got it all wrong. There was always more between us.

I'm done fighting that there is. Stop pushing me away. I'm not going anywhere, and neither are you."

"You just want to control me—"

"No, I want to love you."

Love? Did he just say, love?

38

LUCCA

Everything is finally falling into place. The house, getting my old job with Julian back. I know Claire is close to giving in, to telling me she wants me, that she wants to give *us* a chance. Last night I let my mouth get the best of me, and I told her something that I had never told anyone.

Love didn't exist in my job or life, not until Claire. I know the risk I took in loving her, and I will do whatever I can to make certain I keep her protected and out of my darkness. She is the single beacon of light in my life. I need her light to balance me because without her... I am a man walking the edge of a knife's blade.

Now that I'm working with Julian again, I have no fears. The biggest of my enemies is now my ally. Everything is back to the way it's supposed to be. All I have to do now is get Claire to admit that she wants this. A relationship, a future, maybe even marriage and kids.

Honestly, I just want her by my side.

The afternoon bleeds into evening, and now that we've

been here for two days, I think it's time we go visit her parents. I stop in the doorway of the second bedroom, the one she would rather stay in than with me. Although I'm not surprised. When I bought this house and had this room designed, it was with her in mind.

"I have a surprise," I announce, leaning against the door jamb.

"What's that?" Claire asks without looking up from her book. She's been trying to prove that she's not interested, but I catch her watching me often, and I know she craves my touch.

"I want to take you out to dinner."

Hope flashes in her eyes. "Like on a date?"

I smirk. "Yes, like a date."

"Where are we going?" she asks, jumping up from the bed.

"It wouldn't be a surprise if I told you, now would it?"

Her bottom lip juts out. "Not fair, Lucca."

"Life is not fair, butterfly."

Her hips sway as she saunters over to me, and I grip the doorframe to stop myself from grabbing onto her. "I was actually thinking maybe we could also see Steven and Tracy tonight. I told them I would visit, and I feel bad that I left the way I did."

"Sure, whatever you want."

Claire cocks her head to the side, giving me an adorable expression that's a cross between seductive and curious. Her heart-shaped face and soft pink lips call to me. We haven't had sex or shared a bed since we arrived here, and I'm developing blue balls.

However, I told myself that I wouldn't touch her again until she's decided. Until she's chosen what she wants, and right now, she's tempting the fuck out of me.

"Whatever I want?" She gives me a seductive smile.

I know what she is up to, and for once, it is me who feels like the prey.

"Don't tempt me, Claire. I've wanted to fuck you across every surface of this house since we walked through the front door, but I told myself that until you make up your mind. Until you're certain about what you want, I'm not going to have sex with you."

Her mouth pops open, and then she says, "Really?" It slides off the edge of her tongue like she didn't mean to give voice to the word.

I don't understand why she finds it so surprising. Actually, I do. I've always taken what I want. Always been in control. I can see why she would be surprised that I'm not acting on instinct.

"Yes, really. We're leaving in an hour." I tap the non-existent watch on my wrist.

"You amaze me, sometimes." She shakes her hair out, and strands of red hair fly everywhere. Her beauty makes my cock want to break past the zipper of my jeans. "It feels like you're changing, but still the same."

I smile. "I just want you to be happy, Claire. I want to be happy with you. Together, side by side. I know you're young, and I've put you through some shit. Life isn't easy or fair, and you had your fair share of heartache, but I've always put your happiness and safety before anyone else."

"Stop twisting me with your words."

"They aren't just words."

"To me, they are."

My smile widens. "We'll see about that. I'll be waiting downstairs for you." I push away from the door and retreat down the hall.

ONE HOUR LATER, Claire comes walking down the stairs in a cream-colored maxi dress. The sleeves are short, and the neckline plunges low, so low that my eyebrows raise, and I consider telling her to turn around and march her pretty little ass back into the closet to find something else.

Luckily, I bite my tongue because as she gets closer, I discover the neckline isn't too bad, not with the two tied pieces of fabric in the front. There's a slit on the dress, revealing a bit of leg, but I'm going to have to get used to letting Claire do this shit. It doesn't mean I can't spank her ass and withhold orgasms from her once we're home, though.

"You look amazing," I say when she reaches the last step.

Her gaze sweeps over me. I'm wearing a three-piece suit, something I haven't worn in a while. It feels nice to be back in my element.

"As do you."

"Let's get out of here before I'm tempted to rip that dress off of you."

"Do not even think about it!"

I smirk and take her hand in mine. Together we walk out to the SUV, and I help her inside. I'm excited to see Claire's face when she discovers what the surprise is. On the way to the restaurant, Claire is unusually quiet and looks out the window the entire way. I want to press her on what she is thinking, but I don't want to push her over the edge.

Everything is happening so fast. I came back into her life. Brought her back home. Got us a house. Told her I love her. I'm sure she has whiplash like she's never experienced.

"Are you okay?" I ask, loud enough for her to hear when we reach the restaurant.

Claire turns to me, a slow smile creeping onto her face. "Yes, just thinking. I'm excited to see this surprise."

"Then, let's go," I say.

We climb out of the SUV and step onto the street. The restaurant is popular as hell, so I had to park about a block down from it. Like a magnet, I'm drawn to Claire's side. I want to grab her hand and hold on to it, but I need her to make the first move.

She walks a few steps ahead of me, and I can't stop myself. Her hips sway in a seductive come-and-get-me invitation that makes my cock stiffer with each step I take. As we approach the crosswalk, I stop, but Claire doesn't. She continues to walk, and I reach to pull her back toward me and ask her what the fuck she is doing when a car comes barreling around the corner without its headlights on.

Fear strikes hard, and my heart stops beating as I barely latch onto Claire's shoulder and pull her back in time. A whoosh of air hits us as the car speeds by, not even slowing down the slightest.

"What the fuck, Claire?" I growl, turning her to face me.

Her big green eyes are huge, her face a mask of fear and shock. I give her a gentle but firm shake to bring her back to the present.

"I..." her lip trembles, "I... don't know. I was just walking, and I didn't hear or see the car. I'm sorry."

My nostrils flare, and my lungs burn, thankful for the air that fills them. *Fuck*. I wish there was a way to fix her hearing. It seems it's getting worse, and I can't help but think of how horrible this could've ended if I wasn't here.

"Shhh, it's okay. There's nothing to be sorry about." I wrap my arms around her and speak into her good ear. It might be too soon, but I'd be willing to go to Julian and ask him if he knows a doctor that can help.

Claire pulls away and looks up at me. "I wasn't trying to kill myself. I swear. I just didn't hear the car, and there were no lights."

"I know. I believe you." I smooth a hand down the side of her head. "Let's get into the restaurant so you can find out what your surprise is."

Claire smiles, but there is a sadness in her eyes. "Okay."

We continue our walk to the restaurant, and this time, I take Claire's hand in mine, refusing to let her go, afraid that something bad might happen before we can get into the restaurant. We're greeted by a hostess, and Claire looks around the restaurant in awe.

"Reservation for Torres," I tell the hostess who eye fucks me to an uncomfortable degree.

"Of course." She smiles, but that smile falls when she spots Claire. I tug her forward, drawing her attention back to me.

She leans into my side. "I don't even want to know how you can afford a place like this."

"If you don't ask, then I won't tell." I smile, not wanting to go into detail on what I get paid to kill people. It's not exactly the best dinner conversation. The hostess turns on her heel to take us to the secluded room I rented for the evening.

"It's almost time for your surprise," I say.

My only hope is to see her smile and feel her happiness. That's all that matters to me.

39

CLAIRE

This restaurant is seriously expensive, I know it even without asking. The servers all wear black slacks and white button up shirts with bow ties. The lighting is dim, candles on each table, and chandeliers hang from the ceiling, for heaven's sake.

The hostess leads us into a private room with a round table in the center. We take the seats across from each other, and a waiter brings us glasses and fills them with water. I'm still a bit shaken up from nearly getting run over, but I try not to focus on that.

"So, what's my surprise?" I ask impatiently when the server leaves.

Before Lucca can answer, the door opens again. The hostess appears with two people following behind.

"Claire," my mom calls, basically shoving the hostess out of the way to get to me.

I jump up from my seat just in time for my mom to wrap her

arms around me. She pulls me into her embrace with a strength I didn't even know she had.

"I missed you, baby." She hiccups into my good ear.

"I missed you too..." I trail off with the word Mom on the tip of my tongue. I've been calling her Mom inside my head for a long time, but I've never actually said aloud. I don't know why I can't bring myself to say it now. She has been more of a mom to me than my biological mom ever was.

Still, something holds me back. Like a small voice in the back of my head telling me not to do it. I know it's stupid, but part of me thinks that once I call them Mom and Dad, they won't want me anymore, just like my actual parents never wanted me.

"Now, let me get a quick hug in before you smother the girl," my dad's deep voice fills my ears. My mom lets go of me, but her expression tells me she is not happy about it. She sits, and my dad wraps his arms around me, pulling me into a bear hug. He places a kiss on the top of my head and pulls away enough for me to look at his face.

"Don't you take off like that again. We were so worried about you," he tells me, his voice filled with emotion and his eyes watery. I've never seen him like this, and knowing I caused him to be this sad has guilt gnawing on my conscience.

"I'm sorry," I apologize wholeheartedly, realizing how selfish I was not to tell them I was leaving. I just couldn't risk them going to Lucca.

"It's okay. It's in the past. We're just so happy to have you back. Let's enjoy dinner." My dad squeezes my arms one last time, and we both take our seats.

The waiter comes in a moment later, taking our drink order

and reading us the daily special while I look at him dumbfounded.

What the hell is Foie Gras and Escargot?

Lucca must be a mind reader because as soon as the waiter leaves, he explains, "Foie Gras is duck liver and Escargots are snails."

Ewe. I won't be eating that.

I refrain from gagging, but Lucca still laughs. "Don't worry, they have normal foods like steak, chicken, and lobster."

"I'll have the chicken then."

"Why don't you let Lucca order for you. He'll order something you like," my mom coos.

"He might need to order for all of us," my dad chimes in with a chuckle. "I have no idea what half of this stuff is."

"Everything is pretty good here. This is my boss's favorite place. We used to get stuff delivered from here all the time."

I take in the conversation between Lucca and my parents, and a pit forms in my stomach. There is a familiarity to the way they talk like they have known each other for a long time, which is a harsh reminder of the fact that they do.

They've known each other for years, probably talked weekly if not daily. They just did all of it behind my back. Of course, I already knew this, but having it rubbed into my face has another tidal wave of betrayal pulling me below water. That and the constant reminder of the letter I found in Lucca's kitchen.

The guilt I felt only minutes ago transforms into anger. I was right not to tell them where I was going because they would have told him. They were always on his side and never on mine.

My mom taps my arm, getting my attention. "Do you like the house Lucca bought for you guys?"

Of course, she knows about the house. I bet the only thing she doesn't know about is the other woman he loves.

"It's alright, I guess." I shrug, annoyed by the way my mom talks about Lucca.

"What's wrong?" Lucca asks, covering his hand with mine.

I pull my hand away before his warmth can seep into my skin. "Nothing."

Lucca gives me a sideways look but doesn't push me any further.

The next thirty minutes are spent pretending I am fine while I watch my parents act like Lucca is my boyfriend, and they are the doting parents approving of him being just that.

"You were right, Lucca, everything is delicious here." The more my mom talks about how great everything is, the bitter taste in my mouth grows. Unfortunately, she is talking a lot, probably because of the expensive wine she has been drinking.

"I wish Carter was here," I blurt out, knowing that it will agitate the hell out of Lucca. Just as I hoped, his whole body goes rigid next to me, and he white knuckles the fork.

"Why would you need Carter if you have Lucca here?" My mom giggles and takes another sip of her wine.

"He is my friend, and I miss him."

"Maybe you shouldn't have left for so long. No one stopped you from calling him," Lucca tells me, annoyance lacing his voice.

"You stopped me. You stopped me from contacting anyone because I knew as soon as I did, they would tell you where I was."

"And what's so bad about that? Lucca only wants what's best

for you," my father explains. "The same goes for us. We only want to keep you safe. We want you to be happy. That's what every parent wants—"

"You are not my parents!" I lash out, making my mom flinch like I slapped her. I want to feel sorry, want to apologize, but the anger boiling inside of me won't let me. They hurt me, and now it's my turn to hurt them.

"Claire, you don't mean that." Lucca reaches for me, but I recoil from his touch.

"I mean it. They are not my parents, and you are not my boyfriend, so let's not pretend we are." I get up from my chair. "Thanks for dinner, but I'm leaving."

Without saying goodbye, I walk away from the table and out of the room. I don't need to hear Lucca's footsteps behind me to know he is there. I would prefer to walk out of here on my own, but it's not like I have a car or a place to stay.

I have nothing. I completely depend on Lucca, and I've never hated that more than in this moment.

I don't stop walking until I'm standing in front of the restaurant and don't know where else to go. Lucca comes up beside me, but I don't look at him. Silently, we walk to the car, where he opens the door for me. I get in, mumbling a thanks out of politeness.

Just as he gets into the driver's seat, his phone rings. I watch him retrieve it from his pocket and frown at the screen. As soon as I see his expression, I know something is wrong.

Can this night get any worse?

40

LUCCA

Tonight wasn't supposed to end like this. After dinner, we were supposed to head home, and spend all evening together, tangled in one another's arms.

"What's going on? Who called you?" Claire asks with fervor.

My mood dove straight off a cliff when I saw Julian's name flash across the screen of my phone. The need to punch something just to punch it pulsed through my veins.

The last thing I want to do is expose Claire to more darkness, to carry her into the pitch black with me, but I'm not given a choice tonight. If I don't do this job right now, then I might as well sell the house and take Claire back to that piece of shit apartment. To let Julian down wasn't an option. He barely trusts me now, and I know I must work my way back up the ladder.

I'm lucky he didn't kill me when he had the chance.

"Hello? What's going on, Lucca?" Claire presses for an answer once more, and I slow and turn down an alleyway. "Was it your girlfriend? Is something wrong with her?"

Girlfriend?

"What the hell are you talking about?" I'm seriously confused by her question.

"I know, Lucca. I saw the note... the letter you wrote and left in the kitchen drawer. I read it. I know you're in love with someone else."

Christ.

"Fuck, Claire. Is that why you left?" Her silence is more than enough to answer that question, and I can't believe I've been this stupid. How could I forget about that fucking letter? Everything is making sense now. Why she left, why she suddenly pushed me away. I figured it was because I took her roughly that night, skipping the roses and sunshine when I should have known there was more to it.

"Claire, listen to me." Just as I stop at a red light, I grab her arm and force her to face me. I need her to get every single word of what I'm about to say. "I wrote that letter to push you away, to make you hate me because I thought I wasn't good enough for you. But I couldn't go through with it, so I never gave it to you. Nothing you read on that piece of paper is true. There is no one else, only you. You are the only person I have ever loved."

"Oh..." Her mouth stays open, permanently forming an O.

Wide-eyed, I can see her brain working, thinking back to the last six months and everything she thought about me that wasn't true. So much wasted time all because I didn't throw the fucking note away.

"I promise you, there has been no one else. I haven't been with anyone else in years. It's only you, Claire. It's only ever been you. Always."

"Lucca... I'm sorry, I should have talked to you instead of leaving." She tries to turn away from me, obviously ashamed of her actions, but I won't let her. I don't care what happened in the past. I only care about today, tomorrow, and our future.

"Don't be sorry, baby. All that matters is that we are together now."

She gives me a smile, but it's weak. "So, what was the phone call about?"

"I have a job to do, something that can't wait. It's time-sensitive." I let go of her and look ahead, through the windshield. I can't bear to look her in the eyes, too afraid to see what might be there.

Disappointment, or maybe even fear?

"A job? Like...." Her voice tapers off, and we both know what she was going to say.

I park the car right outside the back of the bar Julian said to go to and turn the lights off. There's a very dim streetlight that illuminates the alleyway, making it possible for me to see anyone who walks out that back door.

Turning in my seat, I face Claire. She's watching me with sadness in her eyes. I have to explain myself before this goes bad, and I risk losing her again.

"When I met you, I was working for this man named Julian. I betrayed him when you were kidnapped to save you. Then when you disappeared, I was pissed and had no idea where you could be. His wife was kidnapped by the same family, and I helped him get her back. A truce formed between us, and he brought me back under his wing. He asked me to do some work for him and earn my way back into his life. He understood why I did what I did, even if he didn't agree with it. If I don't do this job, if I let him down, there is no getting away. I'm in the mob, and there is no way out, Claire. I don't want to scare you or bring you any more pain.

After tonight, you will never be brought into my darkness again."

"Are you going to kill someone?" Her throat bobs.

"Yes," I tell her, unable to lie. In a second, she'll see me do it, so what's the point in hiding it. "I need you to stay in the car, though. Do not get out. No matter what you see."

She looks mortified but nods her head, yes.

My stomach knots and tightens to the point of pain. I reach across the car and into the glove box, pulling my gun out. The blood in my veins pumps a little faster, and a spark of adrenaline ignites as I lift the weapon.

It feels perfect in my hand. Exhaling, I allow myself to sink into the role of being a killer and reach for the door handle.

Claire's hand grabs onto my shoulder, halting me. "Please, be careful," she says, her entire body tight.

"I'll be fine. Stay in the car, please," I say and push the door open. Right as I step out of the car, the backdoor to the bar opens, and the person I'm looking for comes stumbling out. I close the door to the SUV without looking back at Claire and approach the woman.

Killing women is my least favorite thing to do. It affects me differently, makes me feel weak and sick. Like I'm a bastard or something.

My boots slap against the pavement with each step I take.

"Hey," I yell, causing the woman to stop in her tracks.

I need to get a good look at her to verify so I don't end up killing an innocent person. I pull out my cell phone and pull up the image attached to the message.

My eyes scan the picture, like I'm taking a photo of it: heart-shaped face, dark hair, green eyes, and full lips. The woman in this picture appears young and happy. I don't care to know what got her to this point in life. Usually, it involves drugs or a debt that was left unpaid, and as sad as it is, someone else's problems aren't my own. In my eyes, this is merely a job.

"Excuse me?" The woman narrows her gaze at me as she whirls around. We're less than five feet away from each other now.

Green eyes that are dull and lacking life. Brown matted hair that could use a washing and brush. Her face is sunken in, and there are dark bags under her eyes.

"Are you Missy?" I ask.

"Depends, who's asking? You looking for a good time, baby?" I want to fucking vomit when she takes a step toward me.

My fingers grip my gun, and I pull it out, pointing the muzzle right at her forehead.

"What the fuck?" she shrieks at the sight of my gun. At least she's not running.

"Wait!" another voice calls, and I realize in an instant that it's Claire. For one brief second, I take my eyes off the hit and turn to find Claire rushing toward us. "Wait, Lucca! That's my mom," Claire yells, and I stagger backward, completely fucking shocked.

Suddenly, I'm caught between hell and a rock.

Her mom?

"My ClaireBear, is that really you?" The woman takes a wobbly step toward Claire, who's shocked, sad expression has me lowering my gun. "I've missed you so much! I looked everywhere for you."

For once in my life, I don't know if I can go through with a kill. I've already killed her father. I don't know that I can be responsible for both of her parents' lives.

It's obvious that Claire's mother never cared about her. If she had, she would've found her. It wouldn't have been hard.

"Your father, he took you from me. Took everything from me," Claire's mother snaps angrily. I look between Claire and her mother. *What the fuck do I do?*

"I... I can't believe it's you." Claire seems more shocked than anything. Like she's looking at a ghost. "Why... why did you leave?"

"Oh, baby, I'm sorry. I didn't want to. But your father... he made me."

Claire frowns, and I want to sweep her into my arms and return her to the car and forget that the second half of this day ever happened. What the fuck am I supposed to do?

"Why? Why didn't you take me with you?"

"I'm sorry, baby girl. I couldn't, but that's all in the past. Come here. Let me at least hug you," her mother croaks.

Claire crosses the space that separates them and wraps her arms around her mother. In an instant, everything goes from bad to fucking worse. Claire's mother pulls a knife from who fucking knows where, and whirls Claire around, pressing the blade against her throat.

My heart does a backflip in my chest, and I lift my gun, ready to shoot the bitch right between her eyes.

"Let her go," I say through my teeth as calmly as I can.

She laughs. "Give me all the money you got, or I'm slitting her throat."

"Mom..." Claire cries out.

"You wouldn't hurt your own daughter, would you?" I ask, knowing damn well that she would. The feral look in her eyes tells me she would do just about anything for some cash, even kill the person she gave birth to.

"Do you really think I care about her?" She presses the blade harder against her throat. Claire gasps and a small bead of blood appears on the blade. "I left her with her father, hoping he would finish the job that the doctor fucked up when I went to get an abortion."

The color drains from Claire's face, and the air around us becomes electrically charged. Something bad is about to happen. I can feel it in my gut; the gush of something ugly fills the air.

"Let her go," I order.

Claire and I lock gazes and without a word said, she slams her elbow into her mother's side. The knife clatters to the ground, and all I can think of is to protect Claire. My goal has always been and always will be to protect her.

I don't hesitate when I pull the trigger. My ears ring as the bullet leaves the chamber and lodges itself right between her mother's eyes. One second later, she falls backward, crumpling to the pavement like a rag doll. I rush to Claire's side and take her into my arms. This is so fucked up, so wrong. All I want to do is take her pain away and make sure she is safe, but I keep fucking up.

"Are you okay?" I ask.

"I... I think so," she says with a hoarse voice.

Shoving my gun into the holster at my hip, I carry her back to the SUV. I buckle her into the seat and rip out of the alleyway, leaving before police can arrive. My heart pummels my chest as I drive us home and park in the driveway.

In the ten minutes it took to get here, she still hasn't said anything.

Her silence is overwhelming, and it terrifies me. I'm scared that I've lost her, that I've hurt her. Yeah, her mom said some really shitty things and held a knife to her throat, but was that worthy of death? I didn't think Claire would think so, but I knew that if I didn't kill her, someone else would've. Maybe I should've let that person carry the weight of the hit.

Now I risk losing everything. I don't regret killing Claire's mom. She deserved to die, for more than one reason, but the most important being that she threatened my butterfly's life.

I can't take the silence any longer and slip out of the car, jogging around to the passenger side door. Claire doesn't flinch or even move as I snake an arm under her knees and another behind her neck and pick her up. I tuck her against my chest, expecting her to sob at any second.

I'm not sure how, but I get us inside the house and close the door. I carry her up to our bedroom, turn on the light, and place her on the bed, not releasing her for even a second as I do.

"I'm sorry for what I did. I'm sorry for hurting you." I'll spend the rest of my life apologizing to her if I have to.

She lifts her head and whispers, "I'm not.""

I'm so shocked by the words, I almost think she didn't say them at all.

"Why? That was your mother, and I've taken both parents from you. I'm... I'm sorry for bringing you into this fucked up world."

Claire pulls away and cups me by the cheek. Her hand is tiny and fragile like glass. Tears glisten in her eyes. Fuck, I don't know what I'm going to do if they fall.

"I'm not sorry I met you that day years ago, Lucca, and I'm not sorry that you killed my father or that you killed my mother. They were never my parents, maybe by birth and blood, but physically and emotionally, they were nothing. Blood doesn't make you family, and I'm the one that's sorry. I should have realized this before today. Tracy and Steven are my real parents. All you did was kill two people who didn't deserve to live."

"You have nothing to be sorry for…"

Claire cuts me off, "I do. I hurt Steven and Tracy. I hurt you, and I'm sorry it took me so long to understand what I have right in front of me. I'm sorry it took me so long to realize I love you. That I've always loved you. I wanted to hurt you the same way you hurt me. I felt abandoned every time you left, even though I knew you were just trying to protect me."

"Fuck." I squeeze my eyes shut. "I wouldn't blame you for hating me, Claire, not after everything that I've put you through."

"Shut up, stupid. I love you," she says, and her lips find mine in the dark, sealing her fate for life. She loves me, and I love her, which means I'm never letting her go.

I pull back from the kiss, my cock swelling in my dress slacks. I want to fuck her right now, but it's not really a good time.

"I hope you know what this means." I smile.

"That we can get a dog?" She smirks.

"No… I mean, yeah, I guess, but that's not what it means. It means you're mine, forever. Do you want that? To be mine forever?"

"Hmmm, let me think about it." She giggles, and the sound warms me all over. "Of course, that's what I want. I think I've loved you since the day I met you."

"Good, because you'll never be rid of me. No matter where you run, I will find you. Mine. Forever. Always."

EPILOGUE

Claire

Time feels different once you find the things that bring you joy in life. That night in the alley changed my life forever. It made me see what was right in front of me, made me realize I had everything I could've ever wanted. All I had to do was open my eyes.

It didn't take long at all for me to meet the man known as Julian. Intense, dark, and brooding Julian. He was the reason we were on the run for such a long time and why Lucca had to hide me. He was also the one and only reason Lucca found me, so while tragic events that involved him ripped us apart, he brought us back together again.

Lucca grips my hand beneath the table while Elena, Julian's beautiful wife, presents the cupcakes she made for dessert. I know if they can be happy and have children in this world, surely we can, too.

Elena beams as she grabs a cupcake from the tray and peels the liner back. "Claire, you must try the chocolate ones. I put little chocolates inside that practically melt in your mouth when you bite into them."

I smile and help myself to one, letting go of Lucca's hand to do so.

"Yes, Elena has become quite the cook, but only after burning the house down a time or two." Julian snickers before taking a drink of his bourbon. Elena glares at him over her shoulder.

"I love cooking too. Maybe we could get together and have an evening of baking?" Fallon, Markus's wife, suggests.

She's quiet and sweet. Markus, on the other hand, is terrifying with his stocky frame and pensive stare. And when he smiles, it's not like he's smiling because he's joyful, but because he just stabbed you in the heart, and he's happy about it.

"I thought you said it wasn't like that..." Markus taunts and elbows Lucca in the side, a shadow of a smirk on his lips.

"At the time, it wasn't." Lucca shrugs.

I take a bite of the cupcake Elena gave me. The delicious flavor of chocolate explodes against my tongue, and I barely stop myself from moaning at the taste.

Damn, that's a good cupcake.

"Right, so how did that happen?" Markus points at my already swelling stomach.

A giggle slips past my lips, and Lucca's gaze becomes icy. I'm twenty weeks pregnant and enjoying every minute. As soon as we found out, we were over the moon.

I wasn't sure that I would ever want kids in this world that we're in, but Julian and Elena easily changed my mind with their children.

"I said at the time, asshole. You want me to kick your ass?" Lucca rests his fist against the table.

"You could try." Markus snickers, and Fallon rolls her eyes at her husband.

"Stop instigating fights," Fallon shoos.

"Boys, there will be no bloodshed during dinner time," Elena adds, pointing her finger at both men.

"Fine, but next time we get in the ring, I'm kicking your ass." Lucca smirks.

"You can try." Markus leans back in his chair unphased.

"How about I shoot both of you, and we don't have to listen to your arguing anymore?" Julian's eyes glint with mischief.

This is easily the best day ever. Never did I think I would be here having a conversation like this. I finish my cupcake, and Lucca and I get ready to leave. We say our goodbyes and exchange hugs, promising to do a girls' lunch soon.

As we step outside, and Lucca helps me into the SUV, my phone rings. Mom flashes across the screen, and I press the green answer key as I bring the phone to my ear.

"Hello, Mom!"

"Hello, sweetie. I wanted to let you know I ordered some clothing for the baby."

I smile, not only because of how caring and supportive they are, but because after all this time, I could finally allow myself to call them Mom and Dad.

"Mom, we don't know if it's a boy or a girl yet," I exclaim.

Lucca and I decided to wait to find out the sex of the baby, to let it be a surprise.

"I know, I know, but I just couldn't help myself. I'm going to send you a picture of the onesie I got. You're going to love it."

"I'm sure I will. I've loved everything you've bought so far."

"I got to go, honey. Dad needs help in the kitchen with dinner. I love you."

"I love you too."

The words used to be foreign, but now they're an everyday occurrence. I know with them and Lucca by my side, I'll never be alone again. They're my family.

"She bought more clothes?" Lucca asks, already knowing the answer.

He navigates the car onto the road, driving us home.

"Yes, she's excited about the baby. Probably more excited than us."

"I highly doubt that." Lucca looks between the road and me. "I didn't think I would ever find love or have kids, but I did, and I'm fucking excited as hell to have a baby..."

"Same. I'm thankful that everything turned out the way it was supposed to."

"You were always meant to be my butterfly..." Lucca says, grabbing my hand and placing a kiss on the top of it. I shiver at the touch of his lips on my skin.

My core tightens, and instantly I want to climb him like a tree. I tell myself it's just the pregnancy hormones, but it's more than that.

"You look absolutely beautiful tonight."

"Only tonight?" I tease.

"I fuck you so much that you beg me to stop. I'm positive you know I think you look sexy as fuck all the time."

He's not lying, his appetite for sex and me is through the

roof. Now that I'm pregnant, he wants me more. As if the fact that my stomach being swollen isn't his fault.

"I know you think I'm beautiful."

"Not just beautiful, but perfect. You're everything, Claire, and I'm thankful that you gave me a second chance because now I get to watch you fly. I get to see you smile, and that's all that I've ever wanted. Your happiness is mine."

"I'm happy because of you." I beam.

"Good, because I'm never letting you go."

And I'm fine with that because I no longer want to be free of Lucca.

EXTENDED EPILOGUE

laire

When Julian offered to let us see one of his doctors, I wasn't sure about it. Lucca urged me to at least go to the consultation appointment. The doctor was excellent and kinder than I expected.

He explained the procedure and gave me time to think it over without being pushy.

That night when we got home, I knew what the choice would be. I wanted to hear our daughter's laughter, to not have to read lips in order to understand things or have someone speaking directly into my ear. The only way I could do any of those things was by going through with the surgery.

The mere thought brought tears to my eyes.

Sitting in the outpatient room, we wait for the doctor. Lucca is nervous, his knee bouncing up and down while he clenches my hand in his. Our little girl is resting her head against his shoulder, watching me earnestly.

She is the best thing to happen to me, aside from meeting her father, of course.

"I love you. Everything is going to be okay. If it doesn't work, then we will try something else. I won't stop until you hear again, just like you could before."

All I can do is smile. We didn't know if the new device would work, but anything was worth trying.

The door to the room opens, and Dr. Rome walks in wearing his white coat. Now is the moment of truth. He smiles at me, obviously sensing my nervousness.

"Are you ready?"

I nod, feeling the urge to throw up. I've never wanted something so badly before. Natalie lifts her head from Lucca's shoulder, watching the doctor intently as he walks closer. Lifting his hand, he presses on something behind my ear.

"Can you hear me?" he questions, his voice booming in my ears.

A slow smile spreads across my face. "Say something." I jerk my head toward Lucca. His eyes are large and excited.

"I love you." The words are like a balm to my scarred heart.

"Say it again."

"I love you, Claire," Lucca repeats himself, his smile so large it overtakes his face. Natalie blinks slowly and feeding off our energy, smiles and coos. Her baby voice fills my ears, and there is no sound quite like it.

My hearing aid from before allowed me to hear but only small amounts. Everything was a whisper, and now, I can hear everything without missing a word.

"This is good. It looks like the surgery was a success." Dr.

Rome beams, flashing his white teeth. "We will need to go over care instructions and such, and I would like you to schedule a follow up just so I can make sure everything is still going well."

"Babababa..." Natalie squeals while reaching for me.

The sound is so loud, I flinch, but still, the smile refuses to slip from my face. I would forever be grateful to hear her cries and laughter.

"Of course, thank you for seeing us on such short notice."

You'd be surprised what money, and a little fear, got you in this world. Julian Moretti had everyone in his pocket.

"It was my pleasure. Let me know if you need anything else. I'll send a nurse in to go over care instructions," he says one last time before waving goodbye.

Natalie practically leaps from her father's arms and into mine.

"Oh, my goodness, you're a daredevil." I brush a few blonde curls out of her eyes before pressing a kiss to the crown of her head.

"The best part about you hearing isn't just the fact that you can now hear our daughter loud and clear."

"Oh, really? Then what is it?"

A mischievous look flickers in his eyes. "It's that you will now be able to hear every moan and grunt I make as I fuck you raw, claiming you as my wife over and over again."

Jesus, hearing him speak now. The deep, rough sound makes me shiver. My core tightening with anticipation.

"Is that a promise?" I smile, holding Natalie tighter to my chest. I have the best life a woman could ask for, and I'm loved by a man who has never given up on me.

"It isn't just a promise, Claire. It's a vow, a goddamn guarantee. You're mine forever, and I'll make sure you hear just how much I love you every single day."

Tears fill my eyes but don't fall. Ever since that night when Lucca saved me from my father, I felt broken.

I'm no longer broken.

I'm happy, whole, and loved.

Thank you for reading Broken Beginnings! If you haven't read Julian and Elena's story yet, you can do so in Savage Beginnings.

Also check out our brand new upcoming book
Devil You Hate

COMING SOON

They call me "The Devil."
Deranged and violent. Gorgeous but frightening.

I'm a business man so when one of my debtors offers me his fiancé in exchange for a debt settled I figure why not, the woman will be a quick sell. Repayment comes in the form of a beautiful but haunted young woman. The light in her tempts the darkness inside of me. Teases it, tortures it.

I want to hurt her.
I want to break her.
I want to keep her.

Lucky for Celia she fails to see that there is no goodness in me and when she attempts to draw me in with her innocence, and sweet naive heart I thrive to show her the cruel monster I am.

Preorder Devil You Hate Now!

ABOUT THE AUTHORS

J.L. Beck and C. Hallman are an USA Today and international bestselling author duo who write contemporary and dark romance.

For a list of all of our books, updates and freebies visit our website.

www.bleedingheartromance.com

About the Authors

ALSO BY THE AUTHORS

CONTEMPORAY ROMANCE

North Woods University
The Bet
The Dare
The Secret
The Vow
The Promise
The Jock

Bayshore Rivals
When Rivals Fall
When Rivals Lose
When Rivals Love

Breaking the Rules
Kissing & Telling
Babies & Promises

Also by the Authors

Roommates & Thieves

***

DARK ROMANCE

The Blackthorn Elite
Hating You
Breaking You
Hurting You
Regretting You

The Obsession Duet
Cruel Obsession
Deadly Obsession

The Rossi Crime Family
Protect Me
Keep Me
Guard Me
Tame Me
Remember Me

The Moretti Crime Family
Savage Beginnings
Violent Beginnings
Broken Beginnings

The King Crime Family
Indebted
Inevitable

Made in the USA
Columbia, SC
03 February 2023